The Vine Witch

LUANNE
G. SMITH

47NORTH

This is a work of fiction. Names, characters, organizations, places, events, and incidents are either products of the author's imagination or are used fictitiously. Any resemblance to actual persons, living or dead, or actual events is purely coincidental.

Published by 47North, Seattle

www.apub.com

Amazon, the Amazon logo, and 47North are trademarks of Amazon.com, Inc., or its affiliates.

ISBN-13: 9781542008389
ISBN-10: 1542008387

Cover design by Micaela Alcaino

Printed in the United States of America

The Vine Witch

CHAPTER ONE

Her eyes rested above the waterline as a moth struggled inside her mouth. She blinked to force the wings past her tongue, and a curious revulsion followed. The strangeness of it filtered through her toad brain until she settled on the opinion that it was best to avoid the wispy, yellow-winged ones in the future.

Unperturbed, she propelled herself into the murky shallows to nestle among the reeds. As her body absorbed the late-season sun sieving through the half-naked trees, she let her eyelids relax. But with the sun's energy came new hunger. She swiped a forelimb across her mouth and considered hunting for snails along the mud bank when a second peculiarity pricked her instinct. Shapes and colors intensified in her vision, and not merely by a seasonal trick of the light. A brown leaf fluttered onto a ripple of black water. A silver fish with pink gills nibbled at an insect just beneath the surface. A dragonfly zipped across the pond, a blaze of neon green.

Her toad brain latched on to the insect's emerald color and held it in its cortex like an amulet even as her nostrils filled with the sudden stink of fish slime and putrid muck. How had she not noticed the stagnant, vile smell of the shallows before? A muddy chill needled her leathery skin, prodding her to back out of the foul water.

The skin. It was time to shed again.

The shudder began involuntarily, as it had once a week since her toad memory began. Her body writhed, compelled by an uncontrollable urge as the outer layer of skin stretched and lifted, sloughing loose from feet, back, and tender belly. Tugging and twisting with her forelimbs, she pulled the spent casing over her head like a woman removing a sheer nightgown. Then she gathered the wad of skin in her mouth and began to swallow. Yes, she must always remember to do that, though the reason flickered just outside her grasp.

She blinked hard, maneuvering the skin deeper into the gullet, when a queer stirring in the bones halted her midswallow. Her insides churned and tumbled, and she coughed the skin back up. A lacerating sting, like claws tearing into flesh, gripped her hunched back. Panic ignited her instincts. *Jump! Back to the water before Old Fox takes another toe with his teeth!* But then her other mind, the one that had been wrapped and tucked away like a jewel deep within her subconscious, snapped awake. The hidden emerald of intelligence recognized the pain for the sign of hope that it was. It had her hold steady even as a fissure opened along her spine, agony nearly splitting her in two.

Splayed toes dug into the mud as four phalanges morphed into five, elongating joint by joint. A human face pressed beneath the speckled skin, forcing the toadish nostrils and mouth to tear and peel away. The metamorphosis accelerated. Shoulders, arms, and stomach grew. Brown hair, slick with a sort of birth slime, coiled down her back. She gasped for air, filled her lungs, and opened her eyes to the world, reborn.

Still squatting in the mud, she wiggled her fingers, testing, then dared to hold them in the sacred pose as if cradling the face of Knowledge itself. Warmth engulfed her. Consciousness reignited. The bonds of the curse disintegrated.

Elena.

The name flashed in her mind so quickly she thought it a phantom whisper. Then memory flooded in. She was Elena, disciple of the All Knowing and daughter of the Chanceaux Valley. And she was free.

As her body woke from torpor, muddy hands trailed over breasts, ribs, and stomach, assuring all was normal—until warm flesh turned pond-water cold beneath her touch. She dared look down, and a strangled scream caught in her throat. Giant speckled legs with webbed feet clung on in horrid stubbornness. She kicked and thrashed, and yet they remained grotesquely fused to her body.

"What demon spell is this?" she cried. But when panic failed her, she took a steadying breath and let her mind meditate on the problem as she always had.

The powerful alkaloids secreted through the skin had eroded the curse over time. Perhaps all she needed was one last jolt to complete the change. Mastering her revulsion, she picked up the spit-up toad skin and stuffed it onto the back of her tongue. The toxic residue tasted of rotted reed grass and bitter herbs, but as the sun haloed in her vision and the poison danced in her blood, she gave thanks to the All Knowing for teaching her well the ways of magic.

After one last agonizing moment, her transformation was complete. Long legs, weak but willing, held her when she stood, so she tipped her face toward the daylight stars to calculate the distance home. Naked, but no longer at the mercy of the sun for warmth, she walked out of the marshland with the hot pulse of revenge beating beneath her breastbone.

CHAPTER TWO

Elena slipped the flimsy shoe back on her right foot and swore to make a fur coat out of the first fox to cross her path. She would never be able to grow that toe back, no matter how many concoctions she came up with. Not even Grand-Mère in her prime could work that magic. If only she had a little Saint-John's-wort or mallow leaf with her, she could at least make a salve to soothe the blisters brought on by covering so many miles in another person's shoes. Oh, to be tucked away in the storeroom again with her tincture bottles, powder jars, and dried herbs and flowers tied up with string. But she supposed all that was gone. She'd have to start again. The thought exhausted her.

Her magic had atrophied, of that she was certain. Manipulating the goatherd's eyesight had been more difficult than it should have been. A quick pinch of ground-up chicory seed blown in the herder's face was all that was needed to fog the memory of encountering a naked woman emerging from the woods, but it had left her shaky and unsure. And though she'd found a half round of cheese in one of the pockets, she debated the wisdom of not having waited longer for someone more suitably dressed to pass by on the road. Now she regretted how the stolen coat smelled of dung, and without the proper undergarments—some things were best left on the roadside—the goatherd's woolen skirt chafed against her tender new skin. But she was nearly home, and she could bear any suffering if it meant she'd soon walk through the front gate of Château Renard and be greeted by the healing hands of Grand-Mère.

If her moon reckoning was correct, it had just turned November, time of the frost moon. And four days since she'd awoken from the curse. But what was the date? Had it been a year? Two? Certainly she hadn't been gone a decade. Though her magic swam weak and watery in her veins, she did not feel the heavy stack of time against her spine. Her hair showed no gray, her legs were lean and strong enough to run, and her teeth did not pain her. If she was right about the time, *he* should still be alive. She thanked the All Knowing for letting her break the curse before he had the chance to meet a kind death by natural causes.

The prospect of revenge buoyed her again to her feet. As she walked, she filled her pockets with dried hawthorn berries, shriveled seedpods, and damp moss. A twist of shriveled celandine leaves, frost-hardy flower heads, the bark off a willow tree—she knew how to mix and grind them all into healing powders. She knew, too, as she sniffed the hardened seedpods of a dried foxglove, the deadly combinations that were possible. Potions that could drop a man to his knees with his heart exploding inside. She'd felt the murderous impulse when she awoke from the curse, but the desire seethed in her veins now that her fingertips caressed the components that would make it possible.

With thoughts of poison rooted in her mind, she bent to pluck a fringed mushroom off a rotting log when a whiff of smoldering grapevine snaked through the air. Despite her dark thoughts, she lifted her head and smiled. She'd caught the scent of home.

Elena ran in her ill-fitting shoes until she came to the crest of the hill. There the trees thinned, the sky spread open, and the rolling hills of Château Renard revealed themselves in the valley below. From afar, nothing looked amiss in the vineyard. It gave her the courage she needed to move closer.

Neat rows of blackened vines, old and twisted like the capable hands of Grand-Mère, greeted her midhill. The winter pruning had begun. Three men worked the field with their *brouettes*, smoke rising from the char cans where they burned the clippings from last year's growth. The ashes, rich in nutrients, would be spread on the ground to feed the roots through winter in the great cycle of life and death. She walked between the vine rows, her fingers brushing the newly clipped edges, the rough skin of the vines as familiar as her own.

"May I share your fire?" she asked of the first worker she encountered, a clean-shaven man with round wire-rimmed glasses and wearing a gray wool flat cap. He startled as if she'd materialized out of the smoke. "I've been walking for hours. My fingers are chilled to the bone." She was cold, but more importantly she needed information before approaching the house.

"Where did you come from?"

She stretched her hands over the smoldering fire. She didn't recognize the man staring back at her or the others who craned their necks to see her better. Where was Antonio? Margaretta? These faces were all new. "Is Ariella Gardin still the matron of Château Renard?" she asked.

"She lives here, yes," the man said, unaware of how he'd eased her fears, "but if you're looking for work, we won't be hiring again until the spring."

She was almost charmed by the man's ignorance. Though given the state of her appearance, she could hardly blame him for his prejudice. She glanced up at the clouds, tapping into her intuition. "You're lucky if you've got an hour before snowfall. Mind you keep those coals stirred so the fire doesn't go out on you."

The man blinked back in awkward silence as she gave her hands a final rub over the coals. With a shrug of her coat she walked toward the house. It was a full minute before the men's whispers of *sorcière* started up behind her and the snip of the *sécateurs* resumed against the vines.

Elena stared at the grand old house as a shiver frosted the secret places inside her. The house, stately with six bedrooms, though certainly no mansion, was showing its age. The roof was missing three tiles above the door, and a sizable crack had opened in the stonework beside the front window. Houses settled and shifted over time, of course, but how much time?

Her knock went unanswered, so she tried the door handle. It resisted as if she were a stranger. There was much reacquainting to be done, she reflected, before slipping through the hedgerow to try the kitchen.

Peering through the back window, she spied an elderly woman in a black high-collared dress standing at the counter. The woman's long hair was pinned up at the sides so that silver curls trellised down her elegant neck. She hesitated, a cup of flour poised unsteadily in her hand, before shaking her head and tipping it into a porcelain mixing bowl. Tears threatened to spill at the sight of Grand-Mère, but Elena quickly dried her lashes with her sleeve and tapped on the door.

"You can leave the eggs on the step, Adela," the old woman said without looking up from her work. "The money is under the pot of geraniums."

Elena opened the door a tentative crack. "You never used to encourage geraniums over the winter. You called them tedious."

Ariella Gardin, grande dame of one of the oldest and most renowned vineyards in the Chanceaux Valley, turned in alarm, a pitcher of milk gripped in her hand. "Who's there?"

Elena pushed the hair out of her face and took a step closer. "It's me."

The pitcher shattered on the tile, splashing milk the length of the terra-cotta floor and soaking their shoes.

Grand-Mère squinted back as if she stared at an apparition. "It can't be." Skirting the puddle of spilled milk, she reached for Elena's hand. The old woman studied the lines of Elena's palm, breathed in the scent of her hair, and then rubbed thumb and fingers together in the space over her head to check for enchantments. Elena endured it all happily.

"It really is you." The old woman held her hands in the sacred pose to thank the All Knowing before embracing her. "I always knew you'd return someday."

"How did you know when I scarcely knew myself?"

Her mentor waved her inside and shut the door. "The All Knowing always favored you."

Elena disagreed about which shadow had been cast over her at birth, but she held her tongue.

Stepping into the kitchen again after so long, she felt a tinge of strangeness, as if she were a guest. She blamed it on the unusual scents swirling among the familiar—the hint of men's pomade, the turpentine of boot polish, and the slightly musty odor of leather-bound books mingling beneath the homey smells of bread and cheese and Grand-Mère's lavender soap. Change was to be expected, but it only added to her unsettled feeling that more time had gone by than she knew.

The old woman pressed her hands to her cheeks in hopeless exasperation as she looked at the mess on the floor. She reached for a cloth and knelt to mop up the milk and slivers of broken porcelain. Before Elena could protest, the old woman sliced her finger on the first sharp edge she touched.

"Let me do that," Elena said, kneeling. "I've startled you. I should have sent a dove to warn you I was coming."

"Just clumsy old age." Grand-Mère surrendered the dishcloth. "Mind yourself. Milk and blood together are a bad omen."

At the prompt, a familiar childhood rhyme floated up in her mind. "Mud and silk, blood and milk, never the twain should meet."

"For if they do."

"Bad luck to you."

"'Tis the Devil you'll greet." The old woman finished the rhyme and sucked at the drop of blood on her fingertip.

"I remember your lessons well, Grand-Mère."

The old woman peered at her before removing her finger from her mouth. "I wasn't sure I'd live long enough to hear anyone call me that again."

They were not truly related, yet Elena's connection to Grand-Mère often felt stronger than the bond of blood, held together by the terroir and magic of the work they did in the vineyard. They bowed their heads together, touching foreheads over the milk, as they often had when she was still a girl.

"I felt a quiver in my left hand when I got out of bed this morning," Grand-Mère said. "I had no idea it was you I'd sensed. It's been so long I thought it was just the change in the weather."

Elena squeezed the dishrag, bracing herself. "How long?"

The old woman thought about it as she stood and dumped the broken shards in the rubbish bin. "Has to be seven years now." Then she turned and squared her shoulders as if finding her own courage. "Where have you been all this time?"

Seven years!

Her heart gave a little kick at the news. She'd never dreamed she'd spent seven winters in that fetid pond, eating moths and slugs to survive. "It was a curse. I only just got free."

"This whole time? I thought maybe you'd . . . started over somewhere else."

"It was meant to be permanent." Her eyebrows pinched together. "Only someone neglected to study their poisons. They miscalculated the counteractive potency of bufotoxins when self-ingested over time."

"A *permanent* curse?" Grand-Mère drew her hand to her heart. "Good heavens, are you sure?"

Elena dumped the wet rag in the sink and took a seat at the kitchen table. Feeling safe for the first time in years, she described her ordeal, including how she'd held on to just enough of her wits to remember to eat the poison-laced skin every day and not gag it back up, even as the curse tried to swallow her memory of being human. While she spoke, Grand-Mère prepared her a simple meal of bread, cheese, and wine.

"A toad?" Grand-Mère was incredulous as she set the plate down in front of Elena. She took the chair opposite, a hand pressed to her cheek. "It's been an age since that sort of transmogrification was practiced. Who could have done such a thing?"

"Bastien. Who else?"

"Bastien?" The old woman's mouth fell open. "But you were going to be married. You were going to—"

"We had a fight." Elena's face flushed with shame. "Once he slipped the ring on my finger, he made demands."

"Demands?"

Elena buried her face in her hands. "He said as his wife I'd be obligated to serve him. That it wasn't my place to refuse."

"Marriage is always a compromise. Often more for the woman, I admit, but—"

"He understood *nothing* about me. He knew I was a vine witch, that I had obligations of my own to uphold, that I couldn't just fulfill his every whim. I'd finally mastered my first exceptional vintage, and he expected me to set all that aside to serve his dreams. The ambition and greed in that man! How could I have been so wrong about him?"

Grand-Mère shrugged diplomatically. "He always did have grand plans."

"I told him I'd rather be a happy spinster than his miserable wife and threw his ring back at him."

Grand-Mère bent her ear forward, as if she hadn't heard correctly. "You broke off the engagement?"

"I had no choice," she said, reaching for the glass of wine. It had been seven years since she'd held a glass in her hand or sniffed the silky bouquet of Château Renard's pinot noir. She gave the wine a swirl and held it to her nose, needing its cleansing power more than ever. "He doesn't like being told no, even when he's wrong. And he cannot abide being made to look like a fool. Not by a woman. I'm convinced it's why he paid some fly-by-night Fay to spellbind me and keep me silent. He must have." She exhaled at the weight of the implication. "Whoever the witch was, she blindsided me in the road just before I reached home. I'd stopped to slip into the shadow world to see how he was faring. She attacked while my sight was focused elsewhere for the briefest of moments. That 'no' cost me everything."

The old woman massaged her temples, as if she suffered from the sudden onset of a headache. "Could have been one of the Charlatan clan. They usually stay north in the city, but they'll do work for hire. Crude lot they are, too, and more cunning than one might give them credit for," she added, rubbing her eyes to be free of the pain. "And not the sort to study how a curse might be weakened by ingesting one's own toxic skin. Which toads are naturally wont to do."

Elena shuddered at the thought of the warty, poisonous skin sliding down the back of her throat. She took a sip of the wine to chase the memory from her mouth, but if she was looking for relief she was vividly disappointed. None of the musky hues of spice and rose petals the Renard vineyard was famous for hit her palate. It was all chalk and mushrooms. An off bottle?

Then a worse thought hit her as she swallowed. What if there was nothing wrong with the wine? What if her senses had been permanently disfigured by the curse? She'd kill him twice.

She lifted her glass in silent panic to study the wine's opacity against the light. She was still forming her fear into words when the back door opened and the worker whose *brouette* she'd shared walked inside. A wet wind followed, billowing the curtains and spitting snowflakes onto the floor tiles. The man shut the door and brushed his wet cap against his trousers before hanging it on the peg on the wall. His brusque entrance had her set aside the sour wine as well as her growing alarm.

The worker halted and apologized for interrupting as he dried the snow off his glasses using his shirttail. He snuck a glance at her while he polished the lenses, and she couldn't help but notice the fine features of his face—the proud brow that tightened in thought, the geometric planes of the cheeks, and a jawline taut from firm self-confidence.

Grand-Mère hastily stood. "This is Elena Boureanu. I'm sure I've mentioned her before." She hurried back to her mixing bowl at the counter and began measuring more flour. "Elena, this is Monsieur Jean-Paul Martel. He's—"

"Yes, we spoke briefly in the field. You must be the new foreman."

"Something like that." He slipped his glasses back on and then pressed his fist under his nose. His less than discreet gesture suggested he'd picked up on the scent of goat dung saturating the hem of her coat. "A pleasure to meet you, Mademoiselle Boureanu," he said curtly, then in a more polite tone added, "I'll let you return to entertaining your guest, Ariella. Let me know when supper is ready."

Once he left, Elena watched Grand-Mère fret over having no more milk in the icebox. With the taste of bad wine still souring her thoughts, she asked, "Have you grown so desperate for good help that workers now have the run of the main house?"

"Jean-Paul isn't just a worker." Grand-Mère's elbows moved up and down as she worked water into the dough for biscuits. "He likes to eat promptly at five o'clock so he can go out and walk the fields one more time before dark."

"Why didn't you tell him who I am?"

The old woman paused to glance at the swirling snow as a gust of wind whipped against the window. Her shoulders fell and her body stilled, as if she could no longer bear to hold them up. "I've made a terrible mess of everything."

She looked to the sky as if it might offer absolution and then confessed all that had gone wrong. The last five seasons at the vineyard had been failures. Either the grapes had been pinched from searing drought or the rain delayed the pickers so the crop spoiled with mold. In the last harvest, dark speckles marred the grape skins, tainting the wine with the taste of burnt cork. And there was nothing Grand-Mère could do, because her mind and magic had begun to fail.

It was little things at first. Forgetting to add a bit of bone to the soil on the full moon, neglecting to hang the bell-charms inside the vine canopy to warn of searing wind, or whispering the wrong words of protection when the cool air dipped toward freezing, leaving the grapes to fend for themselves. Grand-Mère waved it all away as she spoke, as if thoughts of growing old pained her. It bruised her ego to admit her vulnerability, but she knew the vineyard had suffered because of her failing powers. It wasn't long before successive poor vintages caused sales to drop, and people began to whisper that Château Renard had lost its way.

Failure to protect the vineyard alone was a disgrace to a vine witch as renowned as Madame Gardin. But the worst thing she'd done to bring ruin to Château Renard was neglecting to pay her taxes. Nature could bend and accommodate a flaw, but the government would have its due. Château Renard, one of the original houses to produce wine in the valley, had found itself three years behind in taxes with no money in the coffer to pay it.

"They threatened to seize the property," Grand-Mère said with a sigh. "Suggested I sell and save what I could of the Renard reputation."

The news was as bitter as the wine. And none of it made any sense. The vineyard had been passed down from one generation to the next for more than two hundred years. Its reputation was built on a history of excellence, a blessed rich terroir, and the steady fostering of dedicated vine witches. "It must be some kind of mistake. A misunderstanding," Elena said, unwilling to believe. "Grand-Père set plenty of money aside to weather a bad year or two."

"I don't like admitting how badly I mismanaged things without your help. I thought I still had the touch, but it seems my brain is as withered as a dried-up old apple."

"Surely you must have been sent notices about the taxes?"

"Well, yes. And I know I paid *some* money. But it was never enough, according to the statements. The whole thing had the smell of rot to it," she said, shaking her head. "Especially when Bastien came around to present an offer on the property."

"He showed his face here? After what he did?" Elena nearly drew blood as her clenched fingers dug into her palms. "He tried to buy Château Renard?"

"He's been buying failed vineyards all over the valley the past couple of years. It wasn't long before he showed up here with cash in one hand and a bottle of wine in the other. *His* wine." Grand-Mère snorted. "It was a very short meeting."

Elena could do nothing but shake her head. Everything that man did led to greed and betrayal. And now he'd tried to buy the very place where her heart, blood, and soul were sewn to the soil. If there was one piece of hope she could hold on to, it was that he'd failed to steal Château Renard.

Elena slid her arm around Grand-Mère's shoulders to comfort her. "It's not too late. Now that I'm home again we can fix this. We'll raise the money somehow."

"No, you don't understand. I sold Château Renard."

"Sold? But that's not possible. To whom?"

"To me," said Jean-Paul as he stood in the doorway holding a bottle of wine and two extra glasses.

CHAPTER THREE

Elena stood outside among the vines, snow falling gently on her shoulders. An unnatural chill had settled in her skin after the curse, and the last place she wanted to be was caught out in the cold, but there was nowhere else to go. That *man* had bought the only home she knew. He'd even claimed her old bedroom overlooking the eastern fields for his own. Lamplight glowed in the upstairs window, mocking her while she shivered in her stolen, stinking clothes with nowhere to go, no place to call home.

Oh, he was a sly one, letting Grand-Mère stay on at the house after he'd paid her debts. Clever him, arranging it so he owned everything yet still benefitted from the prestige of her family name and perceived blessing. Mortal men. What flaw was it in their ape brains that convinced them their schemes were paramount to everyone else's?

She shouldn't have yelled those insults at him before storming out perhaps, but without the house, the fields, the harvest, how would she ever start over? She'd been pledged to the Renard vineyard since she was five years old. She was Château Renard's vine witch. The terroir and she were one. If she no longer had that to depend on, how would she ever reclaim the life Bastien had stolen from her?

Elena stared up at the house in tears. She couldn't tolerate the thought of that imbecile man buying the vineyard and allowing wine to age in spoiled barrels. Couldn't he taste the moldering mushrooms in every sip of that swill he'd made? Grand-Mère might have lost her touch, but it was hard to understand how things had gotten so bad. Even if he didn't know how to sterilize a barrel properly with burning sulfur, Grand-Mère did. No, something more was at work. It wasn't just the barrels. The grapes themselves were tainted too. She could still taste the corruption on her tongue.

But the problems of the vineyard weren't hers to worry about anymore.

Unable to stare at the void of her uncertain future any longer, Elena instead did what she always did. She leaned into her intuition. Walking a little farther down the vine row, she placed her hand on one of the oldest canes, one planted by Grand-Père when he was still a young man with a new wife. The vine, black and gnarled with age, had already hardened off in anticipation of winter, but she knew the vitality that ran dormant in its veins. She closed her eyes and held on, concentrating as she tapped into the life source inside the vine and inside herself.

Though her magic wavered at first, their energy mingled deep in the vascular system flowing under the hardwood. After a few slow breaths, she located the plant's pulse. The vine was worn out, no question. Not from neglect or deficiency, but . . . something else. She leaned in, barely breathing, her senses heightening as she slipped into the shadow world. Following her third-eye vision, she detected a black thread of energy running from root to cane. Lifting her gaze, she spied a pattern of spells and hexes interwoven over the vines. Yet none of them were strong enough to account for the melancholia she sensed deep in the roots. This was a profound grievance, a lament that echoed within a hollow space inside her. She yearned to understand its pain, but the feeling pulled back, vanishing under her touch. She let go, and her energy disconnected from the vine.

She was still recovering from the experience when Grand-Mère approached from the house, carrying a woolen shawl. "I always wished I'd been born with shadow sight. Such a remarkable talent."

And a vulnerability, Elena thought, remembering too well how she'd been ambushed while in her trance state. After her return home, she couldn't help feeling she'd been blindsided yet again.

Grand-Mère offered the shawl, then rubbed her thumb and fingers together, reading the air. "It's bad, isn't it, the spellwork? I can feel the electrical charge from the magic every time I step outside. I tried countering a few jinxes, but nothing I did ever seemed to make any difference."

Elena wrapped the shawl around her shoulders. "It isn't just one. There's an entire network of spells over the vineyard. But I don't think the usual charms would work to stop them anyway. There's a black aura running through the center. A reverse curse to thwart any attempt to fix it."

"Ingenious. Bastien warned me there'd be repercussions for not selling."

"It's why we fought," she said as her eyes scanned the vineyard for further evidence of spells. "He wanted me to sabotage his neighbors' vineyards. And not just the usual mischief everyone does. He wanted hexes. Vicious magic that would do real damage. He had this grand plan to squeeze the weaker vignerons out so he could buy their land and double his holdings. I defied him by refusing. Threatened to expose his intentions. But apparently he found someone else to do it for him."

"Ah." Grand-Mère absorbed the confession and glanced up at the snowflakes swirling above their heads. "I should warn you he's come up in the world since you've been gone. His plan seems to have worked. He owns more property than anyone else in the valley now. He even brought on a bierhexe to oversee his place. She'd be the one behind the spellwork."

"A bierhexe from the Alps working a vineyard? I didn't think they had any interest in our type of work. It explains the complexity of the magic, though. But it isn't just the hexwork that has me concerned. There's something else wrong with the vines. I can't quite sort it out. A type of melancholia. Not a spell exactly, and not a disease." She ran her finger over the nub of a freshly clipped branch, finding no further clues.

"You belong here, Elena. It's in your blood." Grand-Mère rubbed her shoulder in a supportive gesture. "Even if the vineyard is no longer mine to give you."

Thinking again about how the vineyard had been lost, tears swam in Elena's eyes. "I would have hawked love potions out of the back of a cart or done palm readings for tourists in the street ten hours a day rather than sell to a . . . a businessman from the city."

"It tore my heart out to sell this place." The old woman looked out at the blackened vines rimmed in new snow. "But do you truly believe I'd hand over my life's work to just anyone? I've been divining harvests and coaxing wine into the world with my magic longer than you've been alive. *And* reading men's intentions. I can tell you he isn't in it simply to make a profit. Even if he is a mortal who shuns witchwork as superstition, Jean-Paul's heart is in the right place. He wants to make wine worthy of the Renard brand. He took your accusation about hijacking my reputation for gain rather hard back there, I think." She rubbed her thumb against her fingers, as if testing the tension wire of his emotions once more. "You may have to apologize for that—he does have his pride—but otherwise he's graciously allowed you to stay as my guest until you find your footing."

"And what will he say when he learns who I am? He doesn't want a witch helping him. He's an outsider who thinks bad wine can be fixed using science, of all things."

"True. He believes he's a victim of bad weather and depleted soil." She scoffed. "If only he were so lucky."

"Come," said Grand-Mère, hooking her arm around Elena's. "He wouldn't be the first man to learn he's wrong about something he's certain about. But for now I have something to show you that might cheer you up."

They left a trail of snowy footprints behind as they walked to the barrel-aging room beside the main house. Elena stomped the snow off her shoes as Grand-Mère opened the cellar door with the key that hung from the chatelaine at her waist. The old woman retrieved an oil lamp from a shelf in the entryway and rubbed her fingers together until a small flame erupted. She remarked it was the only real magic she had left and then touched the fire to the wick. Soft lamplight bloomed above a darkened ramp. "After you," she said.

The air grew heavy with the smell of damp earth, smoky oak, and a ribbon of vanilla sweetness as they descended inside the ancient corridor. The powerful combination of scent and memory mingled in Elena's heart and lungs, feeding her spirit. Before curses and bad luck had got their hold on her, she'd vowed to anyone who would listen that the scent of a wine cellar was its own healing magic. She inhaled deeply, drawing in its power.

The sound of their shoes scuffing against the flagstone floor echoed off the walls as they entered the main room of the cellar. Encased in yellow stone five hundred years earlier, the carved space formed a large rectangular room with a low-hanging arched ceiling. A hand-forged iron lamp hung from a chain in the center overhead, while plain white candles had been jammed into the mouths of empty wine bottles and placed atop several of the forty oak barrels lining the walls. A room untouched by time. The space soothed Elena's uncertainty in a way she couldn't have understood or anticipated the last time she had stood among the barrels.

Grand-Mère blew air off the tips of her fingers, lighting the overhead lamp, then motioned for Elena to follow her to the back of the cellar. "I know you're probably eager to open the barrels, but it's not why I brought you down here."

Three small rooms had been added to the original corridor over the centuries. The largest housed select bottles of prime vintages the way a library showed off its books. It also doubled as a place where a wealthy patron might stand at a table and taste the merits of the latest pinot noir. The second room provided storage for the curved wands used for stirring the lees, a wine thief or two for suctioning samples of fermenting wine, and extra rakes, brooms, and baskets. But at the back end, tucked away behind the barrels, was a small room with a heavy oak door. She dared not get her hopes up.

"Jean-Paul has inquired about it several times," Grand-Mère said, "but I told him I lost the key years ago. Anyway, he thinks it's just another storage closet with a few old plungers and some busted barrel rims." She nodded at Elena. "Go ahead. Give it a try."

A tingle ran up and down her skin as she stood before the door. Elena could almost feel the synergy waiting to converge. She put her hand over the lock and whispered her secret word. "Vinaria."

Nothing.

The curse was still siphoning off the lifeblood of her magic.

"Try it again."

She nodded and took a deep breath of cellar air, concentrating her energy on her palm against the lock. "Vinaria," she commanded.

To her relief, the lock gave a click and the door swung open.

Inside, the room looked the same as she'd left it, with bottles, jars, and dried herbs lining the built-in shelves on one wall. The worktable, which took up half the space, still held her scale for measuring pinches and dollops and the small burner with the glass beaker she used for reducing her concoctions to their purest form. On the shelf, a granite grinding mortar had been propped up as a bookend to hold her half-dozen spell books with the gold-embossed spines. The pestle was draped by a sheer spiderweb speckled with dust. The rescued belongings blurred in a watery mosaic in her teary vision.

"I was certain it would be gone."

Grand-Mère lifted the lamp to better show off the upper shelves. "I've dipped into a few jars for a spoonful of this or that over the years, but otherwise everything's just as you left it."

Elena twisted the lid off a jar of rosemary and sniffed at the contents. A bit off its potency but still viable. The dragonfly wings still shimmered in their bottle, as did the beetle shells and flakes of mica. The beeswax had grown brittle and hard, but it softened in her hands almost immediately. In truth, most things seemed workable again as she looked around. The sale of the vineyard was an abomination, but if this Jean-Paul fellow could be convinced of her value, perhaps her plans could still be salvaged too.

"It's possible to get the vineyard healthy again," she said, believing so with all her heart after seeing her belongings. "With luck we may even see results by harvesttime."

"Since when has luck got anything to do with it?" Grand-Mère smiled and set the lamp on the worktable. "I'll leave you to get reacquainted with your things. Come up to the house when you're ready. I'll have a guest room made up for you."

But she did not return to the house. She spent hours inventorying the bottles, balms, and ground-up herbs she'd left behind seven years earlier. She flipped through books, wiped down the worktable, and sorted out a trunk containing her old clothes. Then, when sleep beckoned, she took out a thick wool blanket and lay down on the flagstones within sight of the wine barrels. Using a trick remembered from childhood experiments with her shadow vision, she placed her ear against the floor and closed her eyes, and soon she was listening to the footsteps of the monks who first worked the cellar. Their voices hummed inside the stones as they chanted their ancient songs in their old, forgotten language.

She breathed in the fragrance of wine and oak and let her body relax for the first time in days. Staying on at Château Renard under these new conditions would be a risk. She knew it the moment that man wiped his feet on the kitchen rug. Yet this was where she belonged. Without the vineyard she'd never gain her full strength back. Nor would she be able to see her revenge through to the end, and only a life for a life would satisfy the constant yearning in her heart. She did not know why the All Knowing was testing her so, but she would have payment for the years stolen from her, and if that meant a few uncomfortable compromises along the way, so might it be.

CHAPTER FOUR

Jean-Paul reached the southern slope of the vineyard as the first rays of light spilled onto the hillside. He enjoyed working in the crisp morning air with the sun shining on his back and his lungs breathing in the autumn scents of woodsmoke, the leaf decay in the undergrowth, and a whiff of musky fox from a nearby den. So different from how he'd spent the last ten years of his life stowed away in a corner office in the city, buried up to his nose in books and legal papers.

The law had its merits but had never been his choice. From the time he was a boy he'd been told he must attend university to fulfill some perceived duty owed to his family lineage. The Martels, after all, practiced the law. They mingled with powerful and beautiful people in top hats at the Palais Opéra. They ate *foie gras* and caviar at Maurice's, drank fine wine at the Moulin à Farine, and spent their summers vacationing along the sunny coast in bourgeois comfort, with the Chanceaux Valley at their backs.

They also succumbed to early deaths. The heart had a tendency to harden off after being forced to survive inside a life two sizes too small, deprived of the oxygen of dreams. At least that's where Jean-Paul's reasoning had led him. The death of his father convinced him he had to make a change before his heart shrank any further. And so he'd escaped to the country, where a man could walk among the dormant vines in solitude and give his dreams a chance to breathe in the open air.

But damn the grapes. And goddamn the wine.

When he first read the news that Château Renard was for sale, he could hardly believe his luck—a once-in-a-lifetime opportunity to own a piece of the valley's history and be part of a renowned winemaking legacy. Certainly he'd heard the rumors that the old woman wasn't functioning at her peak anymore, but making wine was a secret aspiration he'd harbored since his first taste of the vineyard's pinot noir a decade earlier. Such musky, sensuous flavors of plum, cherry, and the perfect underlay of oak and flint. He would re-create that bouquet or die trying.

But something always went wrong. For three years he'd blamed himself whenever he caught someone tipping their head slightly to the side, as if controlling the urge to wince in disappointment at the way the latest Renard pinot hurried over the tongue, vanishing as a jammy afterthought. Yet he also suspected the old woman knew more about what had gone wrong with the vintages than she'd let on when she sold him the place. He'd hoped his invitation to let her continue living at the house would provoke her into sharing what she knew about the trouble so he could fix it, but she'd merely shrugged and blamed the disappointing harvests on jinxes and bad luck.

The entire valley was obsessed with witches and their so-called influence in the vineyards. He knew most of the big vineyards employed a witch to infuse her brand of magic into the wine as a sort of signature. It was outright charlatanism. An old-world custom bound up in superstition that the locals used to sell their wine to impressionable tourists. But he'd read enough books to know a good wine didn't require the aura of magic to make it taste amazing. His research told him the winemaking process should be no more difficult than getting the pH levels in the soil balanced, harvesting the grapes at peak sweetness, and allowing the fermentation to do its job. Alas, none of that had worked since he'd taken over, but he still held out hope that things could be turned around. If only the damn weather would cooperate.

He stoked the coals in the *brouette*, then took out his clippers to finish pruning the last row of young vines. Knowing he had the ability to shape the next year's growth by trimming the canes back gave him a sense of optimism. It was one of the small things he thought he was doing right. He relished the feeling as he stood alone, master of his fate on a brisk morning.

"You're too accommodating."

He turned with a start to find the Boureanu woman standing behind him. How did she do that? Twice now he'd not known she was there until she stood within arm's reach. "I beg your pardon?" he asked, trying and failing to mask how she'd caught him unaware.

"The drainage system you've set up to feed the new vines will spoil them," she continued, running her hand over the hard canes. "The roots are like children. You can't pamper them or they'll get lazy."

He straightened to look at her, noting with relief the change in her appearance from the night before. She'd found some proper clothes, though they struck him as oddly out of style. The bodice had the distinct pigeon-breasted fullness the women in the city now seemed to shun, and the black wool skirt dragged the ground without so much as a peek at her ankles. But her hair was an attractive improvement, cascading around her face and down her shoulders in a tumult of soft waves rather than the frenzy it'd been when he first saw her. He was glad she hadn't pinned her tresses up in a pompadour. And, thank God, she now smelled of lavender soap.

He cleared his throat, feeling the need to assert himself. "The vines require all the extra care they can get in these uncertain conditions. I'm not losing another field to drought this spring."

"You have to let them find their own way in hard times. They'll be stronger for it."

He pointed the clippers at her. "*If* they survive."

"They will." She knelt down beside the base of a vine and swept the snow away. Scooping up a handful of wet earth, she rubbed it between her palms, then held the soil to her nose. She closed her eyes, as if remembering a pleasant dream. It smelled, he knew, of flint, oak, chalk, and fire.

"At least the soil isn't the problem," she said, opening her amber catlike eyes again. "The calcium and lime components are still intact." She looked up at him in a most disarming way, as though she could penetrate his heart and mind with a look. "I wanted to apologize for yesterday," she said. "To come home and find the old place had been sold . . . it caught me by surprise. I may have said some things to you that weren't fair. I'm sorry."

The way she stuttered through her apology suggested she wasn't in the habit of being wrong. He nodded, more than willing to let the matter go. "And I'm sorry you didn't receive word earlier. I did try to find Madame's relatives at the time of the sale, but there were no records of anyone alive. If I'd known she had a granddaughter, I would have written you at the time to let you know she was welcome to stay and not to worry."

"She's not really my grandmother. Not by blood anyway."

"Oh? I just assumed."

"I've always called her Grand-Mère, but she's more of a mentor." Elena snapped off a dried grapevine and passed the broken end under her nose before tying a purple string around it. The move struck him as a nervous gesture a child might do with their hands. "I was brought to live at the vineyard when I was five. As an apprentice to Madame Gardin and her husband, Joseph, after my parents died."

"You were sent here to learn the wine business as a child?"

"Among other things."

He had a hard time imagining the woman standing before him as ever having been a child. There was a flinty edge to her that defied any sense of innocence. "But you *are* like a granddaughter to her. I can see that."

"We have a strong bond." She tossed the vine in the *brouette* and watched the string catch fire. "That's why I returned. The vineyard is the only home I've ever known."

Jean-Paul glanced over his shoulder at the house. He knew better than to ask anything as personal as where she'd disappeared to all these years. Yet he was put in an uncomfortable position to have this stranger, so intimately familiar with the land, suddenly return out of nowhere and call the vineyard home. Certainly he'd had no problem letting the old woman stay on at the house after the sale. He didn't want to be accused of throwing Madame Gardin out in the street in her old age when she had nowhere else to go. But what was he to do with this woman? She was trouble. He knew so the minute he laid eyes on her in the kitchen and felt the heat rise in his temples. And yet if she had grown up learning from the old master—Joseph Gardin himself—she must know a trick or two about making wine with these finicky grapes.

"The weather isn't the only thing giving you trouble," she said, as if reading his thoughts. "But it isn't too late. I can help, if you'll let me."

The way she'd shown up at the house as though she'd been living rough, the ferocity with which she'd stared at him when she learned the vineyard had been sold, the hunger in her eyes now as she waited for an answer—all tore at him as he considered her proposal.

"Unfortunately I was telling the truth yesterday when I said I wasn't hiring. I can barely afford to pay the two field workers I have now."

The woman wrapped her shawl tightly around her body, as if guarding herself before she spoke. "Sometimes there is more to making wine than what we can see and measure and taste. That's the part I can teach you. I can work as your partner. Share with you what I know about making the kind of wine men would pay a ransom for. And in exchange all I require is a voice in the process and a roof over my head. And perhaps some of Grand-Mère's cooking."

Jean-Paul smiled at her last comment even as he knew he had to say no. He'd read every book on winemaking he could get his hands on, attended seminars given by the famous Yemeni brothers, and toured the vineyard at Bastien du Monde's, the most successful winery in the valley. He'd studied all he could about drawing out the subtleties of various grapes. He already knew the science of making wine.

Yet this cat-eyed woman, who claimed with granite confidence she could restore the vineyard's reputation, had him mesmerized.

He already understood the techniques of the craft, from pruning and planting to pressing and bottling, but could there be some secret to transcending from ordinary to superb? Some ancient wisdom passed down from generation to generation that would always elude him if he turned her away?

He might believe wholeheartedly in his methodology, but even he wasn't fool enough to ignore how instinct and intuition played their role in the process too. And in his heart of hearts he wanted to make *great* wine. If she knew even half of Monsieur Gardin's secrets, and if she was willing to work side by side with him in the field, she'd be worth her weight in *coq au vin*.

He extended his hand. "All right. Room and board in exchange for your help."

"Just one more thing," she said. "I wish to be a silent partner, at least until we get the grapes through veraison. It would be better if certain people didn't know I was helping you just yet. Or that I was back at the vineyard."

Ah, she meant Du Monde. He would never admit to eavesdropping, but he'd heard more of her talk with Madame than he'd let on. He could only guess at her reasons for wanting to avoid the esteemed vigneron.

"I should add an addendum then too," he said, his negotiating skills dull but hopelessly ingrained from his years of law work. "I believe in science and innovation, mademoiselle. I've already told the other workers I won't tolerate the superstitious nonsense they do at the other vineyards. No luck charms, no evil-eye amulets, and none of that widdershins business before stepping into the field."

She raised one eyebrow at him, and he waited for her to argue like the rest of the workers had. Instead, she swallowed whatever had irked her, nodded her agreement, and held out her hand. With grudging admiration he shook it, feeling her fish-cold skin in his grip as they made their pact.

CHAPTER FIVE

The spine, stiff from neglect, creaked as Elena spread the Book of Shadows open on the worktable.

"Hush," she said and turned the pages until she found the notes she was looking for. As she read, marking her place as she went, the book finally relaxed and sighed under her trailing fingers. "I missed you too," she said and continued reading.

Alternating between doubtful frowning and optimistic lip biting, she wrote out a list of possibilities, at least for the first of the vineyard's hexes she'd identified. She hoped to unravel them all one by one, as if untangling a child's game of cat's cradle that had gone horribly wrong. And she had to do so without the new owner suspecting she was using witchcraft.

She'd thought at first that would be the hard part, but the kink in her magic still prevented her from all-out spellcasting. Incantations tasted like dust in her mouth. And though she'd been able to maintain a trance state the night before, she suspected she might be suffering from a form of psychic cataracts that clouded parts of her shadow vision. How else to explain the inability to identify the cause of the melancholia in the roots?

Her magic was unsteady, but perhaps the weakness was like a strained muscle and she just needed to get moving again. Or maybe it was like a hand falling asleep and she'd feel a prickling pain take over once the magic rushed back in. Hadn't she felt a small jolt of . . . something . . . when the wishing string caught fire and the mortal agreed to let her stay despite his prejudices, sealing it with his hand pressed to hers?

That man. A cloud of privilege had risen off him like morning fog the moment she'd confronted him in the field. He was a peculiar one. City raised and book fed, intelligent and generous, yes, and yet malnourished when it came to a belief in the profound. He'd been taught to believe in only what he could see, feel, hear, taste, or smell. There was a time she wondered what it was like to live with such confinement of spirit, until she found herself held captive inside another creature's skin.

Was that what it was like to be a mortal?

An unexpected pang of sympathy for the man crept up on her as she wiggled her toes inside her soft slippers—well, with the one notable exception. Though Old Fox had nearly eaten her alive, she was glad for the physical reminder of what she'd endured. The ache kept the fire of revenge burning, stoking the hard coal of hatred that smoldered day and night within her. And for that she would hide her magic from the mortal and let him continue believing the world he saw was the world he lived in.

A page in the spell book rippled softly, as if disturbed by a breeze. "Yes?" she asked, and the words "strand of wolf's mane" shimmered on the page in iridescent green ink. "Ah, of course. Clever book. You found it."

She sorted through the upper shelf to locate the woolly stuff. If dipped in sheep's oil and twisted with a braid of cotton to form the wick of a candle, the smoke from the flame would repel the miasma that had been allowed to creep in over the fields each night. The Toussaints from the Alden River valley had used that particular spell on Château Renard before to stifle growth. Grand-Mère should have been able to counter the jinx on her own, but the old woman must truly have lost her edge to let the damaging fog linger over the property for so long. For humans, old age stole their hearing, their sight, or their mind. But when Nature was unkind, witches lost their intuition.

Not finding the wolf's fur stored with the jars of teeth and claws where she'd expected, she searched through the drawer until she located a paper envelope labeled "Hair, Tails, and Whiskers." She found the necessary strands inside but was curious to see what else Grand-Mère may have misplaced. Half a dozen envelopes were stacked inside the drawer. One contained dried owl pellets, another the tail feather of a nighthawk, and one held a pressed primrose, sealed between wax paper. All useful for adding to various potions, but not kept where she preferred to store them. She removed the remaining envelopes from the drawer to see what other mysteries they held, when a stray slip of paper fell out from between them onto the worktable.

More potent than anything she'd yet handled, her fingers trembled as she picked up the faded and brittle scrap of paper. On it was an ink-drawn illustration, a stately house centered under a bold font that read "Domaine du Monde," the wine label for Bastien's premier red, the wine she'd helped coax into existence for him just before she was ambushed.

She'd felt the yank on her conscience to confront him the moment she returned to the valley. Even now she had to grip the edge of the table to keep from running down the road and throwing a curse-bearing brick through his front window. Time and patience, she reminded herself. Revenge allowed to ferment would carry the most power. But as she stared at the house on the label, she felt her resolve slipping. There *was* a way to see the place without actually going there. This, too, she'd resisted, but the longer she stared at the illustration, the stronger the impulse became to give in to her curiosity until she found herself drifting over the line into the shadow world.

Her vision darkened, the walls fell away, and a sepia sky opened above as sight and sound distorted at the edges of her consciousness. Her mind flew her to an abandoned stretch of road in the valley four miles away. The château where she'd spent countless lazy afternoons believing she was in love materialized out of shadow. The sight struck her as familiar yet strange. The years had changed the house in unexpected ways. The main structure was as she remembered, but a pair of grand turrets now anchored each side, and a new balustrade encircled a second-floor balcony, where a stargazer might search for an impressionist's vision of the night sky. A fence surrounded the property now too—cast iron embedded with amulets and protective spells, topped with fanciful metal finials. As Elena walked past the gate, she felt as if lightning itself had been channeled into the metal. She'd never encountered anything like it. The woman's spellwork was even better than she'd thought. Most witches would need a lifetime to master such a graceful enchantment.

Lamplight from a window at the top of the east tower drew her spirit eye upward. A woman's silhouette crossed in front of the glass. She could understand why a bierhexe might be persuaded to work at a successful vineyard. For some, power was the only elixir that mattered. And Bastien had that now. It radiated off everything he'd touched, though she wondered if the witch behind the glass knew what Bastien was capable of if he didn't get his way. Had she compromised a part of herself for him?

Just then the window darkened. A face peered outside. Another's third-eye vision pierced through the veil of shadow, searching for an intruder. She knew she couldn't be seen, at least not in her physical form, but she shrank from view anyway. Still the intensity persisted, as if a psychic lantern swung its light over the yard, searching. It was her first encounter with one of the northern beer witches, and so far the rumors of their striking abilities proved true. The bierhexe's perception practically assaulted with its vigilance. To know Bastien had that kind of protection put a frost on Elena's hopes for easy vengeance, but she'd never give up. Not until her heart got the peace it deserved.

Elena flew back into her body and opened her eyes. The wine label had dropped from her hand. She picked it up again, slipping once more into the trench of pain of his betrayal. With tears brimming, she held the label to the candle flame and watched it burn and curl at the edges until the paper crumpled into a pile of ash. After allowing a single tear to fall onto them, she swept up the remains and sealed them in an envelope. With a florid swipe of her pen, she labeled the outside "bitter ashes" and stashed it away in the drawer. Then she flipped the pages of her spell book and turned her mind to the study of poison.

CHAPTER SIX

Grand-Mère and Elena wheeled a *brouette* out to the field and made a show of pruning the old vines on the east slope while Jean-Paul hitched up his horse and wagon. At last he pulled onto the road and headed for the village. A trail of woodsmoke seeped out of the *brouette* as they waved their *secateurs* in his direction. Once he was out of sight, Elena removed the tallow wicks from her satchel and set to work on her counterspells.

Four twists of wolf's fur, one for each direction, sizzled and burned at her feet as she and Grand-Mère stood in the center of the property. She recited the spell from her book, the words flat and shapeless in her mouth, and a veil of smoke lifted from the wicks and spread over the vineyard. And though a breeze teased their skirts and rain threatened to dampen their uncovered heads, the spell seemed to hold the smoke in place above the field long enough to swaddle the dormant vines with its protective magic. To the passerby, the winter vineyard looked no different than when filled with drifting smoke from the char burners, but to any witch with her nose in the wind it was a warning that Château Renard was no longer a dumping ground for anonymous hexes.

"Well, that's one spell undone," Grand-Mère said, holding her hands in the sacred pose to thank the All Knowing. "Finally the leaves should be able to breathe deep again when they unfold this spring."

Elena watched the wicks burn down to the ground, worried about the compression of time. "How often does he go to the village?"

"Once a week, generally. Sometimes more if he has business to tend to."

That wouldn't be often enough. Not if she wanted to untangle all the spells interlaced among the vineyard before the growing season began. "I don't know how I'm going to keep hiding the spellwork from him. He's going to find out he's working with a witch, and then what?"

"He's been living with me for three years and hasn't caught on, though I'm as useless as a mortal these days, so that's not saying much."

Grand-Mère dug around in the *brouette* and pulled out a clay container the size of a small gourd, the surface inscribed with a circle that had arrows pointing out from the center in the four cardinal directions. It was one of four witch bottles the two had brought with them to ward off disease and negative energy caused by malicious spells belowground.

"Your senses are merely worn around the edges some," Elena said, removing a flagon of an old vintage she'd stashed in the *brouette*. She uncorked the top and poured a small amount of wine into the witch bottle. To that she added a snippet of Grand-Mère's hair, one strand of her own, and a nail clipping belonging to Jean-Paul, which he'd left beside his washbasin.

The old woman's fingers twitched as she watched the process. "You could always keep him spellbound. That is how you got him to agree to let you stay on until harvest, isn't it?"

Elena cast a sheepish eye up at her mentor. "I didn't use a spell *on* him. That would be illegal. I merely brought a wishing string with me and tossed it into the fire while we spoke."

"Must have been a strong wish to come true so quickly." Grand-Mère handed her another bottle to bury. "Of course you were always good at getting what you want."

Could the old woman even doubt it? Elena's veins practically ran red with wine from Château Renard. How could she wish for anything else but to be part of the vineyard? Its terroir was her blood, its mist her breath, its soil her bones, its harvest her unborn child. But covenants were covenants, and spells cast on mortals were strictly prohibited, though everyone fudged the rule now and then. Stars above, she'd never expected to encounter a winemaker in the Chanceaux Valley who didn't wish for the services of a vine witch. Insulting. She couldn't imagine how stunted life must be in the city to form such an attitude toward magic. All that stone and steel must obstruct the mind's eye.

Half moons of dirt rimmed her fingernails as she patted the soil above the buried bottle. She said a few quick words in the name of the All Knowing, then stood and pointed to the next location. As they walked, the smoke from the tallow wicks settled, highlighting the filaments of energy crisscrossing the field. Though she could sense such things even without the help of the smoke, Grand-Mère needed help. Elena took her hand, creating a circuit so they could both see the extent of the hex magic as it materialized like a spiderweb after a light rain.

The old woman inhaled sharply. "Good heavens, I had no idea it was so extensive."

"It's impressive, isn't it?" Elena had them climb the hill to the highest point in the vineyard. "The spellwork is daunting, but there's a degree of elegance to a few of them that one can't help but admire. See the multidimensional layering holding up the shadow spell over the rows of chardonnay? That's no easy maneuver."

"So he got the bierhexe to do what you wouldn't?" Grand-Mère rubbed her thumb and fingers together, trying to feel as well as see the magic.

She nodded. "Based on the shadow her sorcery cast, I'm almost certain it's meant to hold the dew on the grapes to make them mold even in full sun. It shifts position as the day progresses to keep the grapes in the shade." Elena paused to dab at the sweat building on her upper lip. "Don't know how I'm going to counter that one yet, especially with the reverse curse complicating everything. If it is her, she's better than good."

"Her name is Gerda. She showed up not long after you . . ." Grand-Mère pursed her lips hard, as if forcing herself to swallow the words she might have spoken next. "We've been introduced once or twice. You'd know her on first sight. A blonde like the rest of them."

"Yes, I've seen her."

"Seen her? When?"

Elena began digging a shallow hole between two of the oldest vines on the property as she explained how her curiosity had gotten the better of her—not the first time she'd slipped into the shadow world for less than honorable reasons. There were days when she'd been so consumed with lust or distrust that she had to *see* Bastien, even when he was far away. During the year she thought she was in love with him, she'd felt as if she were under a spell herself. As if she'd been given a potion that seeped into her veins, crept into her heart, and set off a poisonous time bomb that later shattered her dreams of love. Before she was cursed, the shadow world had become an obsession, a distraction, a means to an end that had nothing to do with the grace of the All Knowing. And then it had become a trap.

"That was a dangerous and foolish thing to do. What if she's the one Bastien asked to curse you? You have a reckless side. You always did."

Elena planted the bottle in the ground, poured an offering of wine on top, and uttered the protection spell. When she stood, she considered what Grand-Mère said and then brushed her hands off. "I don't think it was her."

Grand-Mère tapped the toe of her shoe on the soil over the buried bottle to pack it down. "How can you be so certain?"

"If this is her spellwork," she said, pointing to the tiered magic, "she's too good at what she does to be playing with old-fashioned transmogrification curses. And certainly not one as ordinary as turning someone into a toad."

The old woman narrowed her eyes. "Didn't seem like such a mundane curse when you showed up two days ago looking like wolf kill." Elena flinched. Grand-Mère had always wielded a sharp tongue when provoked. "You should be more careful. Even if she didn't catch you watching her in the shadow world, there are Bureau spies everywhere keeping an eye out for transgressions." To prove her point, she snapped her fingers and a tawny-haired rabbit jumped out from between a vine row as if its tail had been lit on fire. "See what I mean?"

"Come, rabbit." Elena pointed her finger at the ground, and the rabbit obeyed, humbly hopping toward her until its nose twitched at her side. She picked up the animal and studied its eyes. Not a hint of shadow in them. The old woman was being unusually paranoid. But perhaps she had a point. "Jean-Paul knows I'm hiding from someone. He's agreed to keep my presence here a secret. I should be fine as long as I keep a low profile."

"Even if you're able to stay hidden, your efforts won't. A witch with her talents will sniff out your magic eventually. She'll know the spells are being dismantled. And when she figures out who you are, she'll tell Bastien. And then what?"

Elena set the rabbit down and shooed it on its way. "Then he'll know he didn't get rid of me as easily as he might have thought."

"Could you defend yourself against her if you had to?"

"My quarrel isn't with her."

"That's not what I asked." Grand-Mère watched the rabbit dart away to a safe distance, then turned back around. "I didn't know how to tell you earlier, but she isn't just his vine witch. They're married. His fight is her fight now. Maybe it would be better if you just let the past go. Start over fresh. Forget any of it ever happened."

Married?

Elena slumped on the ground. He'd found affection when she'd tasted nothing but bitter loneliness for seven years trapped in that creature's skin? He'd enjoyed love's warmth while she sat in mud so cold it chilled her blood until her heart barely beat at a normal rhythm again?

To avoid Grand-Mère's scrutiny, she plucked at the rabbit hairs left behind on her skirt and tucked them in her pocket. "Her part doesn't matter."

"Depends on what you intend to do to him."

Elena picked up the spade and dug a fourth hole, then stuffed a bottle inside. "Did you know there's a spell for making a poison that moves like a snake through the blood?" she asked, pouring out the last of the wine over the dirt. "The potion is designed to avoid all other organs but its one true prey. When the elixir finds the heart, it slowly wraps itself around the beating muscle, squeezing until the blood vessels burst. I'm assured the process is agonizing."

Grand-Mère blinked as a line of sweat dampened her forehead. "Stars almighty, Elena, that's dangerous magic you're playing with."

"So was the curse that landed me in a swamp to eat moths and snails for seven years."

"Blood will tell, I swear," the old woman muttered, then shook her head. "You'd do well to remember a threefold reckoning awaits those who do intentional harm."

Oh, she knew the cost. She'd weighed and balanced it against the pain of doing nothing a dozen times. Yet her need for retribution always proved the thumb on the scale, tipping her mind toward murder. What other recourse was there for having her prime years stolen from her? She should be married by now. There should be a son and daughter learning the art of the vine at her hip. The vineyard should have long ago come under her direction. *Her* wine should be in the cellars of the finest connoisseurs on the continent. Instead she was alone, groveling in the dirt, cleaning up other people's messes.

Grand-Mère drew her shawl up over her head and wrapped the ends around her shoulders, as if suddenly chilled. "What is it you're planning exactly?"

"I'm going to kill him," Elena said, then threw the empty wine bottle in the burn cart and watched it blacken and smoke. "A life for a life."

Grand-Mère covered her mouth with her hand and turned away just as the jingling, clanking sound of glass jars being jostled in a wagon bed aroused their curiosity. On the road below, a covered mule cart rolled by with two women at the reins. They glanced uphill, their noses in the air, and waved.

"Greetings," called the first as she halted the mule.

"Merry meet," said the second, forcing a smile.

Witches.

"Charlatans?" Elena whispered, noting the city accent. It wasn't their real name, of course, but one they'd earned through a tarnished reputation.

"The two oldest sisters, by the look of them. What on earth are they doing here? I'll have to say hello."

Elena wiped her hands on her skirt, cautiously wondering if the Charlatan sisters could be acquainted with Bastien. Though she didn't know them, they seemed just the type he'd seek out for his dirty work. The old woman had already headed downhill, so Elena draped the end of her shawl over her face and followed, wanting to know more about their intentions.

As she and Grand-Mère drew closer, a pair of jars trembled slightly in the cart, clinking together like champagne glasses. The witches smiled.

"Greetings. What brings you out our way?" Grand-Mère asked, wary but not unfriendly.

The sister closest, the one wearing the embroidered flower jacket with the faded needlework, answered, "We're headed to the village. Festival day we're told. Caught the scent of your smoke as we passed. Hex fire, is it?"

"Remedy."

"Ah." The woman smiled wider, revealing a row of tea-stained teeth as she bent forward to get a look at Elena. "In that case, might be I have what you need for a good cleansing spell," she said and lifted the tarp covering the back of the cart. "Or a little revenge." Her eyebrow lifted when she caught Elena's eye. "Nothing like a little newt's eye tonic to slip into your favorite rival's drink, eh?"

On top of their reputation as cheats, they were black-market peddlers, too, judging by their wares. Alongside the silk scarves, silver bangles, and charm bells for sale were dozens of mason jars filled with ill-gotten ingredients. Keeping her shawl drawn over her face, Elena took a closer look, spying heart-shaped gizzards, strips of fenny snake, a collection of bat ears, and a bear paw and gallbladder set. Old World novelty stuff. Medieval quackery. And a tragedy, given most of the items carried little potency for any spell she knew of. Nothing more than a cartload of cruelty for the sake of duping occult-loving mortals and gullible witches out of their money.

She was hoping Grand-Mère would tell them to get their disgraceful cart out of their sight when the jars clinked again.

The second sister, who used an obvious enhancement spell to keep her long golden hair curled in perfect ringlets, crooked her finger. "Two-for-one special, if you're in the market. Fresh too. Dug them out of their holes myself just this morning."

Grand-Mère and Elena both leaned in to see what they had buried in the back of the cart. There, perched side by side beneath the seat, were two hedgehogs bottled up in separate jars with holes poked in the lids for air. They pawed and sniffed against the glass, desperate to be free.

"What are you keeping them for?" Grand-Mère asked.

"Me, I skin them and sell the quills along with my voodoo dolls," said the second sister. "City folk'll buy my souvenirs by the armload on market days, but I can always get another pair if you've got a stew brewing to throw them in. I know where the little *hotchi-witchis* like to hide."

The sister showed her fake smile again, and Elena's disgust hit a flashpoint. "I'll take them."

"With pleasure, if you've got the coins."

Elena reached in and removed the bottles by their necks. The witches demanded their money again as she checked each animal for shadow. When she detected none, she gently laid their bottles on the ground.

The witches grew more agitated but kept their stained-teeth smiles. "I said you've got to pay for them first."

Elena knelt and freed the hedgehogs from their glass cages, then rose up. "How about I give you a case of boils on your face instead? Have you no conscience, trapping and selling animals for profit?"

The witch sisters lost their smiles. "Oh, always so high and mighty, you vine witches. Not above stealing from a pair of defenseless cart women, though, are you?" The golden-haired witch took a shriveled badger's foot from the wagon bed and spit on the ground in a feckless attempt to throw a hex. "I want my money."

Elena felt a warning pinch from the spell. "So be it." She reached in her pocket as the sister righteously nodded. But instead of coins, she took out the rabbit hairs she'd collected earlier and a leftover strand of wolf's fur. She quickly twisted the hairs together, drawing up the magic she had left in reserve, then recited a favorite childhood prank. "Hunter and prey, be on your way," she said and blew the hairs at the mule's feet. The animal took off, dragging the women's cart behind as the spell kicked in. The Charlatan sisters fought to hold on to their seats and rein in the mule, but it was no use. His legs wouldn't stop running as long as the wolf's hair chased the rabbit's, which ought to last a good twenty minutes or more.

"You'll be sorry you done that," shouted the golden-haired witch as she held on to the runaway cart. "May your fields rot before the harvest!"

But Elena wasn't sorry, not one bit, as she watched the wagon disappear over the hill. On the ground the hedgehogs sniffed and darted, uncertain which way to go. She whispered where to find some grubs under a fallen log and gave them a gentle nudge in the direction of the forest. She straightened as they scurried off, feeling the weight of the old woman's stare against her back.

"You know I couldn't let them kill those poor creatures."

Grand-Mère scoffed. "This from the woman plotting murder?"

The schism in her intentions baffled even herself for a moment. "Yes, well, some mortals are a different animal altogether, aren't they?" she answered, hardening her heart again before turning uphill to gather the *brouette* and head for home.

CHAPTER SEVEN

Jean-Paul shut the door to the post office and removed his cap, tucking it under his arm. He'd already included the cash for the catalog item in an envelope, which he produced from the pocket of his tweed jacket. All he required was the correct postal code and a stamp. The clerk met the request with a sardonic glance over his spectacles before bringing out the large reference book and letting it thud loudly on the counter. The man ran his finger down the page in careful examination before stopping and tapping it on a probable candidate. Jean-Paul quickly wrote down the number on the envelope, nodded his thanks, and then slid the letter forward. With luck he'd have his new vinoscope in a month.

He'd dropped his change for the stamp on the counter and turned for the door when the clerk stopped him. "Ah, Monsieur Martel?" he said, reading the name on the envelope. "Hold on. I believe I have a letter for you as well. It arrived a few days ago. Yes, here it is," said the clerk after sorting through several slots on the wall behind him.

He accepted the letter, noted the return address and formal handwriting, and retreated to the farthest corner of the post office lobby to read it. He knew before opening the envelope that it was from his mother. The correspondence began well enough, greeting him with the usual pleasantries about the weather, her arguments on the righteousness of the Union for Women's Suffrage, and complaining about the ghastly condition of the city's underground transit system as if it were a black-sheep relative gone astray yet again. He nearly smiled at the familiar news from home.

Then he read the next paragraph. The real reason his mother had written.

> Your uncle sends his regards. He wishes to inquire when you think this wine business of yours will be concluded so he can make future plans. He's had his eye on the Eichman building for years now, and it has finally become available for lease. There are, apparently, two corner offices, one of which he'd gladly provide to his nephew and law partner if he were here. Given the circumstances, he's been quite generous overall with this folly of yours, but he deserves a partner dedicated to the law and serving the practice your father created.
>
> In other news, I thought you might be interested to know that Madeleine has remarried. She's expecting a child in May. So you see, there is no reason to avoid returning to the city any longer.
>
> As always,
> Mother

Jean-Paul crumpled the letter and shoved it in his pocket.

"Bad news?" asked the clerk.

"Merely an expected disappointment," he replied and slipped his flat cap on.

The clerk scratched at his nose and shared instead his own interesting tidbit of information. "They've found another cat," he said while sorting a stack of letters into their proper slots. "Head and tail gone like the others. Up on the county road above the Le Deux estate this time."

"Another one?" He recalled the other grisly finds reported over the years. More than a dozen since he'd moved to the valley three years ago. Sometimes a rabbit, sometimes a small dog, but most often a cat. Everyone speculated who might be behind the deplorable acts, and yet no one ever seemed to state the obvious. "Tell me, why doesn't anyone ever confront the locals at the vineyards who claim to be witches about this?"

The clerk turned around, his forehead creased. "The vine witches? Why would they have anything to do with butchered animals?"

"Because they profess to be *witches*? Who are known to deal in the *occult*?" He'd overemphasized his words, speaking slowly, though his answer did little to convince the clerk, who returned a blank stare.

"Is that what they teach you in the city? Truth is, we've barely had a whiff of trouble with malevolent witches around here since the 1745 Covenants were signed. Why, my own grandmother was a vine witch and wouldn't have harmed a soul. You want to know who I think is behind it? Those university boys who ride out here on the weekends to raise hell with the local girls. Them with their séances and Ouija boards. Who knows what mischief *they* get up to after dark."

Jean-Paul let the issue rest. He always underestimated the sharp distinction the villagers drew between the so-called vine witches and the wicked witches who haunted his childhood dreams—the old hags who wouldn't think twice about wearing a dead cat around their necks if it pleased them. The witches his nanny had warned him about quenched their thirst with human blood, stirred crow's beaks and frog's eyes into deadly potions, and stole babies out of cribs to roast over the fire for their evening supper. Naturally, he wished as a grown man the world could be rid of such superstition. They were living in the age of technology—automobiles, the *cinéma magnifique*, electric lights that turned on at the flip of a switch. A man had just flown across the Channel in an airplane for the first time, for God's sake. Now there was some real magic to behold!

Not wishing to alienate himself further from skeptical locals who already viewed him as an outsider, he nodded as though the idea of college students killing cats for fun on the weekend had merit. He wished the man a good day and left.

Outside, the street bustled with traffic from people preparing for the weekend, a minor local holiday to recognize the siege of some long-forgotten castle. The celebration meant little to him, though he was told often enough if it were not for the victory the town would not be standing. Still, he couldn't help but join in the festive mood as he walked along the sidewalk.

Normally he would visit the feed store to order grain for the horses or perhaps duck into the shoemaker's shop to have a pair of boots resoled while he roamed the hardware store for a new shovel or spool of wire. He might even flip through the pages of a Boddington's catalog and order seeds for a spring garden. But with the letter from home and talk of dead cats still rankling under his skin, he felt the need for a distraction. Turning down a quaint side street he rarely visited, he let his nose lead him forward. Vanilla cakes, cinnamon and sugar, and a hint of toasted almond drew him to the door of a decadent-looking bakery catering to tourists and housewives alike.

He stepped inside the tiny shop, setting the bell above the door jingling. A woman with a cord of black hair secured atop her head by a blue satin scarf, her cheeks brightly rouged, popped out of the back room. She wore gold hoops threaded through her ears, making her a dead-ringer for the bohemian women depicted in those art nouveau posters so ubiquitous in the city at the time of the Great Expo. She brushed flour from her hands and smiled when her eyes found his, the sort of coy-at-the-corners smile Jean-Paul understood immediately. He felt her appraising eye follow him as he surveyed the cakes and tarts in the glass cases.

"I wondered when you'd find your way to my shop," she said.

"Beg your pardon?" He was certain they hadn't met before.

"Took you longer than most. How long has it been? Three years since you bought the Renard vineyard, and not once have you paid me a visit. I've been ravenously curious to know what your taste is." The woman tapped the glass above a tray of petits fours. "Macaron? Éclair? Chocolate mousse? Hmm, not the madeleines, though. No, I think those might have left a bad taste once."

He had been contemplating the coconut cake, wondering if Madame and Mademoiselle Boureanu would approve. He looked up at the shopkeeper, unsure if the mention of his ex's name had been mere coincidence or something more. *Had* they met before? Could she know him from the city? Know Madeleine? Perhaps she knew him from gossip in the village. He hoped not.

Her flirtatious smile wavered. She excused herself and ducked in the back room, a quizzical expression overtaking her face just before she disappeared.

Just as Jean-Paul thought it prudent to leave without purchasing anything, she returned carrying a tray of small tarts still warm from the oven. "Never ignore a hunch," she said, setting the tray down. She cut a slice for him to sample. "I have an inkling you're going to love the taste of this."

Despite his desire to leave, the fresh-baked smell captivated him, and he reached for the sticky tart. One bite and the full complexity hit him. The pastry tasted of fruit and nuts, butter and brown sugar, and the rich spices of cinnamon, nutmeg, and cardamom, all heat-seared by fire. Sweet, yes, but also sophisticated, heightened by a hint of salted brandy. Not unlike a well-aged wine, he thought, the way the flavors evolved on the tongue. He'd never tasted anything like it. His mouth demanded more, the desire tunneling deep into his core until he thought he might buy the entire tray.

"It's fantastic. What is it?"

"Well, isn't that interesting." The woman narrowed her eyes as if trying to see something past his head. "My fig and praline tart. Haven't made any in years. But something told me to dig out that old recipe again this morning."

Jean-Paul swallowed, then licked the crumbs off his lips. "I'll take them all, if you could wrap them up please."

The shopkeeper was about to say something when the doorbell jingled, diverting her attention. She dropped their conversation to greet the new customer.

Gerda du Monde, Bastien's wife, and the most prominent of the village's self-proclaimed vine witches. She stood in perfect silhouette in a pale-blue hobble skirt that hugged the soft curve of her derrière, while in her grip she elegantly brandished a matching lace parasol poised as a walking cane. A single plume of ostrich feather graced the brim of her musketeer-inspired hat, as stylish as any woman on the rue de Valeur out for a day of shopping. And just as well perfumed, as the scent of lilacs gently mingled with the shop's fresh-baked aromas. There was a time after he'd first arrived when her appearance stirred a curious "what if" desire in him, with her perfectly coiffed hair and steady blue eyes. Even now, standing in a bakery with his mouth full of tart, she carried an allure that was difficult to ignore.

"Tilda, whatever have you been up to? Those aren't any of your usual treats." The woman peeled off her gloves as she peered over the glass case to better see the pastries being boxed up on the counter. "They're for you?" she asked, turning to Jean-Paul. "How remarkable."

The shopkeeper slipped the final tart in the box. "I was just telling him how I hadn't made these in years, and then suddenly this morning I got one of those nagging impulses. You know the kind? And, voilà, in he comes and buys them before they're even cooled."

"Indeed." Gerda looked at him with the same odd stare that went slightly over his head. He felt a blush coming on, wondering if perhaps he'd committed a faux pas by ordering so many of the freshly baked goods. But he really couldn't help himself.

"What do you think the timing means, madame?" asked Tilda as she tied up the box with string.

Bastien's wife tilted her head, thinking it over. "Perhaps a long-lost love has returned? Or an old acquaintance has suddenly become more than just a friend. Oh dear, you and Ariella Gardin haven't decided to elope, have you?" The women giggled.

"I'm sorry, what does my choice in dessert have to do with long-lost love?" He handed over the coins for the tarts.

"Well, that's Tilda's specialty, isn't it? Love is the main ingredient in her treats." The woman pointed to the name painted in gold letters on the storefront window: **Pâtisserie d'Amour**. "Not a love potion, per se. She can't make a person fall in love with you. But she does have a particular talent for matching a person's appetite for love with an equivalent sweet treat. She's quite good at it. When Bastien and I first met, he was in here every day for Tilda's spicy *lebkuchen*. So charming that he would crave something of my homeland. Whoever your lucky lady is, she must have quite the dark and mysterious side to her, judging by the delicious scent of those tarts."

"That's it! I remember now. I used to make those tarts for Bastien when he'd buy them for . . ." Tilda stopped talking a second too late, her eyes white with the horror at what she'd just let slip. "Oh, but that was before you moved here. Years and years ago."

Gerda's admiration for the bakery dissolved into a poisonous stare aimed at its owner. Jean-Paul took the awkward moment as his cue to leave. He bid the women good day, grabbed his purchase of tarts, then left as quickly as he could. Back on the street, he turned the corner into the alley and spit the taste of the fig and praline out of his mouth. Bad enough he had to endure superstitious notions from the locals about witches and dead cats at every turn. He certainly didn't need love potions cooked into his food. In fact, the entire day had left a bad taste in his mouth, he decided, and tossed the tarts in the rubbish bin along with the letter from home.

CHAPTER EIGHT

Two months had passed since her return, and the counterspells, at least the ones Elena had been able to summon the energy for, seemed to be holding. Little by little she was ridding the vineyard of its invasive hexes, plucking them out like weeds. Yet the deeper melancholy persisted in the oldest vines despite her efforts to understand and treat the affliction. She flipped through the pages of her spell books again, hoping one of them might reveal some forgotten wisdom. She began to suspect there was an altogether different level of magic at work in their veins, something older than even her spell books understood.

She suspected, too, that Grand-Mère knew more about the trouble with the vines than she let on. There were mornings when the ice hung on the windows when she would catch the old woman staring out at the fields, muttering a plea to the All Knowing under her breath. They were the chanted words of someone afraid of the future, as if a spiteful god wielded the passing of time like a scythe in the hand. Had a fear of death nipped too close to her heels? Something was bothering the old woman, but Elena couldn't find the right words to confront her about it. Time apart had allowed a tangled wall of tension to grow between them. Perhaps it was just ordinary cobwebs in the relationship, the inevitable result of years of disuse, but something blocked the easy flow of energy they once had.

Elena convinced herself it was also why she hadn't told Grand-Mère the entire truth. She knew more about the witch who had cursed her than she let on. She'd spied one important detail before falling from shadow vision into the hex-void of the transmogrification curse. She'd spotted a pocket watch—small and made of silver, with a green dragon's eye on the cover. The unusual timepiece practically winked at her as she collapsed on the ground at the hem of the witch's robes. It was a distinct detail in the small world of witches, and one she hoped might help her find the traitor who'd thought nothing of stealing the life of a sister for the right price. Bastien, after all, wasn't the only one who deserved to feel the sting of revenge. But until her veins thrummed with the pulse of her full magical power again, there was little she could do to satisfy her heart.

Still, she could use the time to refill her supplies. She was dreadfully low on even the most essential of potion ingredients. Her mind made up, she closed the spell book and picked up a basket. She might not be able to perform complex magic yet, but it was no reason to be unprepared when her strength did return. She banished the notion that it might not ever return out of her mind as she closed the storage room door behind her.

As she exited the cellar, she met Jean-Paul in the courtyard as he brought the plow horse in from churning the soil between the vine rows. She didn't need to see his face to know he was angry. His aura blazed to rival the setting sun.

"What is it?" she asked. "Has something happened?"

"This," he said, reaching into a bag he'd slung on the side of the horse. He produced one of her witch bottles caked with mud. "Care to tell me what this is for?"

Lie or tell the truth? She didn't expect to be torn over which was the right way to answer. "It's to protect the roots." *There, not a lie.*

"Oh? And does it contain some sort of slow-release fertilizer I've never heard of?" He opened it and gave it a sniff, though he was obviously mocking her now. He tipped the bottle and poured the contents out at her feet. The wine and strands of hair splashed on the cobblestones. "I specifically said I wouldn't tolerate this sort of nonsense."

Nonsense?

How to tell him that the vines on the crown of the hill had been exposed to a spell encouraging black fungus and wouldn't survive the summer if those bottles were not kept in the ground? "It's an old custom," she said, choosing the lie after he'd splattered her skirt with the remnants of her wasted work. "Joseph Gardin would never face a growing season without first paying homage to the earth, sky, sun, and water. Every grower knows that the hope for a good crop begins with humility. It's like an offering to the gods of wine. Harmless, but hardly nonsense."

His eyes narrowed at the mention of Grand-Père, the look of a man zeroing in on knowledge he wanted for himself. His respect for the old vigneron ran deeper than she'd first thought. And though she didn't regret the lie—he'd just undone a day's worth of work, after all—she did regret she couldn't be candid with him about someone he obviously admired.

Joseph Gardin, as everyone knew, had been the best vine witch ever to work in the valley.

She waited for the lingering influence of her wish to strum through his heart until his posture relented.

"On second thought I suppose it was just a bottle of wine," he said, backing down. "I can appreciate the symbolism in the gesture. Even a modernist like myself has a soft spot for the old Romantics and their reverence for nature. We'll toast Monsieur Gardin at dinner tonight to make amends for spoiling the custom."

"I'm sure he would appreciate that. Until then I'm off to gather a few supplies for a project I'm working on." She swung the basket in her hand for emphasis.

Jean-Paul glanced up at the darkening sky. "Will you be all right walking by yourself?"

His genuine concern for her safety disarmed her. Odd how he could win her over in the most unpredictable moments. "I'll be fine," she said and even managed a smile. "I'll return before dark."

"Maybe I should accompany you."

To see the worried expression on his face, as if she were a mere defenseless mortal in a dangerous world, made her almost sorry she'd had to use the wishing string on him. He wasn't truly bewitched, but he wasn't capable of seeing her for what she was, either—a witch who experimented with poison in her spare time so she could kill the former lover who'd betrayed her.

"No, that won't be necessary," she said and then saw he'd taken her answer as a rejection. "But perhaps next time?"

"Of course. Well, I'll leave a lamp burning for you in the courtyard." With nothing left to say, he shoved the witch bottle back in the bag and led the horse toward the stable.

Elena tucked her basket in the crook of her elbow and headed out the gate, wondering why she'd said that last thing. She had no reason to spare his feelings. Did she?

For someone who didn't approve of spellcraft, this handsome mortal was very good at the charm business.

CHAPTER NINE

Jean-Paul had not lived with a woman for three years, not since his fledgling marriage had been allowed to fall apart under the new secular law. Now he lived with two. Yet when he'd first bought Château Renard and invited Ariella Gardin to continue on at the estate, the arrangement had felt little different than sharing a home with an elderly aunt. They complained about the weather when it rained, gossiped about the neighbors when it didn't, and on Saturday evenings he endured her gentle teasing about being a bachelor as they ate their supper together in the kitchen with a glass of red wine from the cellar. Sometimes he'd wished he'd had the house to himself, of course, but most days he was happy for the company. With two women now coming and going in the house, there were days he barely knew how to navigate the hallways without feeling like a guest who'd overstayed his welcome.

From the first night, the Boureanu woman had slipped off to sleep in the cellar workroom—the room Madame had long claimed was a storage room full of useless broken equipment. During the day she came and went inside the main house as if she owned the place, but at night she always retreated to the workroom. Peculiar for a woman to want to sleep in such spartan surroundings on her own, but on reflection everything she did was slightly strange.

His curiosity had, of course, boiled over. While she and Madame went to finish pruning the old vines Monsieur Gardin had planted, he had tried the door to her room. He'd found it locked, as usual, and for a moment considered breaking the door down. He gave it a hard shove with his shoulder, testing, but the solid oak door might as well have been a tree still rooted in the ground.

He swore the house hummed with her energy. Even now, as she sat at the dining room table with Madame, a pile of charts and maps spread out under the light of a work lamp, a wave of static electricity skittered along the hairs on his arm. He never quite knew what to make of the phenomenon. Or of her. She completely disarmed him, and yet not in the way a woman normally did. Despite Madame Gardin's chiding, he had courted a few women from the village. He wasn't shy around a woman if he was touched by desire. He would charm her with witty compliments, smile and take her to dinner, and more often than not accept an invitation to her bed. But this was something different. Despite the awkward revelation that he found Elena oddly attractive—and not because some woman who baked sweets for a living claimed to know his taste in lovers—he'd fought the impulse to act. He likened it to obeying the same instinct that warned one not to pick up a scorpion by the tail. Her allure held hints of danger, which, if he were honest with himself, was part of the attraction, but the reasonable side of his brain knew better from experience. And for the better part of four months now, he'd resisted the temptation.

"Is there something you wanted?" Elena asked, looking up at him with her feline eyes. "You've been staring for five minutes."

"Was I?" Knowing he had, he took a step toward the table. "I was just curious about the calculations. Is that an astrolabe?"

She paused before responding. "I'm helping Grand-Mère work out the cycles of the moon and planets so we can know the best days for planting and harvesting in the growing season."

"You mean like an almanac? Don't be ridiculous. I can send away for one easily enough."

The older woman exchanged a look with the younger one. "Yes, those farmer's almanacs are handy to consult for some things," Madame said. "But this one will be a little more detailed. I would have made one for you years ago, but without Elena's help I could never sort out all the intricacies with my failed . . . um, eyesight."

Odd. He'd never heard Madame complain about her eyes before. He leaned in closer to examine their notes. His brows tightened as he read a few of the entries:

- New vines are best planted when the moon, Jupiter, and Venus are in conjunction at 45 degrees.

- Mix sheep's bone and charred beetles into soil two weeks after the last frost on the twenty-second day of April.

- Pinch back leaves when first lacewings appear on the last day of May.

Jean-Paul scratched at the static electricity sparking against the back of his neck, wondering why anyone would believe the stars dictated the daily business of humans on earth. He was disappointed to see them cling to their superstitious beliefs, especially two such intelligent, talented women. Country folk were often stubbornly behind the times, he knew, but one day in the near future he was going to drag the vineyard into the new century. Perhaps even invest in a hydraulic-powered winepress. But for now, he sat in his favorite chair and buried his face in *Le Temps*.

He'd just begun reading an article about demonstrators in the city decrying the number of public executions when a gust of wind slammed against the house, whistling through the cracks in the doors and shimmying the windows. The women's heads lifted in alarm when their papers rustled on the table. "A north wind at the south door," Elena said to the old woman with a note of concern.

Madame, showing the same worry, got up to peek out the window. The rattle of metal and hissing steam clamoring down the road followed. She craned her neck to get a better view, then backed away in alarm. "It's Bastien in that confounded contraption of his. And he's got *her* with him. What will you do?"

"It's too soon," Elena said in a panic. "I'm not ready."

Jean-Paul didn't miss the unspoken communication that also boomeranged between the women. Then Madame did that strange thing she does when she gets nervous, rubbing her thumb and fingers together as if tasting the air with her touch, while Elena mumbled a few foreign-sounding words and doused the work lamp. A trail of smoke snaked over the table, concentrating in the place where she'd just been sitting. It appeared to make a perfect outline of the shape of her body before dissipating.

Jean-Paul stood and folded his newspaper. "Du Monde? What would bring him here unannounced?"

Elena collected her charts and pens and, with arms full, reminded him about their agreement. "I'm not here, remember?" He gave a distracted nod on his way to the door, recalling her outrage when she'd heard Du Monde had once tried to buy the vineyard. He nodded more firmly, and she escaped up the stairs at the back of the house.

Moments later, a black automobile, its front end sloped like the nose of a goose, chugged into the courtyard. White smoke billowed from the engine as the automobile rattled to a stop in front of the door. Madame "hmphed" from behind the window as Du Monde stepped out, waving his hat at a cloud of angry steam. His passenger smoothed a strand of blonde hair back in place under her fur-trimmed black hat as she waited expectantly for her door to be opened. After a troubled glance at the engine, Du Monde did just that, walking around to the other side of the vehicle to take his wife's hand. She stepped out of the automobile and shook out her black damask coat with the matching fur trim. Of all the women in the village, she was the only one who might shrug off the rural life at a moment's notice and slip into a fashionable city salon. As if expecting an audience, she strode up to the house, an obsidian-and-silver walking stick held in her grip like a scepter. Jean-Paul wiped his palms against his trousers and opened the door to greet the couple.

"Welcome. To what do I owe this unexpected surprise?" he said, meeting the pair in the courtyard.

Du Monde removed his hat. "You must excuse the intrusion, Monsieur Martel. I'm not sure what happened. One minute the damn thing was running smooth as a kitten, the next it's fuming like an alley cat trapped in a rubbish bin."

Jean-Paul shook his hand when offered. Though not strangers—they had twice been introduced at a meeting of the village wine council—it would not be accurate to say they were friendly or even on a first-name basis. But one thing they shared was an appetite for the roaring age of new technology. Automobiles, to be precise. Not the wind-up steam confound-its of his father's day. No, these new engines could rev up to sixty-five miles per hour. This very model had won the Grand Prix three years earlier doing precisely that. Bastien, who had been there to witness the race, had relayed the excitement of the final lap over cigars and glasses of port at their last council meeting. Jean-Paul was rightfully envious. In his old life he, too, would have been there to see it.

With a sigh he greeted Madame du Monde more formally and then took an appreciative walk around the vehicle to get a glimpse of the engine. "They'd just added the electric headlamps when I left the city. Must be a dream to drive."

"It never met a rut in the road it couldn't stay away from," Gerda du Monde said, peeling her gloves off in anticipation of being invited inside. "Honestly, they're little improvement over the pleasant Sunday pace of a double-team and carriage, if you ask me."

He resisted the urge to argue. "I'm sure it's just overheated. Please come in and sit while she cools down."

"My wife or the car?" Du Monde guffawed at his own joke and then ducked a chastising slap from his wife's gloves.

Jean-Paul extended a hand toward the front door and escorted the couple inside to where Madame waited. The old woman stood as if poised for battle, though he hoped there wouldn't be a confrontation. He rather liked Du Monde, or at least admired all that he'd accomplished.

"Welcome—do come in," she said, though her smile appeared forced against the sagging lines in her face.

Gerda du Monde offered her hand. "The esteemed Madame Gardin. A pleasure to meet again."

The women shook hands. As far as he knew this was the first time Gerda du Monde had come to the house, yet something familiar traveled between the women. He saw it in their eyes, their body language. Daring. Defiance. Respect. When their hands parted, Madame rubbed her thumb and fingers together at her side before excusing herself to prepare some refreshments for their guests.

Jean-Paul led the couple into his sitting room, where the whiff of kerosene smoke lingered in the air. Gerda inspected the space with keen eyes that searched from the coved ceiling to the fringe on the oriental rugs. Her hand trailed over the chair where Elena had been sitting moments before. She drummed her fingers three times before returning to her husband's side.

"You keep a lovely home," she said. "There's evidence of a woman's touch. Not a bad thing for a single man."

He motioned to the padded leather chairs near the fire. "Most of the furnishings are Madame's. I didn't bring much with me when I left the city," he said, taking a seat on the flowery upholstered sofa.

"It's just the two of you in the house?"

He pinched the seam in his trousers, straightening the fabric as he crossed his legs. "Yes," he said, avoiding her eye.

Her stare trapped him in his seat so that he could not move. He feared any twitch might reveal the lie. He didn't know why he owed Elena such loyalty, but he'd given his word and he meant to keep it. Especially after he'd seen the fear creep over her face when she understood who was coming to the front door. He quickly changed the subject.

"So what new surprise will Domaine du Monde have for us this season?"

"We're aging a fine blended red," Du Monde said, eager to brag after the compliment. "One of our best. Gerda's full talent is truly on display with this barrel. It will be our entry at le Concours des Vins, I am almost certain."

"Ah, of course. No doubt another grand champion wine. You do the valley proud."

Du Monde tilted his head in obvious feigned modesty and squeezed his wife's hand. "We've done well together." Then, likely realizing he was not in a position to offer a similar compliment, commented where he could. "Er, I noticed as we drove up that you'd dug out half an acre of chardonnay on the north end of the property. Those were new, weren't they?"

"Rot." He gave a small shrug. "Seems to affect one patch or another each year."

"Madame Gardin doesn't have a cure for it?" Gerda inquired, apparently perplexed.

"A cure?"

"For the roots. Any working vine witch ought to have the counterspell. It's all part of the game, isn't it?"

He blinked back at her. "Game, madame?"

"Oh, come now. Everyone does it. A little jinx here and there to keep the competition on their toes. I myself had to rid three acres of aphids in January, if you can believe it. Perhaps you've found a new vine witch to work the property. Someone who can take care of it?"

Jean-Paul had no immediate response. His good manners fought against his intellect's desire to put the irrational woman straight on the matter. But he was getting better at holding his tongue. He understood he was the outsider. A man from the city, with city ways and city thoughts he must keep to himself to get along in the country. "I'm afraid we run a simple winery here."

Du Monde put a hand on his wife's arm. "Come now, *ma petite*. You know Madame is retired now. Monsieur Martel is dedicated to working the vineyard on his own terms. He's a man of science. He even believes he can measure the precise moment when the sugar in the grape is at its peak."

"But of course he can."

"Yes, but he tests it by reading the color on a piece of paper."

Gerda scrunched her nose at her husband. "Is it a form of scrying? I've never heard of it before."

"It's not magic, it's a . . . what do you call it?"

"It's called a pH test, a way to measure the acidity in the grape to determine the best time to harvest."

"Ach, quatsch," she said, her native language bleeding through. "What does science have to do with wine? The only way to know if a grape has reached its proper ripeness is to taste it, feel the juice run in the mouth, grind the bitter skin between the teeth, check the color of the seeds. After that it's a matter of intuition. There's only so much vine work Mother Nature can bear without the assistance of a witch. We're the midwives of good wine, from conception to delivery."

Jean-Paul was just forming a retort in his mouth when Madame returned carrying a bottle of wine from the cellar. He held back his remark and then shrank a little inside, worried she might offer his most recent vintage out of some misguided sense of vineyard hospitality. He knew it was an inferior wine unfit for the palate of the great vigneron of Domaine du Monde. Madame uncorked the bottle, a sly smile forming in the corners of her mouth. He understood the old woman's stubborn pride in thinking Château Renard was still one of the great vineyards in the valley, but he appreciated the enormous gap that stretched between his best effort so far and that of the man sitting across from him. And yet, as Madame well knew, etiquette demanded he offer Renard wine to his guests, so he must swallow his sour grapes with humility.

And then he recognized the faded label on the bottle.

She poured the garnet drink into crystal glasses, and he sat up a little straighter. The wine danced and sparkled in the glass as it passed from host to guest in front of the lamplight. Gerda accepted the wine graciously, a slight wrinkle forming between her brows. It deepened when her nose passed over the top of the offering. She gave the wine a swirl, and Jean-Paul knew if there was ever magic in the world it was in that glass of perfectly blended seven-year-old pinot noir. Madame knew it, too, as her perceptive eyes watched for the reaction.

Gerda took the wine into her mouth. Her cheeks hollowed slightly as her tongue slid back and forth, tasting. An average customer sipping the wine for the first time would commonly raise his brows in surprise at this point and remark about its uncommon smoothness. A connoisseur would sniff and then describe the robust and complicated layers of velvety plums, smoke, and currants on the tongue. But the self-proclaimed vine witch said nothing. Not in words anyway. Yet her face betrayed that first moment of insecurity one feels when they know they've been outdone. If she could have spit it out, he believed she would have spewed the contents on the rug. She swallowed instead, as if it were a tadpole in her mouth rather than one of the finest wines ever produced in the valley. He was witnessing the taste of envy.

Du Monde, on the other hand, approached his wine as a man forced to take his medicine. But as he swallowed, his tongue most certainly pressing against the soft palate in his mouth to be sure of what it had just tasted, he sheepishly avoided looking at his wife, as if he'd just been caught kissing another woman. He did, however, glance at Madame, who confirmed his suspicions with the slight upward flick of her eyebrow.

"One of Château Renard's finest vintages, madame." Du Monde raised his glass in a gesture of admiration. He took another sip, nodded approvingly, and then set his glass down. "Thank you for serving this particular wine. In truth, it makes what I'm about to propose even more significant."

Madame straightened, holding her head at a tilt. Jean-Paul, too, tensed slightly, drawn in by the curious phrasing.

"Monsieur Martel, as I'm sure you are aware, I am a businessman as well as a winemaker." He paused to formulate his next words. "Perhaps providence stranded me outside your door today. You see, I remember this vintage distinctly. It bested my first solo entry in le Concours des Vins. That was the first time I understood what it meant to create something truly magnificent and have the world take notice. And, if I may be brutally honest, it may have been the last time Château Renard produced such an exquisite vintage."

"Bastien . . ." The word came out as a growl of warning in Madame's throat.

"Monsieur Martel, you are a lawyer by trade, if I'm not mistaken. A man who understands the art of negotiation."

"Please, call me Jean-Paul."

"Of course. Now that we have shared wine, we can be direct with one another. You have been in the wine business for three years, have you not? And in that time you have had, shall we say, three years of disappointing harvests." Du Monde gave a slight shrug of his shoulders. "Surely we can agree it is not a forgiving trade for the novice."

Jean-Paul squirmed in his chair, wishing to defend his efforts at the vineyard but knowing in his heart the man across from him was telling the truth. He only wished the wife didn't stare at him so intently. He swore he could feel her thoughts pressing in on his own.

"And," Du Monde continued, "I have it on good authority there is a law firm in the city that would eagerly like to see the return of one of its brightest associates." He paused to see if his compliment had landed. It had. "So, given the balance of one against the other, I have a proposition for you."

Du Monde finished delivering his proposal, and the room went silent except for the sound of Madame's glass hitting the table.

CHAPTER TEN

Elena crept up the stairs mindful of every creak underfoot. She hadn't been in the attic since her return, but it was the farthest away she could get from the others without climbing on the roof. She opened the door, and the stagnant air swirled as if for the first time in years. Only a few bars of weak light filtered in through the vents under the eaves, giving the space an abandoned feel. The odor of wet wood met her as she pressed a hand against the exposed ribs of the angled ceiling to avoid hitting her head. A leak in the roof tiles perhaps. There was little money to spare for house repairs, but it was beyond her talents to stitch rotten wood back together. She set her star chart and astrolabe down atop a discarded chair and made a mental note to discuss it with Jean-Paul once the intruders had gone.

Sweeping a cobweb from her forehead, she cursed Bastien for once again forcing her to squat in a dark and damp place she didn't want to be. Why would he show up at the house unannounced? She pressed her nose to the vent and peeked at the car with the nose like a mechanical goose still wheezing in the courtyard below. White steam billowed up, but there was something false about the way it wafted, as if crafted by illusion. The artifice made her think of her hasty smoke spell, and she worried it wouldn't be enough to rid the room of her aura's imprint. Bierhexen were like bloodhounds, able to sniff out the faintest hint of magic. Was that the reason Bastien had brought Gerda? Elena's heart pulsed harder. Did he already suspect she'd returned to the château? How could he know? Unless Jean-Paul had betrayed her. Would he? The thought made her ill, and she sank onto an old trunk, where she sat with her head in her hand.

Below, the front door rattled shut. Muffled voices, smothered beneath two levels of house, echoed up between the walls, but the words disintegrated before she could make them out. And she couldn't very well use her second sight to listen in on a witch as sensitive to magic as a bierhexe. She'd be discovered in an instant. Resigned to her confinement, she stewed a few moments in idle thought, wondering if there was at least a spell she could conjure to drop a chandelier on Bastien's head. But even such thoughts were dangerous. The witch might easily pick up on the negative vibrations. No, she couldn't risk the discovery. Not yet.

Left alone, Elena shivered. It might not be a pond of black muck she found herself in this time, but the frost of betrayal felt eerily familiar. The curse had embedded a permanent chill in her skin that she couldn't shake off, even in a room as stifling as an attic. Not willing to suffer one more second because of that man, she knelt on the floor and flipped the lid open on the trunk to look for a moth-eaten shawl or old blanket she could use. Instead she found a chipped cup and saucer wrapped in paper, a stack of old wine labels tied up with string, and a pair of candlesticks with two malformed candles that had softened in storage. Seeing the wicks were still intact, she brought them out and set them on the floor. She risked a quick snap of her fingers to light them, then rubbed her hands over the heat of the flames before sorting through the items again.

The trunk was full of Grand-Mère's personal items—objects boxed up and put in storage to make room for the château's new owner. She felt a tinge of guilt when she opened a book and discovered old photos of Grand-Mère and Joseph in intimate poses of early love. Arms around necks, lips pressed to cheeks, smiles shining on one another as only true love can project. When guilt began to turn to envy, she replaced the photos between the pages and closed the book.

Pushing aside an old hatbox, she found a lace tablecloth with a wax stain that would do for a shawl. As she shook out the cloth, a colorful sheet of paper flew out. A handbill for a carnival. She wrapped the tablecloth around her shoulders, then tipped the paper to the candlelight to better see the details. Marked in bold red and gold ink, the advertisement promised exciting fire-eaters, knife-throwers, clowns and grotesques, and a woman who did somersaults on the back of a pony. And in small print at the bottom, beside the image of a mustached man in a striped turban, it highlighted the return of the "All-Seeing Fortuneteller to the Kings and Queens of the Continent."

It was an odd memento for Grand-Mère to hold on to. The old woman had never once taken her to a carnival as a child. And she'd done her share of begging when the acrobats and ponies showed up for that one precious week during the summer, as any child would. The oddity tugged at her instinct enough that she didn't replace the flyer in the trunk right away, reading it again for a clue as to why an elderly woman would stow it alongside her other keepsakes.

Two floors below, the voices grew more distinct. They'd moved to the main salon. Eager to know if she could hear more, Elena crept to the end of the attic where the chimney stood. The hollow interior, she discovered, made a remarkable conduit for sound. She closed her eyes and heard Jean-Paul direct his unannounced guests to sit in the leather chairs. They were directly below her in front of the fireplace. She pressed her ear full against the chimney and listened again. And then Bastien's unmistakable bravado rose up through the brick and mortar, his voice reverberating off her tightly coiled emotions.

As raw as the day he'd accused her of putting his needs second, his voice sent a shock wave of pain spiraling to her core. The man who'd stolen her life was sitting directly below her, bragging about his good harvest, his champion wine, and the unmatched talent of his vine witch.

His *wife*.

Like the building of any good spell, the pain began to churn inside her, mixing, binding, reforming. It stirred, waiting for her intent to hurl the flow of energy. Temptation warmed her fingertips. She could almost justify using the magic to harm him, but then the feeling fizzled. The heat subsided. The magic went damp inside her. The vigor gone.

The carnival flyer sat crumpled in her hand. She shook her head and asked the All Knowing for patience. It wasn't time yet. She wasn't ready. Revenge would come as sweet as honeysuckle on the tongue when the moment was right. Until then, Bastien would have no hold over her. She would not allow it.

She took a deep breath and leaned forward. With her ear to the bricks she clearly overheard a woman speaking about the ripeness of grapes. The bierhexe. Grudgingly, she agreed with the witch's observations on midwifery.

Then the voices quieted. The pause felt too long, too awkward for conversation. Grand-Mère must have brought out the wine. Yes, that was it. They were tasting. Swallowing. Forming critiques on their tongues. But what had Grand-Mère served? Certainly she wouldn't pour them any of the swill Jean-Paul had produced. The man had good intentions, but his efforts were pitiful. The thought made her cringe with embarrassment for the château. But then she felt it, a tingle at the base of her neck, a finger-light frisson that spread along her hairline. It was something she only felt when someone tasted her wine in her presence.

"Oh, Grand-Mère, you didn't," she whispered, though she smiled as she said it, remembering the last vintage she'd bottled. The grapes had been exquisite. Some said it was better than Grand-Père's champion red.

Eager to hear their reaction, she wrapped the tablecloth tight around her shoulders and pressed her ear even tighter against the brickwork. Her thumbnail firmly embedded between her teeth in anticipation, she listened and smiled with pride. Not a word out of the bierhexe. No criticism or praise, merely the reward of silent envy. It would have been enough to know it vexed her, but then Bastien spoke. His words were full of admiration. Praise. Humility. It confused her. Had she misheard? Misjudged him? Was it even possible? She missed what he said next, but then Grand-Mère cautioned him with a verbal warning in the form of his name. What look did he have in his eye to make her wary?

Oh, but it wasn't the look in his eye. It was the greed in his heart. His hunger to own and control everything. She could feel it coming. His sweet, luring words were nothing but vinegar in disguise. His aim in visiting, the reason the car had conveniently broken down—it was all done so he could turn out his pockets before a vulnerable Jean-Paul and negotiate for the one thing he'd always coveted. He wanted to own Château Renard.

The proposition struck like a match to the wadding keeping her anger under wraps. Her temper caught and flared until she could no longer control it.

With the tablecloth still wrapped around her shoulders, she climbed the ladder out of the attic and ran down the stairs, her heart pounding with fear, but determination too. What weak magic she commanded she used to shore up her confidence. Her hair flew back from her face as she stormed into the salon to confront Bastien and tell him Château Renard was not for sale. Not to him. Not ever. Not as long as she lived and breathed.

But he was gone. The room was empty except for the scent of lilacs that trailed behind the woman. Outside, the automobile started up on the first try. Elena flew to the window in time to see the couple chug down the road as the light faded from the sky.

With nowhere to hurl her swelling anger, her magic found the nearest inanimate object, shattering the half-empty bottle of wine on the table in front of Jean-Paul.

CHAPTER ELEVEN

He'd seen champagne bottles burst spontaneously before but never a wine bottle. And not one that was nearly empty. There must have been a flaw in the glass. A crack. Or perhaps the atmospheric pressure had dropped too quickly.

Jean-Paul had also seen Elena fly off in anger before, but she looked near deranged as she stood at the window, wrapped in a tablecloth, her fist banging against the glass as Du Monde drove off. No consolation would allow her to believe the man had graciously left so that his offer might be given proper consideration without further unnecessary pressure.

Then she turned on him.

"You cannot sell Château Renard to that man. I won't allow it."

He bent to collect the shards of glass. "*You* won't allow it?" Du Monde's offer had, in fact, rankled his pride, and he was in no mood for an argument with a woman over business. "It's no longer your place to decide such a thing," he said and hoped that would be the end of it.

Elena shot across the room and scooped up the glass with her bare hands. "Oh, but it is my place." She muttered some child's verse under her breath, then tossed the broken pieces of glass into the fire. "And this vineyard is not for sale," she countered. "Not to that man, not to anyone."

Too late, Grand-Mère raised her hand to stop Elena.

The glass fizzled and turned to smoke in the flames, as if it weren't glass at all. More evidence there was something inferior about how it was made, he decided. And also evidence there was something wrong with this woman. Who disposes of broken glass in a fireplace?

"I don't know what to make of you," he said, finding the will for a fight after all. "You turn up on my doorstep dressed in rags after being gone for years, yet claim the château is the only home you know. You ask me to keep your presence here a secret, presumably from the man you just ran away and hid from, and yet you storm down the stairs to confront him the moment he shows up on the doorstep." He took a step toward her. "Do you play me for a fool?"

Elena narrowed her eyes at him. "I realize you're limited in what you can see and understand—"

"Oh, yes, by all means insult me too."

"But I am as much a part of this vineyard as the vines themselves. I do have a say."

He picked up his glass of wine. "Do you know why a man like Du Monde wants to buy Château Renard? For the terroir. To own grapes grown in soil capable of creating something this divine. It's also why I bought the vineyard. Here, taste it. See what a *real* vigneron is capable of creating with this plot of soil."

"I don't need to taste it."

He swallowed the wine after she refused, savoring the sensuous aftertaste, until the inevitable feeling of defeat followed. "But the grapes won't yield," he said. "Not for me. I don't know how to re-create this. I don't know if anyone can. So, yes, there are days I'm tempted to sell and admit I'm no winemaker. Maybe that time has come, but it's for me to decide, not you."

"*I* can do it."

He looked her up and down full of doubt as she stood wrapped in an old tablecloth with a candle wax stain on it. "Yes, you're supposed to know all the old master's secrets. I'm sorry, Elena, but your bold promises are beginning to wear thin."

"Your problem isn't a lack of knowledge. Or bad luck. Or even bad weather." She picked up the fireplace tongs and sorted through the ash in the fire. "It's a lack of vision," she said and fished out a perfectly round piece of melted glass. A lens, really.

Madame spoke up from her chair. "Elena, are you sure you want to do this?"

"He needs to know the truth."

"What truth?"

She blew on the glass, then dropped the lens from the tongs into her hand. It should have burned her skin, but she didn't even flinch. "If you are serious about wanting to make wine this good again," she said, flipping the piece of glass in her palm, "follow me and I'll show you."

There was a new assurance about her, as if she'd been hiding before and only now stepped into her true skin. Her confidence lured him outside as he followed her to the vine rows south of the house.

She shrugged the tablecloth tighter around her shoulders and nudged her chin toward the field. "Look out there and tell me what you see."

Dew saturated the evening air, settling as glossy droplets on the budding vines. He sighed as he pulled his collar up against the mist. "I see vines starting to leaf out. Acres of work yet to be done. And potential. Always potential for the next harvest."

Her eyes relaxed, though she kept the rest of her face controlled. "Yes," she said. "And yet there is so much more. Hold this to your eye and take my hand."

He checked over his shoulder to see if Madame was watching them. "Is this really necessary?"

"It's the only way I know how to show you."

"Show me what?"

"Everything," she answered and extended her hand.

Reluctantly he locked his fingers with hers. Her cold skin repelled him at first, but she held on tight, as if she would not let this moment out of her grasp. With her other hand she gripped the ancient vine in front of her, then mumbled a few words of nonsense while pretending to go into a trance. He knew then he'd been a fool. He should never have followed her outside. Should never have come to the country to work with these backward, superstitious people in the first place. Maybe Du Monde was right. Maybe he did belong in the city with his books and ledgers and blessed logic. The admission sobered him. He held the woman's hand, opting to appease her long enough to avoid further confrontation, but then he was going inside to get drunk and give serious consideration to an asking price for the vineyard.

God, she really was beautiful, though. It was almost as if her skin shimmered in the mist.

Her eyes opened. "Don't watch me. Use the lens to look at the field."

He hadn't realized he'd been staring. "What is it I'm supposed to see exactly?" But as he held the glass to his eye, the change became evident.

An iridescent fog hovered over the vineyard, glimmering to rival the northern lights. On the hillside, moisture clung in a crisscross pattern like a giant net suspended above the vines, while blue sparks skittered along the ground. "What is this, some kind of trick?" He lowered the lens to examine it, wondering how she'd made a kaleidoscope out of a melted shard of glass.

"The spectral cloud hanging over the acreage nearest the château is some sort of sun-blocking spell meant to promote mildew. I imagine you lost some grapes last fall to fungus, yes?"

"We had to hand sort the entire acre to salvage what we could."

"I'm working on a counterspell, but a reverse curse is complicating things. Unfortunately it's had years to morph without interference. I'm still tracing its origin."

"Reverse curse?"

"Yes, and the other effects you see . . ." She nudged him to raise the glass to his eye again. "I still have to counter the jinx on the hill and the static in the soil. And then there's that fellow. There, see him? Sitting on the stump in the middle of the row. We have a gargoyle living among the old vines, the ones Monsieur Gardin planted for Grand-Mère's birthday. The wine you poured tonight came from those vines. It was the last vintage I brought into the world before I . . . went away."

He pressed his eye closer to the glass. "How are you doing this?"

"I'm merely showing you what I see every day."

He tested the vision several times with and without the glass. A beast with leathery wings and pointed ears opened its eyes and shifted on its feet before yawning. "This can't be happening."

"So disrespectful, I know. This one appears to be harmless at the moment. But I'm guessing as soon as the grapes are ready to be harvested, it's his job to piss on the clusters as they go into the baskets so they'll be sour for the press. That is, if I don't find a way to banish him first. I'm sorry—he should have been dealt with years ago, but Grand-Mère hasn't been able to keep up by herself."

The gargoyle twisted his face around to sneer at them before tucking his head under his wing to go back to sleep.

Jean-Paul dropped the lens and crossed himself. "This isn't possible. I'm drunk on spoiled wine. Or . . . or out of my mind with fever."

"I assure you you're not. It's merely magic. Or, if you prefer one of your scientific terms, you're getting a glimpse of what's found at the end of the spectrum, outside the range of what your mortal eye can see."

"No, this can't be happening." He jerked his hand loose of hers, and the vineyard appeared as it always had. He rubbed his eyes and looked again to make sure. But still he doubted his sanity.

"I'm a vine witch, Monsieur Martel. Château Renard's vine witch specifically. And while you've been operating under the impression that bad weather and worse luck have been conspiring to hurt your vintages, I'm sorry to say it's mostly been ignorance combined with an abundance of sabotage due to my prolonged absence. Grand-Mère's spectral vision just isn't what it used to be."

"Madame is . . . ?" Jean-Paul's thoughts swam in drunken circles inside his skull. "No, it's all just superstition. How can any of this be real?"

She gestured to the sky with eyes cast up. "How can it not?"

His feet seemed to float beneath him. He worried his knees might buckle in front of this woman. He needed a drink. He needed a priest. God almighty, he had to be rid of her. Without another word he turned on his heel and returned to the house, slamming the door and shutting out the world behind him.

CHAPTER TWELVE

The cellar felt tolerably warm after standing outside in the cold spring air for so long. Elena threw off the ridiculous tablecloth and lit three fat candles, enough to give her strong light to read by. She hadn't followed him to the house. He was angry. Scared. He needed time alone to wrestle with his doubt. She'd expected that. What she hadn't anticipated was her own need to huddle in a safe space. The spell to alter the broken wine bottle in the fire had depleted her energy, yes, but at the same time something fervent swam in her humors.

His hand.

The heat from his skin still tingled on her palm. She'd felt a tiny flame of magic ignite inside her at his touch. Her heart ticked faster thinking about the spark. Her blood was still more water than fire, but for the first time since she'd awoken from the curse her power flowed toward healing. Despite her doubt, a full recovery might be possible. But how was it possible?

She flipped through her grimoire, ignoring the book's incessant sighs and riffling pages suggesting she read up on love potions. Instead, she stopped on a passage explaining the static transfer of electricity from one body to another. Could that truly be all it took to revive a cursed soul? A little body heat? And what about the change she'd noticed in the vine itself? The deep melancholia she'd discovered the night she returned had felt like an anchor tugging her to the bottom of a black sea. But moments ago, with the first leaves ready to unfold, she'd detected a subtle shift, its mood no longer cloaked in gloom. More than the normal tilt toward spring that always swung on the hinge of hope, this change had coincided with the one inside her. But what particle of unseen fate had brought the change?

Lacking any clear answer, Elena turned again to the study of poison. A paragraph on the slow and painful death caused by ingesting castor beans proved so fascinating, she almost didn't register the clattering of horse hooves across the cobblestones. So he'd left. At a gallop. He was more frightened by the revelation than she'd realized, but she'd best not intervene. He'd have to come out of it on his own terms. Closing him out of her thoughts, she turned her full focus on the spell book. If her strength truly was returning, she could begin distilling the poison. Eyes skimming over the complicated steps she would have to perform, she studied every ingredient and subtlety of the concoction until ribbons of misshapen candle wax pooled on the workbench.

And still he hadn't returned.

She stared again at her palm. The sensation of his touch hadn't subsided. If anything, it grew as she thought about Jean-Paul again. He was stubborn and prideful, but not so much that it closed him off from accepting the truth about her. He'd circle around in time. But where could he be? She cared more than she wished to admit, but knowing he'd come home when he was ready, she snuffed the wicks and went to bed, as startled by what had transpired between them as he must be.

In the morning she retrieved the milk bottles off the back step and carried them inside to Grand-Mère. The kitchen, normally abuzz with prework bustle while Jean-Paul finished his breakfast and read his *Le*

Temps, was quiet as a funeral. The man's chair sat empty, and his work boots slouched unworn near the door. He hadn't come home.

"You knew he was a nonbeliever." There was no accusation in Grand-Mère's tone; she merely stated the obvious as she entered the kitchen still tying her apron. "It's a lot to accept for a man with strong convictions of his own. How do you want your eggs?"

"We might have lost the vineyard to Bastien if I hadn't told him. Besides, we're past bud break. The fruit will be setting on the vine soon. I have to be able to do my spells in the open if I'm ever going to rid the place of that woman's hexwork."

Grand-Mère waved a hand, dismissing the idea. "That man wants to make wine. *Good* wine. He doesn't want to sell. At least he didn't before he learned the place was overrun with witches." The old woman shrugged. "And anyway, it's already lost to me. And you."

"You shouldn't talk like that."

"Why not? It's true."

Elena puffed air out from her cheeks and pushed her empty plate aside. The vineyard couldn't be lost. It just couldn't.

Hours later, with one eye constantly watching the road, she and Grand-Mère attended to the chores. She prodded the plow horse out between the vines to finish churning up the rocky soil and loosen the year's compaction. The earth had to breathe again to encourage new growth. Were men any different?

After a midday meal of broth and bread, she ducked into the cellar to top off what the angels had stolen for their share from the barrels over the week and to test the progression of last year's wine. It was a chore she did not mind doing alone, though she'd grown accustomed to Jean-Paul's company and his close observation of her as she swished the wine in her mouth, tasting, sensing, and deciding best how to counter his missteps. His absence echoed in the stillness when, certain the plum undertones would never mature in the barrel, she thought to ask him what moon phase he'd harvested in. He wouldn't have known the answer, but she enjoyed watching his face struggle with the logic of her questions. Of course, now she could explain the importance of the moon's tug on the grape skin for rounding out the full flavors just before picking. If only he were there.

But by late afternoon, it was clear either the man's fear or his ego wouldn't allow him to come home. She went to the cellar and dug out the burlap sack she'd stuffed behind the back barrels. She thought she'd rid herself of any need for the goatherd's clothes again, but now she was thankful she'd stashed them instead of burning the garments with the rest of the rubbish. Taking the bundle with her, she returned to her room and changed into the stiff woolen skirt and blouse. She slipped her feet into a pair of clumsy sabots and tied a red scarf on her head. She'd given the clothes a rinse in lavender water before tying them up in the burlap sack, but it only added a flowery stench to the lingering odor of dung.

Pleased, however, with the effect of the clothes as a disguise, she retrieved her bolline—the work knife she used to cut herbs—and tucked it in the leather belt she'd added. She picked up the threadbare cloak and then tapped on the kitchen door.

"I'm going to the village to find him," she announced, slipping the cloak on over the ragged skirt. "He can't stay afraid of the truth forever."

"You'd be surprised what a stubborn man is capable of." Grand-Mère looked her up and down and frowned. "Why on earth have you put those rags on again?"

"I don't want anyone to recognize me yet."

"Well, I'll wish you luck. Though, if you ask me, wearing that pretty blue dress of yours would be more potent than magic to lure the man back home."

An hour later Elena stood on the road overlooking the village, rubbing her sore foot where the wooden sabot pinched the nub of her missing toe. From where she stood the town looked much the same as it always had. The abbey's bell tower rose above the tile roofs like a compass pointing at the sky, while at street level the cobbled stonework buildings bore the burnished patina of centuries of wear. But smaller changes disoriented her once she reached the main street. There had been a metalwork sign—a dragon with elaborate grape clusters draped about its neck—that hung over the door of the first shop after the bridge. A bit of whimsy, something from childhood she had always looked forward to seeing on her trips to the village. When very young she'd imagined the dragon winked back when she said hello, and once she mastered her magic, it actually did. But the sign was no longer there. Nor were the Aucoins who ran the shop inside.

Elena raised the hood on her cloak over her head and turned her face toward the empty shop glass as a man approached on the sidewalk. She didn't yet know what to expect from the village and its inhabitants. Would they recognize her? Would they wonder where she'd been? Would they even remember? The man, a banker as she recalled, didn't even tip his hat as he passed, presumably taking her for the goatherd she pretended to be. Confident of her disguise, she limped past him to the place where the road split—one fork bending uphill toward the respectable shops and businesses, the other descending to the more unsavory end of the village, where there were no streetlamps to chase away the shadows.

At the top of the hill she spied a gentleman's tavern. A man wanting to hide from the truth might spend a night and a day drinking in a place like that, she reasoned. Taking a deep breath, she opened the door and peered inside at the half-filled room ripe with the aroma of onions and garlic and sour beer. A handful of men in patch-worn corduroy jackets and dingy white shirts with tab collars loitered at the bar, smoking hand-rolled cigarettes and lifting warm glasses of beer to their mustached mouths. A few cocked their heads in her direction, but none let their eye linger for long. Not seeing Jean-Paul among them, she was forced to try the bistro, the general store, and the one small hotel, where she asked for him by name. But all shook their heads, saying he had not been in town for a week or more and, anyway, it was no business of a goatherd's what a gentleman like Jean-Paul Martel did with his time.

She had never felt more like a stranger. The disguise had done its job, but she'd had little need for the charade. So many faces were unfamiliar to her. Three new houses had been built on the hillside, a perfumery had opened where a flower shop used to be, and a wine merchant on the corner sold bottles from Domaine du Monde that advertised "tastings."

And then there was Pâtisserie d'Amour. She knew without entering that Tilda still ran the shop as its secret magic wafted out the door.

The smell of fresh-baked *pain au chocolat* hit her full in the face. The scent intoxicated, filling her with the same warmth she'd felt the night before. Temptation drifted under her nose, stirring a craving inside her like she'd never known. She yearned to taste the buttery sweetness in her mouth, feel the warm chocolate melt on her tongue, and lick the flaky crumbs from her lips. It frightened her how much she wanted to give in because she understood how the magic worked. Tilda's magic wasn't a love spell exactly, but if you caught a whiff of one of her confections and found the lure impossible to resist, it meant she'd tapped into your tastes and desires. But the craving only took hold if there was someone in your thoughts. Someone you were falling in love with. Someone basic and good and reliable, yet filled with surprising stubbornness.

Elena began to cross the street toward the shop, her will not her own, when a horse and wagon thundered past, forcing her to step back. That moment of disruption wrenched her loose from the spell, and she backed away from the pâtisserie. Covering her nose and mouth with the end of her cloak, she darted off the street and into the nearest refuge.

Elena shut the door to the post office behind her, thankful for the mundane scents of polished wood and paper dust. As she regained her bearings, she decided to question the postmaster. Perhaps Jean-Paul had stopped to check on his mail, and maybe he even mentioned where he was off to next. Two women stood in line to collect their letters, so she perused the notices on the wall while she waited. Curiously, she found it filled with several pleas for information on missing pets.

"There's been another one," the clerk said after the other women exited.

She turned, still holding her cloak over half her face. "Another?"

"Killing, that is. This one out near the Lambert place."

"Who's dead?"

The man looked up from his work to study her over the tops of his glasses. He straightened and blinked twice in sober appreciation. "Ah, you're not from around here." He removed his glasses and gestured broadly with them toward the notices on the wall. "The animal killings. Cats, dogs, rabbits, sometimes a fox turns up. Blood drained right out of them. Puts people on edge the way it's been escalating lately. People are starting to say they're ritual killings."

Horrified, Elena glanced at the notices on the wall with new appreciation. As she read, a shadow crossed her vision, nudging a dormant memory to the forefront. Gooseflesh rose on her skin as she recalled another of Grand-Mère's rhymes from childhood.

Toss crone's teeth and mystic rune
'neath Jupiter and crescent moon,
Cast your lot into the fire
Thou spinning heart of dark desire,
Bow before the one bedeviled
On cloven foot and fetlock beveled,
Pas de chat, around you go
Dance before the carrion crow,
Once you've done the *Danse Démon*
By blood and bone your fate is sewn

"Démon dansant," she whispered. But it was just a fable. A story to scare children. She shook her head to clear it of the frightening image before

approaching the counter. "I'm looking for Jean-Paul Martel. Have you seen him today?"

The man scratched his balding head with a pencil. "No, he hasn't been in for a few days. But if you're hoping to talk to him about offering your services at the vineyard, you'll have a tough time with that one. City man. Nonbeliever. The grapes suffer because of it, if you ask me."

"My services?"

The man slipped his glasses back on and smiled. "My mother worked at La Domaine Blanc as their vine witch for decades. I have her vision but, alas, not her talent with the wine." He shrugged, as if life worked out the way it was meant to in the end.

A faint purple aura peeked out of his shirt collar, confirming his heredity. Trusting he had a sympathetic ear, Elena tapped her finger on the counter and dared to dig deeper. "How long has the animal killing been going on?"

"There was only one poster on the wall when I arrived five years ago. Back then people occasionally mentioned they'd found a dead cat in the road on their way to the village. About a year ago it began happening more frequently. Now it's almost weekly. If you ask me, it's just college boys fooling around with the occult. But they'll find themselves on the brute end of karma's bad side one of these days. And when they do, they'll be lucky if they don't lose a few vital parts themselves."

University students? Possibly. They'd always flocked to the village on their summer breaks, accosting any woman in a fringed shawl to read their palm or sell them a love potion. Some, though, did go looking for more, like hex stones and evil talismans to use on their enemies. The sort of items a certain pair of witches liked to hawk out of the back of their mule cart. Her skin still prickling from a roused instinct, she thanked the clerk for his help and stepped back onto the street with no better idea of where to find Jean-Paul than when she'd started. How could no one have seen him? Unless he never came to the village after their fight.

Her mind tumbled over demons and dead cats as she turned left at the next street corner. A block later she turned left again, letting her feet lead her far from the center of the village to the low road, where the gutters fizzled into open sewers and dogs with matted fur slinked between overturned rubbish bins. The ugly business with the dead animals still nipped at the heels of her instincts as she walked past the barrel maker, farrier, and laundry shop at the end of the lane. At last she stood at the mouth of a desolate alley upwind of the last establishment in town. It meant something, all those killings. She felt it in her blood. And if Jean-Paul genuinely didn't wish to be found, then perhaps there was another way to salvage the trip to the village. After all, he wasn't the only missing person she was looking for.

The old building had barely changed in the years Elena had been gone. And probably hadn't in the two hundred years it had been standing. Or leaning, rather. The dilapidated tavern and flophouse known as Grimalkin & Paddock's had rightfully been kept at arm's length from the rest of the village. It was the sort of place most mortals never heard about. They didn't dare venture into the grubby dead-end street overrun with rats and sewage and transient witches.

These were not the sought-after vine witches who tended the vineyards and stirred the magic inside the grapes to encourage the wine. No, the spirit folk who limped through Grimalkin's existed on the fringes, dabbling in the junk arts like erectile potions, cures for warts, and penny jinxes to inflict a rival with a case of pink eye, which they hocked on the high street to the gullible on festival days. And occasionally there were witches who practiced the darkest shades of magic out of sight of the All Knowing's eye. Summoners of murder, whisperers of ambition in powerful men's ears, and perhaps conjurers of transmogrification curses.

Yellow gaslight gleamed inside the tavern. Yet even the glow had a dingy quality, diminished to a greasy haze from the buildup of smoke and grime on the windows. Elena emerged from the alley thankful she'd worn the old goatherd's clothes. On the main street the clothes had made her invisible among the well-heeled villagers, but here she'd be scrutinized with third-eye vision by the aura readers, psychics, and overly curious. The clerk's quick observation earlier had her dim her spectral glow to better match her appearance and mask her true identity long enough to ask a few anonymous questions.

The hinges on the enormous door screamed like a wounded man as she entered the tavern. She skirted the small crowd seated near the fire, keeping her head down. A few raised their noses, squinted their eyes at her, and then turned their attention back on their mugs when she proved unremarkable. Having passed the first test, she sat in an alcove built for two at the back of the room. A stub of candle fused to the center of the table flickered to life as a dangling cobweb floated above her head on an invisible wave of warm air. Nearly a dozen witch-folk huddled over meals of lumpy soup and frothy brew, despite the early evening hour. Though it was nearing dusk, many, she knew, were only beginning their day, as their work often called for the cover of darkness. She looked from face to face, hoping for a spark of recognition or a sense of déjà vu, but the only sense of the familiar she picked up on was a fellow vine witch, past her prime, seated in the corner. She sipped a glass of garnet wine, smacking her tongue as she tasted. Elena inhaled the whiff of cherries, black currants, and dark coffee. A Château Vermillion? No. The minerality was wrong. More likely it was one of Bastien's new labels. His scent was everywhere lately.

She'd just brushed the unwanted thought aside when a gray-haired woman with gray skin and pale-gray eyes approached her table with a quill and parchment in hand. Madame Grimalkin.

"What'll you have?"

The red wine tempted. "Gin . . . and information."

"Can you pay, *étranger*?"

Elena set three coins on the table. Madame Grimalkin nodded and slid the change into her apron pocket.

"The gin I can manage, but the information depends on what kind you're after."

"I'm looking for someone."

"Aren't we all?"

The gray woman held up two fingers to the rotund man polishing glasses behind the bar and called for the gin. She took the chair opposite, eyes squinting as if trying to decipher the aura around her newest customer. "You haven't been in here before—I'd know. Give me your palm."

Elena tried not to stare at the woman's gray teeth as she opened her hand on the table. It was all part of the ritual, of verifying her identity to see if she was who and what she claimed to be. She hoped the woman didn't read anything into the dampness that slicked the shallow crevice of her lifeline.

The woman made a soft rumbling noise in the back of her throat as her third eye probed the edges of Elena's thin disguise. She cradled Elena's hand in hers, dragging her fingernail over the open palm and tapping briefly on the lines for the heart, mind, and fate. After tilting her head one way and then the other, she looked up with an unnerving grin. "I'd say you know your way around poisons. And you're searching for the person who cursed you."

Elena shivered. Even she wasn't that good at palm reading. "How did you see that?"

The old woman let go of her hand and laughed. "That you've been working with poison? I can smell the bitter residue of freshly ground foxglove leaves on your fingertips. As for the curse, your hands are even colder than my husband's. That part never goes away, I'm afraid."

The bartender, widemouthed and slit eyed, waddled to the table with two shots of gin held on a tray. The old woman stroked his arm before he left, purring words of thank-you at him. "He's been living with cursed skin since before you were born. Never did catch up to the witch who done it. What makes you think you can find your special someone?"

"I heard a rumor there've been dead cats turning up on the roads. Could be someone trying their hand at blood magic."

The woman bristled at the mention of the cats. "It's a dark heart behind that business, and no question about it. Whoever's doing it turned their back on the covenants years ago."

Elena picked up her glass and swirled the gin until a blue arc of light ran through it. "Curses go against the covenants too. Could be the person who does one sort of dark magic might just as easily do the other." She leaned in, hoping not to be overheard. "The witch I'm looking for wears a long blue robe and carries a distinct pocket watch on a silver chain."

"Distinct how?"

"It's got a green dragon's eye with a yellow slit on the cover. She might work the high street on festival days reading cards for tourists, or sell potions out of the back of a wagon."

"Sounds like you're looking for one of the Charlatan clan."

She'd discounted the idea after meeting the sisters, thinking them too coarse and ignorant to pull off a transmogrification curse, but maybe that was just her pride misleading her. Maybe their interest in the occult ran deeper than the novelty junk they sold on their cart.

"Are they customers of yours?"

"We get all types in here." Madame Grimalkin spoke behind a whisker smile of indifference. "Can't say as I've ever noticed any of them with that particular trinket, though."

"Would you tell me if you did?"

She tapped the base of her glass on the table, then locked eyes with Elena. "We make a decent living, me and old Paddock. 'Cause we don't ask no questions. Let people come and go as they please, as long as they pay their bill. Which is why I don't ask why a goatherd has no goats with her." She paused to look over her shoulder at her husband behind the bar. "But witches that go about cursing each other are the lowest, and I spit on 'em."

"So you'll keep an eye out?" Elena slid another three coins on the table.

"A pocket watch like that ought to be easy enough to spot on the sly," she answered, taking the money. Elena was about to thank her when the old woman cut her off. "But let me give you a word of advice, goatherd. Whether it's the Charlatans mixed up in this or not, the type of witch that deals with the foul stuff like what's going on out there with those cats don't bother with the sort of curses you walk away from alive. Best not to go asking too many questions, if you value what skin you have left." Madame Grimalkin swallowed her gin in one gulp, then stood. "Now if you'll excuse me, I've got other customers to attend to."

Elena sipped her gin and peered over the rim of the glass at Madame Grimalkin as she walked away, a definite nervous twitch in her step. She was encouraged, though. Even if it wasn't one of the Charlatans, the witch who cursed her still might be inclined to put her feet up in the sort of tavern that didn't ask questions. But what then? She had a plan for Bastien, but what of the witch who'd done the actual spellwork? It would take a little more innovation to get past a conjurer who prospered off forbidden spells. And for that she would need all her strength.

Elena rubbed her palm, reminded of how the touch of Jean-Paul's hand against hers had heated her blood, making the magic spike. It was true the cold had gotten into her skin after the curse, but she no longer believed, as Madame Grimalkin did, that the affliction had to be permanent. Even thinking about him stirred a curative pulse inside her that sent a warm thread running through the veins. So odd that a mortal could affect her and her magic that way.

Drawn out of thought by the sensation of being watched, Elena took a sip of her gin and scanned the room. A bearded man in a black frock coat and monocle kept looking up, but he appeared to be working on a sketch in his lap. So many witches were drawn to the arts, unable to resist the temptation of seeing their spellwork preserved in paint and charcoal. But he was not the one ruffling her senses. It was another, wearing a broad-brimmed hat pulled low over his eyes. He watched her from a secluded corner by the front windows. He thought he was concealed in shadow because he'd snuffed his candle out, but the weight of his stare on her neck overwhelmed like the panting breath of a dog. Unable to intuit his intentions, she tossed one more coin on the table and walked outside, eager to get home and learn if Jean-Paul had returned. She took two steps in the muddy road before her plans were thwarted.

"It isn't just cats," the man in the hat said, catching up to her before the door shut. He proved no taller than a broom handle when he sidled up beside her. He tipped his hat back to reveal a full-moon face and wisps of tawny hair that poked out over his ears. His eyes, a chalky sort of blue, traced the outline of her weakened aura. "Couldn't help overhearing your conversation in there," he said as he handed over a business card adorned with moons and stars.

"You're with the Covenants Regulation Bureau?"

"Inspector Aubrey Nettles. I'm investigating the spate of grim incidents you referred to in there. Thought I might ask you some questions."

"By 'overheard' you mean you used a cochlear charm to listen to a private conversation."

Inspector Nettles flicked a speck of invisible dirt from his coat sleeve, ignoring her accusation. "Would you mind telling me what your interest is in blood magic?"

"I don't have any interest in it. I'm simply curious about the dead cats, like everyone else."

"Yet you seem to think it has something to do with you, mademoiselle . . . ?"

She couldn't afford to disclose her name. Not yet. "I'm looking for someone, that's all. I thought they might have passed through the tavern recently."

She tried to walk away, but the man followed, dogging her heels.

"Like I said, it's more than cats that are showing up dead." He had to double-step to keep up. "There've been rabbits, squirrels, a badger even. Hearts cut right out of them. Not a drop of blood left in the bodies." Elena stopped in her tracks. "Ah, so you do know something about the dark arts, then." The man bared a cold smile, knowing he'd touched on magic she understood. "Not something your average goatherd has reason to be familiar with."

He was right. It wasn't common knowledge, by any means. Blood magic was the darkest form of spellcasting, absolutely forbidden by the covenants. Few books even existed that described how it was done. But then Elena was no ordinary vine witch. Her shadow world vision alone was an extraordinary talent, but it had made her all the more curious about the things she couldn't see. When she'd mastered the divine arts while still in her teens, she sought out the magic she hadn't been taught. Not to use but to understand. For even knowledge itself was a form of magic in the eyes of the All Knowing. At least that was the argument she'd used on Brother Anselm to gain permission to study *The Book of the Seven Stars*, the only surviving reference held within the abbey that mentioned blood magic. Even then, she'd had to beg. The book had been locked up for nearly two hundred years out of an abundance of caution, ever since the Covenant Laws were officially signed and sealed.

Elena clenched her tattered skirt in her hands and remembered her purpose. "I'm just worried for my goats, is all. Don't want no harm coming to them, or me, out on the hills at night. I was hoping there's an amulet that could protect me and my animals."

"You seem vaguely familiar to me. Have we met before?"

The man peered at her hard enough with his third-eye vision that she felt it pierce her solar plexus. She had to get rid of him; he was getting too curious. And she knew from experience a man like him could easily be in Bastien's pocket. Casting a spell using the small reserve of magic she'd recovered was going to hurt, like swallowing with a sore throat, but she had to try or risk exposure. She couldn't use anything direct. A member of the Bureau would have potent charms to fend off an attack. Something off-body, she decided, as she spied an object on the ground that might do.

In the alley across the lane, a cat screeched bloody murder.

"You don't think?" she said with convincing alarm.

The inspector cocked his head to the side, then told her to stay put while he stepped into the lane to have a closer look. While Nettles investigated the phantom cry she'd tossed off with a flick of her brow, she bent to pick up a black feather poking out of the mud. She placed it on her open palm and took a deep breath. With one eye on Nettles she muttered the necessary words, tolerating the hollow pain that welled beneath her breastbone.

"Feather black on pinion hollow, take to the sky, let your brothers follow." She blew on the feather to send it airborne, and a moment later a flock of blackbirds dropped out of the sky, swooping and diving straight at the inspector.

CHAPTER THIRTEEN

Jean-Paul extinguished the candle flame between his moistened fingers. A small but nagging pain had settled above his right eye since he'd sat down to read. Now, in the diminished light, he closed the book, removed his glasses, and rubbed his brow. He'd found some answers in the volume the monk suggested, but, as was often the case, they only created more questions in his mind. Still, his fear had settled, replaced with a guarded curiosity that held like a shield wall against full acceptance.

After leaving a donation in the box on the altar, he exited the small abbey library and thanked the monks on the way out. They crossed themselves and wished him a safe journey home.

Yes, he ought to get home. But to which one? Where did he belong? That was one of the new questions he'd come to face after waking up in a different world than the one he'd fallen asleep in. The one he found himself in now was full of mystery and magic. Unseen powers. And threats. And yet his old life had perils of its own. The dull progression of an ordinary life that chipped away at a man a day at a time so that he didn't see the damage done until he found himself sitting alone in a house with nothing to show for it but the slow ticking of a clock on the wall.

He'd grown up hearing the stories about the Chanceaux Valley, of course. Everyone did. Just stories, he'd thought. Superstition. Quaint country folklore. He'd even seen the witches plying their trade in the country villages as a boy, with their potions, palm readings, and tarot cards spread out on tables outside the bistros. Christ, he'd even had his fortune told to him once. A raven-haired woman with jeweled fingers whispered to a small dog on her lap, then flipped over three cards as he walked past. She'd locked eyes with his ten-year-old self and warned him about wearing other men's shoes. He'd laughed at the woman, while his father, in a holiday mood, had chucked a small coin in her cup.

That was before his introduction to the wine.

A decade later, returning as a young man exploring the world available to a bon vivant on summer break from law school, he'd set about sampling the varied wines of the Chanceaux Valley. Even then he'd hoarded a case of Château Vermillion's vintage '99, impressed by its structure and the smooth inebriation it brought on after one glass. The first Du Monde reds he'd tried were bold yet immature, but he saw the promise and audacity and so collected those too. A bottle of Domain Da Silva was so good it got him into the bed of a foreign heiress visiting the valley on holiday. And later, when he better understood the seduction of wine, he'd courted his fiancée Madeleine with a bottle (or was it two?) of Mercier-LeGrande, '02. He'd thought it the finest wine he'd ever had the pleasure to drink. The fruit, the alcohol, the residual influence of the terroir were in perfect balance in that particular vintage. He didn't think he'd find anything to compare. Then a friend introduced him to Château Renard, a small vineyard at the base of the hills that had made a name for itself with its self-assured old vines. He'd tilted his first glass in front of the glow of an electric lamp, noting the warm ruby color as it stirred alive against the artificial light. He'd swirled the glass, then pressed his nose inside the rim to sample the bouquet of black currants, a hint of woodsmoke, and ripe figs. The wine itself flowed like velvet in his mouth. It aroused the smooth sensuality of being inside a woman in the midst of lovemaking, the confluence of pleasure and attraction, the taste of lust on the tongue.

Magic. Yes, even then his instinct had called it that. The wine was hers. It had to be.

Thinking of her brought back the image of the creature she'd shown him in the vineyard, the strange fog, and the eerie glow hovering over his fields. Torn, he glanced back at the threshold of the six-hundred-year-old abbey. He'd still been drunk when he'd shown up in the middle of the night and pounded on the door, demanding to speak to someone, anyone who could explain what the hell he'd witnessed. He didn't see how it could be possible. There were laws of physics. Doctrines of religion. The empirical evidence of the senses. But they'd all been rendered useless by what he'd seen.

The monk who answered the door, Brother Anselm, had patiently let him in and led him to the kitchen. It had smelled of bread and vinegar from a day's labor of baking and scrubbing. The monk set out two mugs of strong tea and a plate of bread and cheese while Jean-Paul described what he'd seen. His hands had shaken as he recalled the gargoyle's eyes opening to look directly at him.

"Was it witchcraft?" he'd asked. "Is she . . . a witch?"

Brother Anselm had tapped his lip thoughtfully with his finger. "We are privileged to have among our population a fair number of them, yes."

"Privileged?" Distressed, he'd pushed his chair away and paced the floor. "You're not afraid? You're not compelled to cast them out?"

"That would be a mistake."

He'd lost control of his senses. There was no other explanation. "But this can't be," he said. "They can't be real."

The monk observed him patiently. "Do you like cheese, Monsieur Martel?"

"I beg your pardon?"

"What about yogurt and bread? I assume you're fond of wine."

"What?" He'd begun to think he was sleepwalking in a drunken dream. "What does that have to do with the madness I saw tonight?"

Brother Anselm motioned to the bowls of bread dough rising on the counter waiting to be baked into loaves in a few short hours. "My job at the abbey, aside from serving God, is to feed its inhabitants. All day I bake, I churn, I clean. It never ends."

Jean-Paul slumped back down in his chair. He'd come to the wrong place. He was going to get a lecture on how expensive it was to run an abbey purely on donations and could the monsieur please see it in his heart to add a few coins to the coffers to help them out. In exchange he'd be given a benediction, a blessing, and a promise to look into the witch business.

To his great surprise, he was instead given a science lesson.

"When I first came to the abbey I asked many of the same questions. Who are these witches? Is their magic dangerous? How could something exist if I can't see it? That, I believe, is the essence of what you're wrestling with, monsieur. And the answer is in the cheese."

He'd begun to question if the old man's mind was gone, but the monk waved off his look of doubt and begged Jean-Paul to hear him out.

Brother Anselm broke open the chunk of yellow cheese he'd set out. "Do you smell that? The ripeness? Nutty almost. A little sour, a little salty. *Les pieds de Dieu*. Do not tell my superior, but the smell of God's feet is heaven to me." The monk smiled. Threw his hands up in mock surrender. "Eight months ago I added milk, rennet, and a little salt together in a wooden vat. Pressed it, shaped it, and put it on the shelf to age. Today I have a delicious cheese to share with a guest. But the flavor, monsieur, that grows from something I did not add."

"You refer to the bacteria." Jean-Paul sat forward, surprised to find himself in the company of a man who'd followed the latest discoveries. "You've read the science?"

"We live a humble life at the abbey, but we do not close ourselves off to the world. Yes, those unseen microbes are what create the rich texture and flavor of the cheese." The monk kissed his thumb and fingertips in exclamation, signifying the magnificent result. "But, of course, now we know how these small wonders occur—miracles in my humble estimation—because men can look through a microscope and see them, track them, but for all the centuries before that, the mysterious process must have seemed like—"

"Magic." And he'd begun to see.

"Precisely. Fairies, elves, gnomes, witches—they've all been credited or blamed. What the eye couldn't see, the imagination filled in. We put names to the unexplained. Cast it as something to either fear or worship. And yet just because a thing can't be seen doesn't mean it isn't real." The monk lifted his palms skyward. "In truth, you could say almost everything I do here at the abbey relies on a belief in the unseen. In my profession we use faith to see; in science it's the microscope. With magic, we don't yet know how to quantify that range of unseen energy. We lack the proper tool. But not so for the witch."

"So you're saying the witches, this magic they do, it's conceivable it's merely a part of the natural world, only we don't yet have the means to measure how it works?" He rubbed his hand through his hair, trying to make sense of it all. "She told me as much. She said she was showing me things that occurred outside the normal spectrum of human vision."

"Ah. Yes. Like ultraviolet light. This, too, I have read about."

Jean-Paul nodded, though not yet entirely convinced. "As you say, these bacteria in cheese are of the beneficial type. But where there is good there is also bad. Like cholera or flu. Also unseen, yet dangerous. What if this witchcraft works the same way? There might be benefit, but could there also be something to fear?"

Brother Anselm steepled his fingers. "The locals won't admit it, won't say a bad word against the vine witches, but malefaction does happen. You've no doubt heard of the devastation that swept through the valley's vineyards half a century ago."

"The phylloxera? Nearly every vine was killed because of the infestation."

"Terrible times by all accounts. But despite official reports, it was no insect that was to blame. It was Celestine, the last witch to be burned in the Chanceaux Valley."

Skeptical, Jean-Paul leaned forward as the monk relayed the story of a young witch who once worked the vines at Château Vermillion. One day she'd found herself with child, the result of an affair with the village mayor. Instead of marrying the woman and claiming the child as he should have done, he claimed he'd been spellbound. Hexed. Spurned, the witch cursed the entire valley. Not every witch can do that, explained the monk. But this one had broken the rules of the covenants and summoned a disastrous, forbidden magic. She nearly devastated the entire valley to smite one man. "So, yes," the monk said. "As with the bacteria, the valley mostly benefits from the witches and their magic. Though it's just as possible for their power to turn deadly under the right, or perhaps I should say wrong, conditions. Bear in mind, however, all witches born after the 1745 Covenant Laws were ratified are absolutely bound by its decree. The consequences of stepping outside the law are quite severe."

At last Jean-Paul had found firm ground to stand on. If there was a covenant agreement, a lawful decree, then there were books and documents he could study. Laws he could test and weigh against the magic he'd seen. Rules and punishments. Finally he could get his bearings and find his way forward in the midst of uncertainty and fear.

As if reading his mind, Brother Anselm waved him forward. "Come, let me show you to our library. There are some books there I think you might find useful."

And that was where Jean-Paul had stayed until the strain of reading by candlelight put unending pressure on the tender nerve above his right eye, as well as his heart.

CHAPTER FOURTEEN

A thousand blackbirds swooped into the narrow lane. Wings dipped and flapped, ugly squawks rattled out of feathered throats, and claws spread open to strike. Or at least the illusion of a thousand blackbirds descending on the inspector filled the darkened space. If Elena had been forced to summon the birds on the main road above, where the setting sun was unobstructed by spells, the translucent nature of their true form would have shown through. But in the dingy lane on the outer edge of the village, her illusion thrived in shadow. The inspector dived for cover, his voice of alarm drowned out by the incessant screeching of the fabricated birds. In the days before her curse she could have conjured real birds and had the man pecked a thousand times. Still, the display was enough. While the inspector ducked with his arms covering his head, she escaped inside the nearest building.

The acid tang of soap and lye filled her lungs as she darted across the launderette. Dodging wet trousers and limp bedsheets hung on a line, she ran for the rectangle of light at the back of the room, where an open door led to an alley. Much to the surprise of the worker scrubbing shirts against a washboard, she dipped under his clothesline and through the exit, shutting the door behind her.

A Bureau man would use every tool at his disposal to sniff out the truth of who she was after the stunt she'd just pulled. And then the entire village would know she was back, including Bastien and his bierhexe. In her weakened state, they'd destroy her.

Her feet fought for traction in the alley as she struggled to return to the upper end of the village, but it was as if her legs trudged through mud. The spell had depleted her last ounce of energy. She'd only made it halfway through the alley when her heart pounded hard enough she had to stop and catch her breath. She leaned against a wooden door under an arched alcove. She needed a plan, yet logic seemed to fly out of her head the moment she formed an idea. If only she could rest.

The inspector burst through the back door of the laundry shop, casting threats into the open alley. He pushed over wooden crates and kicked at abandoned barrels in his way, shouting for her to show herself. He couldn't have been more than a block behind her.

Why had she come to the village? She should never have taken the risk. But then she thought of Jean-Paul, and her resolve returned. She pulled the work knife from her belt. Blood raced to her temples, throbbing in sync with her panicked heart. The inspector taunted her to come out in the open as he rattled door handles and pounded on doorjambs. A boot sole thudded against a wooden plank. The sound of frustration. But it was not followed by a stomp up the alley in her direction. Not yet. She pushed her back flat against the door and calmed her breathing until her heartbeat normalized again. Stupid man. Why couldn't he have minded his own business instead of eavesdropping on other people's conversations?

Two quick breaths later, desperation incited her to act. Gripping the knife, she jiggled the door handle, forcing the lock with the tip of her blade. The door gave way and she squeezed inside, clicking it silently closed behind her. She didn't need to look up at the brick oven and copper mixing bowls to know where she was. The intoxicating aroma of butter, chocolate, and sugar hit her full in the face.

Of all the shops in the village, she'd broken into the kitchen of Pâtisserie d'Amour.

Her head reeled at the scents, her mouth watered with want, but fear overrode her craving. With her cloak pulled over her nose and mouth, she staggered through the curtain into the main shop, skirting past the glass case full of macarons, custard tarts, and freshly baked croissants. Tilda, her head wrapped in a blue silk scarf, looked up from a tray of *pain au chocolat* fresh from the oven. Elena gave a heartbreaking sigh at the sight and averted her eyes as she stumbled for the front door, narrowly avoiding the seduction.

"Thief!"

Tilda chased her to the door with her spatula held like a weapon, shouting her accusation into the street for everyone to hear. Shop owners, the postmaster, and even a pair of waiters stuck their heads outside to see what had happened. Elena dared a quick look over her shoulder before darting into the road to maneuver around a couple strolling arm in arm on the sidewalk.

In her desperation to escape, she didn't register the rumble of the engine rattling along the cobblestones. Didn't see the headlights bearing down on her.

The driver slammed on the brakes, locking up the wheels. The rubber tires skidded on the stones as a woman shrieked in warning. The horn sounded and the goose-nosed auto jolted to a stop a mere foot from Elena's body. The hot gasp of the engine exhaled against her legs as she froze with her eyes dead set on the driver.

A cloud of steam roiled up from the car's engine. The man rose out of the driver's seat, waving his hat to clear the air. Seeing how close he'd come to hitting her, he gripped the windshield and leaned forward to inspect the front of his car for damage. "Blast it, goat woman, what were you thinking running into the road like that? Didn't you see me coming?"

She'd already felt the rough chafe of his voice against her heart, having listened through the bricks, but she wasn't prepared to meet him face-to-face in the street. To look into the same eyes that had once stared deep into hers and claimed everlasting love. Eyes that quickly betrayed her after a sideways glance toward his new lover: ambition. Eyes she now wanted to scratch out with her bare hands.

He continued yelling at her, more worried about his confounded machine than whether he'd injured a pedestrian. Seven years he'd had her cursed and left for dead, and he couldn't even be bothered to look up after nearly killing her a second time. But she thanked the All Knowing the man was such a self-centered ass. It might just give her the small chance she needed to escape. She wrapped the end of her cloak back over her face and turned for the opposite side of the street.

"You there, stop! Someone stop that woman."

Nettles. The inspector sprang out of the pâtisserie, eyes on his prey. Despite the weakness in her legs, the doubt in her heart, and the closeness of the growing crowd, Elena ran from the car, away from the inspector, desperate for a way out. In her panic, her clumsy sabot caught on a cobblestone and she stumbled, tearing her skirt and scraping her knee. The postmaster beckoned her forward, showing her the open road behind him. She got to her feet and lifted her hem, ready to run, when a firm hand grabbed her by the arm and spun her back around.

CHAPTER FIFTEEN

Jean-Paul's mind swayed over everything he'd read as he nudged his horse onto the village's main road. As the sun went down he realized he'd been gone nearly twenty-four hours. Scratching at his new beard confirmed it. But she could have no quarrel with the way he'd reacted. The world had changed, not him. Though that wasn't quite true. For good or bad, he would never be the same after the things he'd seen.

He gave the horse a kick to hurry the beast along when he noticed a commotion on the street ahead. A crowd had gathered in a circle to gape at what he assumed was yet another traffic accident. He fancied the new automobiles and nearly bought one himself when he still lived in the city, but they were unquestionably a danger in these country villages. Twice now there had been a collision between a car coming down the main road at top speed and a horse-drawn cart stubbornly plugging along at last century's pace.

It occurred to him he'd been the cart most recently, nearly run over by the revelation that the witches of the Chanceaux Valley were no mere superstition invented to draw in tourists. They were real. Their magic was real. Even the thing he'd seen. To say he'd been blindsided by the revelation would be an understatement. And yet he'd walked away from the collision mostly unharmed.

Twenty-four hours ago, in a rare moment of uncertainty, he'd considered selling Château Renard so he could be done chasing after some phantom vision of the perfect wine. He'd been ready to tell his mother the dream had withered. He'd return to the family law practice. No questions would be asked, and his days would go on as they had before, his life shrinking like a raisin until he died early like his father. But that was the difference, wasn't it? He felt alive here. Expansive. Creative. His work meant something to him. He felt it in the exhaustion of his body, the clarity of his thoughts, the unexplained happiness he took from seeing a leaf unfurl fresh and green and full of potential. It fed his soul, his mind, and his heart. He didn't make good wine yet, but he would. With her help, by God, he would.

Elena. A witch. It must be true. And yet the prospect no longer frightened him. At least not as it had. The revelation was astonishing, certainly, but no more so than discovering some never-before-seen creature on an uncharted continent. Something rare and deserving of protection and understanding.

Now, if he could just get past the crowd on the street so he could get home and explain to Elena the fool he'd been.

CHAPTER SIXTEEN

"Got her."

The musty scent of the wine cellar clung to Bastien's coat, his hair, and his breath, swirling around Elena as she struggled against his grip.

"Let go of me."

The inspector muscled his way between a pair of gawking waiters. "Hold her for me. Thank you. Pardon me. A matter of CRB business. If you'll just let me pass."

Panic squeezed against her lungs. She was caught. Trapped under Old Fox's paw again. She had to get away. If only she hadn't used up all her strength on that useless illusion. She struggled against Bastien's grip, unable to conjure even a spark to jolt him off. But then she remembered the knife in her belt, and an animal instinct kicked up from some secret place deep inside her. She wrapped her fingers around the haft, willing to cut off her own flesh to be free if she must. Or, more gratifyingly, Bastien's.

The inspector, out of breath, doubled over with one hand pressed on his knee while he held up his badge with the other. "Inspector Aubrey Nettles. Hold her please."

Emboldened by the weapon, she turned and faced Bastien head-on. "I said let me go."

"Elena?" He blanched as if he stared at a dead woman.

Nettles straightened. "You know this woman, monsieur?"

"She's my . . . or, rather, she was once my fiancée."

Elena tried to yank her arm free once more, but Bastien held on as if afraid to lose her again. "I was never your anything," she said, staring at the place where his heart should be, fingers tightening on the knife.

The inspector leaned in, ready to take her into custody, but Bastien waved him off. "Where have you been all this time? What happened to you?"

The hatred she'd been cultivating for this one moment finally erupted, and she bared her teeth at him. "What happened? You ruined my life with that damnable curse of yours, and you have the nerve to ask me what happened?"

"What are you talking about? What curse?"

"Do you have any idea the hell you put me through? For seven years my mind had to tread water inside that creature so I wouldn't lose who I am. I was nearly eaten alive."

"Look, I admit I was angry when you left, but I would never—"

"All because I said no to your scheming and lying. Do these people know all the deceitful ways you've profited?"

Bastien pulled Elena a fraction closer, squeezing her arm as he took in her disheveled appearance. "What happened? Who did this to you?"

Her body began to shake. The knife handle grew slippery in her hand. The crowd hovered closer. This wasn't how she'd planned her revenge. If only she could plunge the blade through his heart and be done with him for good, but pressed against him she couldn't summon the nerve. Her magic wouldn't rise. And she was no common murderer who drew blood with mortal tools. She slid the knife back into her belt and pleaded one last time: "Let me go."

"Bastien?"

The crowd parted as if moved by an unseen hand. A stately woman stepped forward like a queen through the open space, wearing a dress made of blue silk and lace. A gift box from the perfumery, wrapped in lavender paper and tied up with string, dangled from her delicate fingers. "What on earth are you doing? Unhand that woman this instant."

"I . . . she . . ." Bastien let go and took a step back to stand beside the woman.

With Elena free, Nettles reached in his pocket for a protective amulet of rosemary and cedar tied with jute. "Careful, this one knows a trick or two. She assaulted me in the alley not ten minutes ago."

"Ach, quatsch." The woman advanced on the inspector, plucking the charm out of his hand and tossing it on the sidewalk. "I think the more likely scenario is the two of you teamed up on this poor creature and hounded her until she was run ragged. Just look at the state of her."

Elena stiffened. She recognized the bierhexe at once—the flaxen hair, the rose-petal complexion, and the air of superiority—but there was something else. An aura of undeniable power. She understood immediately why the men obeyed her. They didn't dare not. But then Elena caught the scent of the perfume wrapped up in the box. The combination of fragrances, though oddly accompanied by a subtle whiff of spoilage, suggested a potion to lure back a lover who'd turned cold. The information opened a small crack in the bierhexe's facade, revealing a pool of doubt that lurked beneath the confident surface.

Their eyes met, and in the speck of a human second there passed recognition, a flinty spark between witches, as each identified the strength and weakness in the other.

The bierhexe swung the perfume box playfully from her fingers and said ever so pleasantly, "Please tell me what this unfortunate woman has done to get you boys in such an uproar."

Bastien flushed. He removed his black felt homburg and pointed it at the inspector. "Yes, Inspector, what do you want with her?"

Nettles retrieved his charm and dusted it off. "I'm investigating the use of illegal magic, and this goatherd knows more than she ought about certain dark practices. I was about to question her about it when she assaulted me and escaped down the alley."

The crowd murmured, pointing fingers and whispering about dead cats. Elena shrugged her cloak tighter around her shoulders, wishing it were armor.

Bastien smoothed his hair back and replaced his hat on his head. "She's no goatherd, you fool. She's a vine witch."

"Her?"

"That's Elena Boureanu. She's a vine witch. And a damn good one too. Or at least she was."

The inspector's eye shifted between Gerda and Bastien, testing. "One of yours?"

"Mine, actually."

Elena turned toward the voice and nearly cried out from relief. Jean-Paul sat atop his horse, his jaw set for a fight. He slid out of the saddle and landed firmly on his boot soles. His eyes raked over her torn skirt and the trail of blood that led from knee to ankle.

"Are you hurt? My God, you are." He flew at the inspector, grabbing him by the lapel. "Explain yourself, monsieur."

"It's concerning a covenant matter." Nettles balanced on the tips of his toes, displaying his badge as Jean-Paul hauled him up by his jacket. "And *she* attacked me first."

Gerda interceded. "She used a small, innocuous charm to defend herself. Its shadow is still circulating in the air." She pointed to where a wispy gray cloud floated at the top of the abbey's bell tower. "It was nothing threatening, Monsieur Nettles. Not even a real spell. There was no law broken. Just an illusion."

Jean-Paul leaned on the inspector. "Is this true?" Nettles admitted as much. "Then you have no more business with her," he said, letting the man go. "Come, Elena. I'll take you home."

"Home?" Bastien pushed the inspector aside to stand toe to toe with Jean-Paul. "What's the meaning of this, Martel? You've never used a vine witch before."

"And I've never made good wine before. But if she's as talented as you say she is, it's high time I got started."

But the crowd hadn't entirely dispersed when Elena took a last threatening step toward Bastien. "I want you to know I came back to ruin you for what you did to me," she said, keenly aware she could show no more weakness in front of the bierhexe. "No more jinxes, no more falsifying the tax records to try and steal Château Renard. We're going to produce wine so exquisite the world will forget about Domaine du Monde. And if you come within ten feet of the vineyard again I will make you sorry you were ever born."

"Elena, it wasn't me." Bastien looked to his wife. "Tell her it wasn't me."

The bierhexe merely stood with the perfume dangling from her grip, her jaw locked, her teeth grinding.

The automobile rumbled down the road as Jean-Paul retrieved his horse. He walked slowly back to Elena, never taking his eyes off her. "What made you come to the village?" he asked.

She patted the horse's neck, letting it get the smell of her. "I didn't want you staying away because you were afraid."

He glanced over the top of the saddle. Inspector Nettles leaned against the post office wall watching them, as if to say he wasn't yet satisfied. "I'm not afraid. Not anymore," he said. "Confused and bewildered, perhaps, but that's not as rare as you might imagine." He put his foot in the stirrup and pulled himself onto the horse.

She smiled at his confession and took his hand when he offered it. Though unladylike, she hiked her skirt up and swung her leg over the saddle behind him.

"What changed?" she asked. She'd not seen him like this before, resigned yet resolute.

"Let's just say I spent the night smelling God's feet."

"Ah, so Brother Anselm is still at the abbey, then. The All Knowing favors him."

"Will you tell me about it? The things I saw? What you do? I want to know everything."

"If you're sure," she said, then shivered as much from her cursed skin as the prospect of what his change toward her might mean.

"You're cold." Jean-Paul twisted in the saddle to speak to her. "Your hands are like ice. Do you want my jacket?"

Her first instinct was to pull back, protect herself, but his body was so warm. And the closer hers was to his, the more the magic stirred back to life inside her. The sensation was tiny, a speck of dust floating in a ray of sunlight, but it was there, still alive, somehow being nurtured by this man's nearness, like no magic she'd experienced before, not even with Bastien in the early days of their courting. She slipped her hands inside the wool pockets of his jacket and said she'd tell him anything he wanted to know.

He tapped the reins, and they left the village behind as the sun went down over the surrounding vineyards.

"My people have been making wine in this valley since the earliest vines were planted thousands of years ago. It's our particular talent. Others excel in similar arts."

"How many witches are there?"

She watched him swallow the word, knowing how foreign it must taste in his mouth. "It isn't just the vineyards. There are witches who are experts with scent, like the perfume sorcerers that work the lavender fields in the south. Others experiment with healing waters and gemstones. And a great many have mastered the art of flavor and texture in food," she said, restraining a smile, "as you've perhaps already noticed in our local pâtisserie."

"It's true about the desserts?"

"Oh, there are bakers who can create a scent so provocative it will make your head reel with passion. Cake so succulent you want to hold it in your mouth and savor each swallow as if it's your last. Some say they are the most dangerous witches of all." She laughed so he would know she was only teasing. "But only if you're in love. Or so they like to say."

"Is that so?" Jean-Paul cleared his throat, and she was grateful he could not see her face turn crimson as she remembered the heady smells of cinnamon and chocolate. "I'd heard rumors about the witches here since I was a boy," he said. "Everyone in the city has. But I always thought it was just a ploy to lure tourists to the valley."

"Some do earn their living off strangers. Most, though, work at their trade the same as anyone else." Elena lifted her head to speak directly to him. "And before you ask why we don't all just cast spells and reap gold out of thin air, you should know there are laws we have to abide by."

"The Covenant Laws. Yes, I read through them last night." He held his hand up defensively as she leaned forward to see if he was telling the truth. "I'm trained in the law," he said. "It's what I do. Or did, rather, in my other life back in the city." It seemed he wanted to say something more, but he took a breath of country air instead, his chest expanding until she felt his back press against her. "And Madame is a vine witch as well?" He shook his head. "All this time, she never once made me suspect she was anything but a little eccentric, maybe a little superstitious. Well, except for that thing she does by rubbing her thumb and fingers together."

"Her magic has worn thin with age. The gesture is how she checks for spells. Like reading by braille, only . . . metaphysically."

"And Du Monde's wife? She's a foreigner, but she's a vine witch too?"

"Oh, no. She's quite different. She's a bierhexe from the north."

"Bierhexe?"

"They're formidable at spell magic, but they don't usually dabble in winemaking. They typically concentrate on potions and curatives when they're not making beer. Think big cauldrons and clouds of rising steam. Though some do venture into wine nowadays. They've done well with the Riesling."

"Am I wrong to think that there are more of your kind here in the Chanceaux Valley than other places?"

"It's the terroir," she said, breathing in the scents of distant rain, chalky soil, and verdant growth springing open on the vine. "I'm not sure there's anywhere else to compare in the world. The place carries its own magic. Difficult for my kind to resist."

He nodded as if he understood, taking in the scenery like a country gentleman out for a bit of night air. The same things had likely lured him to the valley. Grand-Mère had been right about him. She saw that now. He had the heart of a true vigneron building inside him.

"I was pledged to the vineyard at Château Renard as a child after my parents died," she said, wanting him to know the truth. "I'll always belong to that plot of earth, no matter the owner."

"Are you saying you were sold into the business? Is that how it works?"

"I'm bound but not indentured. I could have easily ended up working on the streets as a card reader or pickpocket if I hadn't been taken in. Madame and Monsieur had no children of their own, no one to take over when they were gone." Elena paused, wondering if she sounded like she still blamed him for losing the title to the vineyard. She no longer did. "When they offered to teach me the magic of making wine," she continued, "it was like planting a new root in old soil. Because I was so young my knowledge was shaped around the unique characteristics of the Renard terroir. That bond is why I'm so protective of it. It's why I can't imagine making wine anywhere else."

They rode a moment in silence before he shifted in the saddle and asked, "What I saw last night. The lights. And that thing."

"The gargoyle?"

"Yes, that. Is that normal? Is there really an entire world I can't see?"

"Not even all witches can see what walks in the shadows."

"But you do."

She looked around, astonished at how quickly her energy had recovered in his presence. She pointed to a wall marking the boundary of an abandoned vineyard on their right. Above it loomed the ruins of a stone castle. Only one turret remained upright. The rest of the fallen stonework sat buried in overgrown moss and ivy. "There, on the hill. Do you see the arch above the old gateway?" He pulled on the horse's reins, and she pressed her hand over his. "Now what do you see?"

He looked down at their clasped hands, then squinted at the distant castle. "Do you mean the blue light? It appears to be moving. I watched a demonstration in the Palais de l'Électricité at the World Exhibition a few years ago that created a light like that. But they couldn't possibly have electricity up there? Why would they?"

"No, it's not electric. Not exactly." She fumbled for a way to describe it. "It is energy, but the source doesn't come from any generator. It's more atmospheric in nature. It's been glowing above that gate since I was a child."

"What's it for?"

She slid her thumb over the back of his hand, thinking about the witch who had cursed her and stolen her warmth. "It was a fort once, and later they kept a few witches there who'd broken the new Covenant Laws. Celestine is the one most people remember."

"I've ridden up there. The whole place is falling apart. There couldn't be anyone there still."

"No, not for ages, but I wanted you to see the ruins aglow with spell magic."

He stared up at the place, eyes focused in morbid fascination, then tucked her hand back in his pocket and patted the outside of his jacket, ready to be rid of the image. "Thank you for showing me."

She wished she could thank him as well for the magic returning inside her, but how to explain the change when she didn't understand it herself? She had her suspicions, of course, but she wasn't yet ready to let those words free. Words carried power, more so for witches, so she closed off the thought. With a sigh, she tipped her face to the evening stars just coming out, mystified at the way the All Knowing sought to bend her life in the one direction she had not thought she'd ever go again.

CHAPTER SEVENTEEN

Tiny green tendrils explored the canopy with curled fingers, eager to find their anchor point. Humans were not so different, Jean-Paul thought, as he thinned the vines to rid them of excess growth. To find your place and hold on—wasn't that what everyone wanted? She'd said the terroir anchored her to the vineyard. There were days he felt it slip inside him—the soil in his lungs, the chlorophyll under his fingernails, the atmosphere crackling with the scent of rain—binding him to the place as well. He could build a good life on it. The grapes would give under her care. He could tender a heritage, one he could pass on to a son or daughter when he was too old to walk the vine rows anymore.

But then he thought of that thing lurking somewhere in the unseen ether and shook himself out of his daydreams. He gripped his clippers and cut. The new tendrils always overshot their ambition, clinging too tight to where it was impossible to remain.

A week later the first fruit appeared on the vine, whispering its promise of a new vintage. Elena spent the morning tying protective charms of amethyst crystals to the trellising. If he hadn't seen what he had that horrible night, he would have put a stop to it. And he never would have let her stir salt into a bowl and chant rhymes to cast out the grotesque thing perched atop the old canes. Instead he went about his light plowing, observing, surmising, and staying out of her way as she walked among the spreading canopy with a bowl and candle held before her. Though ready to jump at the first hint of trouble, he trusted in her ability to flush the gargoyle from the unseen world. And though he would not know with his own eyes if she succeeded, he thought he might feel the difference. Likely the assumption was his mortal ego at work, but there were moments just before dusk he thought he could sense the thing watching him.

After an hour she put aside her tools.

"Will it come back?" he asked.

She lifted her chin to the sky as if listening for a particular sound. "Only if summoned, but I'll know if he steps foot inside the vineyard again. He'll run screaming from the salt curse I wove around the perimeter. Gargoyles aren't so different from slugs."

Her smile disarmed him, and he forgot again there was anything to fear from the supernatural. "Come, let's get inside before the rain pelts us."

"You're predicting the weather now?"

"Madame warned me this morning there'd be a downpour."

He walked beside Elena on the path, still uncertain if he should take her hand. It wasn't only his aversion to the manifestations he'd seen that prevented him from pursuing her, not when the thought of kissing her distracted him daily to the point he could hardly concentrate on anything else. But he couldn't deny the barrier that stood between them. Love with this woman would be a master class in complication.

And so he slid his hands in his pockets, held back by the restraint of logical thought.

His mind was dead set on the matter, but the constant torment the desire created between his head and his heart had him half believing she'd put a spell on him. He'd seen the love potions the street witches sold on market day. He'd always assumed the vials contained a shot of Vin Mariani or, more mildly, a spritz of lemon verbena oil. Harmless fun when you needed to believe your heart's desire could be won with a swig and a wish. But that was before he knew the potency of real magic. It was against the covenants, of course. She couldn't put a spell on him or any man without his consent. But what if *he* had willed it? There was a brief moment after he first learned the truth that he'd wondered if her powers included the ability to read minds. A damning notion if true.

To test the idea and know if he needed to guard his thoughts, he'd decided one evening to let his natural mind wander as he sat across from Elena in the salon. He began at her ankles, then inched his thoughts up along her calves, her thighs, and the soft curve of her derrière, but the only person in the room to flinch from the improper entertainment was himself, left to adjust the crotch of his suddenly too-tight trousers. He thus faced the astonishing confirmation that he was under no spell and there'd been no unintended invitation to manipulate his thoughts. The mundane truth was that he was utterly, completely enchanted by this woman.

Attraction was its own powerful potion, able to conjure unsolicited desire out of thin air.

Elena kicked mud from her shoes and then entered the kitchen as he held the door open for her. He'd hardly followed her inside when Madame slumped to her knees and clutched her chest.

Elena ran to the old woman and put her arms around her. "Grand-Mère, what's wrong?"

"Don't you feel it?"

"Feel what?"

The old woman glanced up at the sky through the window. She swallowed hard. "Like last time, only worse."

Jean-Paul shook his head in confusion. "Is she ill? Shall I fetch a doctor?"

"She has premonitions. She feels the warning in her chest when it's strong enough." Elena glanced at the gathering clouds. "Last time she suffered this badly we had a killing frost. We lost half of the vineyard that year."

"Frost?" The threat sent a jolt through him. "Can't you do something? Say a spell to keep it off the vines?"

Elena ignored him and hurried to the parlor. She pulled the almanac she and Grand-Mère had made out of the drawer and spread it open on the sideboard table. Her finger traced over moons and stars, suns and symbols. She double-checked dates and forecasts.

"Is it true?" asked Jean-Paul. "Can you see it in your calculations?"

Elena shook her head. "No, there's nothing to warn of frost. Unless we missed something. A sun flare could throw off a prognostication, but that's rare. And it's too late in the season for a serious threat." She tapped her fingers on the almanac before returning to the kitchen. She gripped Madame by her shoulders. "What do you sense now?"

Madame's head wobbled atop her neck, uncertain. "It's getting closer."

Losing even a quarter of the vineyard would ruin him after three bad years already. "If it's frost, we should prepare," he said, tired of waiting. "I'm going out to set up the char cans for the fires."

"I'll come with you." Elena followed him out the door, her eyes searching the horizon. She got as far as the center of the courtyard before she stopped and called out. "It isn't a frost."

He swung the workroom door open and lowered the bellows and a box of candles to start the fires. "I'm not taking any chances. I'll walk the fields all night if I must to keep the fires going."

Elena stared at the road. "It's not a frost."

The tone and certainty of her voice the second time she spoke made him set down his tools. With one hand pressed to the door's edge, he peered around the corner to see what had her frozen to the flagstones. A black coach-and-four, the red crest of the Region of the Chanceaux

Valley emblazoned on its side, headed straight for the château. Even without the power of premonition, he knew its approach was as threatening as any storm front bearing frost. In that one vision he saw more than just lost crops. An instinct he rarely gave credence to shouted up from the deepest well inside him that something terrible had happened. Was still happening.

He joined Elena in the center of the courtyard, standing shoulder to shoulder as they faced the danger bearing down on them. The coach rattled around the last bend in the road. Three helmeted men on skeletal motorbikes followed at a rumble. The driver lashed his team with the whip from his high perch and then made straight for the gate. The wheels gyrated under the weight and speed of the careening coach, yet it held to the pavement without tipping.

He threw a protective arm around Elena, ready to pull them both to the ground to avoid the speeding coach if he must. The driver shouted "Halt!" and the horses responded, coming to an unnatural stop a yard in front of them. The motorbike riders circled, then shut off their engines.

"Reckless fool, you nearly ran us over," Jean-Paul shouted as the three bikers surrounded him and Elena on the cobblestones. The coach driver sat silent, his face forward, eyes as placid as the dead.

The cab door opened and the Chanceaux Valley constable emerged, his uniform cape flapping in the wind as he descended in one graceful stride. He wore a look of mild concern as he straightened his gold-corded *kepi* and glanced at the couple. "You are Monsieur Martel?"

Jean-Paul swallowed. "I am. What business do you have at the vineyard, Constable?"

The policeman, a captain as indicated by the bars on his shoulders, flipped open a small notebook. "And you are Mademoiselle Boureanu, a vine witch employed at Château Renard?"

Elena telegraphed her growing fear with a nervous sideways glance at Jean-Paul before answering. "Yes. What is this all about?"

The constable ignored her and signaled instead to the bikers. They set their helmets on their motorcycles and then spread out in the courtyard at his command. The captain clicked his heels together with military precision, took a regimented step to his left, and held open the coach door. Inspector Nettles poked his balding head out, smiling at them with all the appeal of a rabid dog. He exited the coach with an air of cockiness until his short legs forced him to jump the final gap from the steps to the pavement. Jean-Paul felt Elena reach for his hand at the sight of the insufferable inspector. He gripped hers back and squeezed.

"Well, well," Nettles said, slapping the collar of his jacket up against the first drops of rain. With a little too much self-satisfaction he walked up to Elena, looked her over in her proper work clothes, and smirked at the change in her appearance. "It seems our conversation is not yet finished after all, *goatherd*."

Jean-Paul took a threatening step closer to the man. "I warned you in the village you have no further business with her."

"Oh, did the constable not spell out the official reason for our visit?" Then he dropped all pretense of civility. "I have a warrant for this woman's arrest." Nettles nodded at the constable, who removed from his vest pocket an official-looking paper with a red wax seal displaying the mark of the magistrate on the bottom.

"Arrest? You can't be serious." Jean-Paul looked to each man's face, hoping Nettles had it in him to make a joke. "On what charge?" He took the warrant from the constable and scanned the document.

"The murder of Bastien du Monde. I think you'll find everything is in order."

The last sliver of sun was swallowed by cloud; the temperature dropped and a north wind gusted through the valley.

"Murder?" Elena gasped. "Bastien is dead?"

"Very, mademoiselle. Found gutted like a cat this morning on the edge of the village."

"Du Monde? Dead?" Before he could stop it, Jean-Paul's mind blamed the witches—the nameless, faceless creatures he'd feared as a child. Then he looked at Elena, so vulnerable as she stood before the law, and had to swallow his shame, knowing how wrong he'd been in the past.

"This is madness. I didn't murder anyone," she said, her arms going limp at her sides. "I haven't left the property in days."

The inspector turned to Jean-Paul. "Can you verify this?"

"Of course. She's been here with me the entire time."

Nettles licked his bottom lip, which on his face translated into a lascivious sneer. "Day *and* night, monsieur?"

He stuttered at the implied accusation. "I . . . no, not at night."

"I sleep in my workroom in the cellar."

Nettles raised an eyebrow. "Among your spell books and potions?"

Jean-Paul frowned and folded up the warrant. "What does that have to do with anything?" He turned toward Elena. "Don't say another word to them."

Nettles ignored him and took a step closer to her. "And do you ever fancy a moonlit stroll alone in the shadow world when everyone else is fast asleep?" Rain fell on Elena's hair, raising a cloud of mist around her. She stared back at the man with cold blue eyes but said nothing. "I suspected as much the moment I first saw you," he said, leaning in. "I have a knack for these things." He straightened and crooked his finger at the bikers. "Take her into custody. And search the premises."

Two of the riders pushed past Jean-Paul to get to Elena while the third strode toward the house.

"Wait. You can't do this. Where is your evidence?" Jean-Paul pushed back and was immediately knocked to the ground by the constable, who'd struck him in the back of the legs with a club. He watched helplessly from his knees as they twisted a pair of thick metal handcuffs around Elena's wrists. His eyes did a double take as a faint blue glow emanated from a circle of runes engraved into each metal cuff.

"The modus operandi is the evidence, monsieur." Nettles tightened the gloves on his small hands, stretching them so the ridges of his knuckles showed under the leather before plucking Elena's knife from her belt. He held it with the tips of his fingers, as if careful not to smudge any evidence that might be found, then glanced down at Jean-Paul in triumph. "Are you at all aware of who I am?" When Jean-Paul did not answer, the inspector lifted a brow as if he yet again was faced with the task of informing the ignorant. "I inspect acts of illegal magic. Constable Girard here inspects crimes against mortals. When the two branches of law enforcement overlap, we have a crime that violates the covenants. In this instance we have a dead mortal obviously killed by a witch. Our victim was found dead by means of a specific form of exsanguination. A ritual only a few skilled witches are capable of."

Elena paled as if reading her fate in the foggy air. "Blood magic."

"Dark, evil magic that runs contrary to the laws of the All Knowing itself, mademoiselle, and for which you will meet a most gruesome fate when judgment is passed."

The inspector's eyes shifted to the house as Madame hobbled outside, clearly distraught.

"Is it true? He was murdered?" She pressed her hand against her chest when she saw Elena in chains. "You can't take her. No, not again. She's done nothing."

"And yet we have multiple witnesses, myself included, who heard her publicly threaten the man in the street just a week ago. I regret, madame, so much shame has been brought on such an old and respected house."

Elena took a step toward Madame but was thrust back by the two men flanking her. "It's all right, Grand-Mère. It's just a misunderstanding. The magistrate will sort it out. I'll be home soon. I didn't *use* anything."

The old woman fretted, pulling at her hair so that it frayed loose from its pins in long white strands that clung to her face in the rain.

"You can't honestly believe she had anything to do with this. We make wine, that's all."

"Inspector!" At that moment, the deputy sent to search the house came running outside, pointing to the wall near the gate. "I could see it from the upstairs window." The young man ran to the wall and then reached atop the capstone with his upstretched hand. When he brought it back down he held a desiccated cat in his hand, one recently drained of blood.

The inspector clucked his tongue at the sight. "Madame, I believe in her guilt with all my heart. Take the witch away."

CHAPTER EIGHTEEN

The stone steps leading up to the witch's tower had been worn smooth at their center, as if a thousand previous feet had trod the same wretched path Elena now took. With her wrists shackled, Nettles led her by the arm and prodded her through the main gate. The blue light of a spell-wall glowed in her shadow vision. She'd been nervous on the long ride out of the valley, watching the vineyards disappear behind her, but now she visibly quivered at the sight of the impending oak door and iron lock before her. How could this be happening? She'd returned home with the intent to kill Bastien, yes, but the thought had never made the leap from her mind to her hand. Not even when he'd stood before her in easy reach of her knife, the temptation slick as sweat in her palm.

The doors to Maison de Chêne yawned open as if prepared to swallow her inside the imposing granite walls of the tower. Was this yet another curse? Her mind careened back to the moment just before the curse touched her seven years ago. She'd been picking stems of eyebright along the road to make a tea when she got home. But she'd let her mind drift into shadow, anxious after her fight with Bastien, when a stabbing pain in her liver forced her to her knees. Locked in metamorphosis, her true self had been bundled and wrapped inside the skin of a toad, the confinement squeezing her consciousness until only the dimmest of mental light shone through the amphibious eyes. From that narrow point of view she'd watched the wheel of time turn round for seven seasons.

Tick.

Tick.

Tick.

She'd had only a moment to grab on to something meaningful, something to trigger memory. Her nose pressed against the grass, the green blades a curtain before her eyes. The stems of the eyebright gripped in her hand. And then another hand reached down to retrieve a dropped pocket watch. A green eye with a yellow slit. With her last wisp of clear thought she clasped on to the color green, making it a talisman if and when she woke again. It was the last thing she saw before sinking inside the curse.

She stared up at the prison gate, the terror of a second imprisonment draining her veins of warmth until she shivered uncontrollably. The prison matron, a middle-aged woman dressed in an iridescent blue robe, cut her a measuring look, then greeted Nettles in a curt yet professional manner. "This is the one?"

"She is. Got her dead to rights on summoning dark magic for murder. We've got weapon, means, and motive, and we even found her with a dead cat."

The matron tapped a thoughtful finger to her lip before turning a wormy eye on Elena. "In that case, welcome to Maison de Chêne. I am Madame Dulac. You will address me as Matron. You will be housed here until your trial. Know that we do not coddle nor cosset, and we do not give in to whims of privilege. We are here to take in the dangerous, the deranged, and the derelict. But I warn you we house only the harmless here. Done so by plucking out the stingers of would-be wasps such as yourself." To emphasize her point, Matron withdrew a yew wand from her sleeve, running the smooth wood through her fingers before pointing it at Elena. "You will not cast spells here. You will not conduct magic of any kind. Be assured any witch caught trying to manipulate the physical matter inside her cell will feel the sting of this queen bee."

"But it wasn't me. I've done nothing wrong."

The matron shook a weary head at Nettles. "Have you ever brought me one that didn't say that?"

Elena shrugged free of Nettles's grip. "You're making a mistake. Someone else murdered Bastien, and they're still out there."

"You should be grateful, you know," Nettles said, brushing his hands free of her. "You're being granted a speedy trial. Seems the higher-ups want to make sure word gets out that we've caught the witch who's been killing cats and conjuring blood magic for who knows what purpose. Though if it were up to me, I'd probably hang you on the spot." Nettles cleared his throat. "Never mind I said that, Eugenie."

"I'm the soul of discretion, Aubrey." The matron locked her lips with a pantomimed key.

Shards of panic needled into Elena's skin. The world had tipped on its axis so that up was down and down was up. To be held captive, cut off from magic, unable to clear her name—she'd go mad if she had to go through that again. Her icy blood retracted from her heart. Damn the consequences. She had to get free. Uttering words she'd vowed never to use as a vine witch, words of shadowy, summoning magic, she bent her wrists to hold her hands in an upside-down sacred pose, ready to unleash hell to escape.

She called on the sun, the moon, and the east wind, hoping to create a tornado of energy out of the torment building inside her. Her hair lifted slightly, as if a gentle breeze had wafted over her shoulders . . .

. . . and then nothing. No destruction, no magic, no escape—only the desperate silence of a failed spell. She stood trembling.

"The magic is stronger with this one than most," Matron said to Nettles. "She got the energy to stir around her. Most can't even finish an incantation." Matron yanked at the handcuffs on Elena's wrists as the runes glowed in neon blue. "But now that you've tried your little trick, you can be satisfied your spells and hexes are of no use in here."

Elena stared dumbfounded at the vibrancy of the magic running through the shackles. The binding spell inscribed in the metal forced the cuffs to grip another inch tighter, zapping her arcane energy completely. She tried another spell, but the more she struggled, the weaker she grew. Defeated, she lowered her head to hide her tears. If the All Knowing had ever favored her, it was in another life.

Nettles doffed his hat and made a quick bow before the matron. "I'll leave you to it, seeing as you have everything under control." And with that he departed, abandoning Elena into the night bucket of the criminal justice system for witches.

She was led down a corridor ripe with the scent of mold and damp straw. A wall of empty cells lined the passage, the cages where the condemned from another era had once been housed. Curiously she could still hear the moans of the tortured and tormented reverberating within the bricks and mortar of the prison despite the shackles. But as her feet passed over the same ground where theirs had trod hundreds of years earlier, a chill snaked its way through her core to the space where she hid her deepest fear, and there it coiled, waiting to strike.

The matron stopped marching when they reached a set of iron bars at the end of the corridor. Inside the cell a chain rattled and feet shuffled in dry straw, as if a stall full of cows had suddenly awakened to the scent of an intruder. The smell that hovered in the cave-like space, however, was worse than a cattle pen. It was the scent of neglect and the absence of hope.

Elena looked up to see an impish face emerge from the shadows and press against the bars. Alert eyes stared out beneath greasy strands of unkempt hair. A crooked smile split a plane of pale skin.

The matron shooed the young woman away. "We have a new prisoner, Yvette. Stand back."

The nymphlike young woman pirouetted out of the way of the barred door. Matron removed her wand from her sleeve and opened the lock with a manipulation spell. Elena knew it. She'd recited the words before when the wine cellar door had jammed, but now the words to the spell swam in her head, slippery as an eel, so that she couldn't wrap her mind around the phrase. After a shove in her back, she entered the cell. The depraved space assaulted her senses with its pungency of unwashed bodies, the hard chill of stone underfoot, and the finality of metal clanging against metal as the door thudded closed behind her.

The runes on the iron bars glowed faintly as the matron poised her wand a second time from the other side. "Hands up," she said, and Elena's shackles slipped off her wrists. The wan young woman with the glittering eyes sprang to the ground to pick them up and then handed them, polite as can be, to the matron. "Shoes too."

"What?"

"Remove your shoes and pass them through." She tapped impatiently on the bars with the end of her wand. "Prisoners do not wear shoes."

The waif greedily picked up the kicked-off shoes, turning them over to casually note the maker's mark imprinted on the bottom. She raised her brow at Elena before forwarding the soft leather lace-ups to Matron.

"Thank you, Yvette. Take care of our newest guest."

"With pleasure," said the young woman, whose placid smile lingered as long as the matron remained within the corridor. Once the guard was gone and the door at the end of the corridor slammed shut, her eyes flashed bright as sapphires in the dim light as they practically devoured Elena.

"Well, well, what have we here?" The young woman circled her just out of arm's reach. "I'd say you've got the look of one of Dubois's light-fingered girls, but they don't throw people in this pit for a little thievery. A Maison de Miel worker maybe? Hmm, no. Your clothes are well made, but they're too plain for fantasy work. And you can't be a carnival kink. I just come from there."

Elena wasn't sure how to respond to the interrogation. She was reasonably certain a "carnival kink" was akin to being a gentleman's *illusionniste*, someone who used magic to carry out sexual fantasies for paying customers. The young woman's black silk stockings with the embroidered fleur-de-lis running up the sides, though badly torn, were a dead giveaway. As was the trace of kohl liner smudged under her eyes and the lingering scent of male musk on her clothes. But the jagged scar along the young woman's cheek suggested there might be a more violent side of the tale. A casualty of her trade? Life in the cell? What kind of hell had Nettles left her in?

"I'm not . . . that is, I don't do that sort of work."

"Oh, too tawdry for the likes of you, is it?" The waif turned puckish, leaning in close enough that her sour breath blew in Elena's face. "Some of us are good enough to make a decent side living at it. Want to know how good I am?" she asked, stroking her finger along Elena's jaw.

"Sit down, Yvette. Not everyone practices their magic while on their back."

A second body, this one seated cross-legged on the floor opposite the only window, leaned forward in the single beam of sunlight. Long black hair framed a brown face and world-weary eyes offering little comfort. The woman wore a faded silk robe of red and gold over a linen tunic and small gold hoop earrings that pierced the lobes of each ear in three places. The scent of charred citrus and incense rose off her skin. Foreign. Old World. Like the spice emporium Elena had once visited in the city as a child with Grand-Mère.

"Oh là là, Sidra, I'm just trying to find out what kind of criminal they dumped in here with us. You'd think you'd be grateful I care about our safety."

"She's a murderer, same as us. End of story."

Elena said nothing in reply as a small wren landed on the windowsill between the bars. It preened and bowed and then flew inside the cell to perch on Sidra's outstretched hand. The sorceress whispered to the bird, and the bird sang back. After a brief exchange she petted the bird's head, then plucked a daddy longlegs out of the straw and dangled it in front of the wren's open mouth.

"How can you talk to the bird? Don't the runes prevent magic?"

"They block spells," Sidra explained, "but not even a place like this can strip away a person's essence. I need no spell to talk to birds."

Was it possible? It must be. Hadn't she heard the lamenting of the dead surface through the liminal space as she passed through the corridor?

Yvette picked up a handful of damp straw and threw it at Elena's feet. "This new one smells like alcohol. Can't stand a drunk for a cellmate."

"It's wine and oak." Sidra pinched a silverfish between her fingernails and offered it to the bird. "It's the scent of someone who works in a cellar."

Yvette scrunched up her face. "You mean she's a vine witch? In here? Never heard of nothing like that before. What reason does a fancy witch like her got to kill someone?"

"Good question." Sidra's eye lingered on Elena a moment before she whispered a last message to the bird. It flapped its wings and slipped out the window. The sorceress tracked the wren's flight through the open sky, unable to hide the yearning to follow.

Elena sat against the free wall and drew her legs up defensively, hugging them to her chest. "I didn't kill anyone."

"Well, you don't get locked up in here for making bad wine." The young woman, who couldn't have been out of her teens, transformed again from ingénue to cunning street urchin, the soft angles of her face hardening as she stiffened her jaw. She inched closer and flashed a four-inch piece of sharpened metal she'd pulled from her hair. "And you don't get to sleep with both eyes closed unless we can come to an arrangement."

The shiv, once an ornate silver hairpin, had been filed down to a deadly point, one Elena did not doubt could draw blood. It was the sort of thing that ought to have been confiscated, but savvy Yvette had somehow managed to smuggle in a little nonmagical protection. Clever.

Elena stared at the point aimed at her throat. "What sort of arrangement?"

Seeing she was going to get her way, Yvette's eyes brightened. "You're going to pay for your side of the cell."

"With what?"

Sidra made a clicking noise with her tongue. "Do we have to go through this every time?"

"It's all right for you in here," Yvette snapped back. "You got that bird to pass the time. What have I got?" Sidra dismissed her with a shake of her head. The young woman turned her venom back on Elena. "A witch like you ought to have plenty of rich friends. Whatever they bring you when they visit they got to bring me too. I want a clean blanket, food, and a change of clothes. And new silk stockings. I can't wear these worn-out rags another day."

"No one's going to bring you those things in here," Sidra said.

"Why aren't they?"

"Because no one's going to waste money on a carnival tramp like you."

"Better me than a dried-up old hag whose neck is about to feel the kiss of *la demi-lune*. Your birds can't save you from fate's hand on the guillotine."

The young woman's waspish tongue had found its mark. The sorceress got to her feet. The rattle of metal followed. Beneath her robe a heavily linked chain attached to her ankle trailed back to a solid metal ring affixed to the wall. Elena worried she meant to attack the young woman as she loomed over the dour pixie. If the chains and bars had not held her back, the sorceress might have annihilated the young woman with a single spell, so threatening was her look. Instead, Yvette scuttled away to the other side of the cell, safe in knowing, for the moment at least, she was the more dangerous of the two. Sidra kicked at the straw, then pulled her scarf over her head. She returned to the wall and faced her back to them to gain the only privacy available in such tight quarters.

"Is that true?" Elena asked the young woman. She risked drawing the wrath of both inmates, but she couldn't help wondering about her own fate. "About . . ." She subtly gestured with her fingers drawn against her neck.

An inkling of regret crept into Yvette's voice as she leaned her head back to stare up at the small square of sky framed by the window. "Her execution is in three days. That's why she's chained."

The chill in Elena's body sank from her skin to the inside of her veins, where it swam in a circle around her heart and lungs so she couldn't get a proper breath. Yes, she had wanted Bastien dead. Yes, she had distilled the poison to do the deed. She had even written a spell to bind it to his stomach so he couldn't cough it back up. She did it all, accepting the consequences to her soul if she followed through. But building doubt had created a wall in her mind that she couldn't get over. His denial, spoken only moments after he'd nearly run her down, had been given time to ferment in her thoughts. He'd always been proud of the control he exerted over others, bragging about having neighbors hexed or competitors' fields jinxed. If he'd been responsible for her curse, he wouldn't have backed away from the triumphant moment when he could finally take credit for it. The realization was enough to give her second thoughts, and so she'd stored the poison in the cupboard above her worktable and focused instead on making a wine so superb it would erase the name of Du Monde in the valley. Only now she was trapped behind bars and accused of killing him, possibly facing the same deadly fate as the women beside her.

After a long silence Sidra leaned her head against the bars and stared into the corridor, where the lamps had long been doused. "Do you hear them? They are crying again."

Elena glanced over her shoulder. She'd tuned out the low wails and pitiful calls for mercy imprinted in the stone, too consumed with her own worries, but Sidra had called the voices up again so that they echoed in the dark as if rising out of a tunnel.

The sorceress gathered her chain to her and then looped it into a neat coil at her side. "That one," she said with a tip of her head, "does not believe me when I say there are voices that echo in the hall. They used to keep me up at night. But now I listen for them. I am sorry for them, though I do not know who they are or why they cry."

She wondered where Sidra came from. Whatever distant land, it was far enough away she'd not heard the tragic history of the valley's falsely accused. "They're the voices of the condemned," Elena said. Her eyes followed the path of a low moan, trailing the sound across the floor to a spot on the wall where a pair of eye-hook bolts would have secured someone by the wrists under heavy irons. "They were confined and tortured here for practicing witchcraft two hundred years ago. Men, women, and children."

"What, you can hear them too?" Yvette shook her head as she flexed her foot and pulled her stocking up. "Then you're both loony, if you ask me, listening to a bunch of dead witches."

Elena recalled the time she and Grand-Mère had traveled to the city to shop for the few rare ingredients they couldn't get in the village—root of turmeric, dried fish bladder, and fine henna powder, which they infused into their yarn with a binding spell. Unable to find the correct shop on the unfamiliar street, they'd stopped to ask directions of a woman sweeping her sidewalk. At their approach, the woman took out an evil-eye amulet from her pocket and spit on the ground before shooing them away with her broom. Elena hadn't understood, so Grand-Mère took her to a café for ice cream while she explained their history and why there were still those who held witches in contempt.

"Only most of those you hear weren't witches." Elena stood and gripped the bars with both hands as she closed her eyes. Instantly she knew what Sidra had said earlier about the place not being able to stifle a witch's essence was true. The energy from the rune spell hummed under her fingers, vibrating through the metal like a pulse that blocked her connection to the All Knowing. She opened her eyes again and rubbed her hands together to rid them of the spell's odd energy. "When the condemned were alive, this place was a regular mortal prison. It hadn't been magicked yet. Any healthy witch would have had no trouble escaping these cells."

Yvette snorted. "Or getting caught in the first place."

Elena agreed and then pictured Grand-Mère. "Though any witch too old or weak to defend themselves would have been as helpless as a mortal."

Sidra shifted on her feet so that her ankle chain rattled against the flagstones. "Or someone who'd been cursed?"

It was as if the sorceress had used a scrying glass to peer beneath Elena's skin to inspect the vulnerability embedded on the underside. She rubbed at the gooseflesh on her arms and nodded as a ghost-thought fluttered in her head. Would she have had the strength to escape the witch hunts had it been her in her cursed state?

"What terrible spell did these lost ones unleash to cause their cries to be etched into stone?"

"They were accused of consorting with the Devil and committing evil acts against their neighbors. And it's true, there were some witches—warlocks mostly—who conjured destructive spells that brutalized a handful of villages. But they weren't the ones caught and put in prison. It was almost always some hapless mortal from the valley who they were able to coerce a confession out of."

"They cry for mercy and"—Sidra tilted her ear—"relief from the pain."

"Many were abused. Tortured. Back then the prosecutors might drag a woman to the river and dunk her head under the water, over and over again, until her lungs were near to bursting. Or they'd shave her head. Or use thumbscrews. Or maybe tear a fingernail loose from the bed and force the injury to throb for hours so that the accused would do or say anything to make the pain go away."

"Tell her about the stones," Yvette said, no longer pretending to ignore the conversation.

Elena nodded. "Some had stones stacked on top of them. With every denial, the load increased until the person either suffocated under the crushing load or they confessed convincingly enough to have the weight lifted off before their lungs ruptured from the pressure. Either way, the law got what it wanted."

"Pain has always been the prosecutor's handmaiden," Sidra said, agreeing. Then she closed her eyes and inhaled deeply as she listened. "The women also say they fear the lick of fire at the stake. Did they burn them too?"

"Yes."

"Alive?"

"Sometimes."

Sidra lifted her head from the bars. "But now in this country they take the head with a curved blade." She stared at the empty corridor with the same yearning with which she'd watched the bird escape. "I would trade places with any one of them to have the fire," she said, then bent to pick up a thin wool blanket she'd been using as a pillow. She offered it to Elena. "Here, you'll need this tonight. And don't let Yvette steal it from you, either."

"What's this for?"

"Where I come from we pay our storytellers." The woman smiled briefly, revealing a row of gold and ivory teeth.

"And where is that?"

"The most beautiful desert of pink and gray sand. Where palm trees sway in the morning breeze, and figs grow as big as your fist."

She wanted the blanket but hesitated to accept it, unsure if there were strings attached to accepting a gift from a desert sorceress. What else might she owe in return?

"Take it," Sidra said, tossing it gently as if amused by Elena's inner conflict. "Honestly, I never feel the cold."

"Thank you." She accepted the blanket and retreated as far away from the commode bucket as she could manage. She would find no comfort wedged between the cold stone floor and the weight of her own fear pressing down on her, but she knew she had nothing to confess. She hadn't killed anyone.

And yet Bastien was dead. Murdered to serve some part in a blood magic ritual, if the inspector was to be believed. Old, dark magic that had mostly flown from the world. And for good reason. How many mortals had died during the witch hunts because they couldn't defend themselves with the same quicksilver thoughts of a malevolent witch? She stretched out under her blanket and thought of the midwives, the herb women, and the poor widowed wretches who'd paid the price for the crimes done by coven witches too cunning to be caught. There'd been some improvement in the aftermath, of course, led by reformist witches sick of the killing. The Great Conclave of 1745 had finally brought all sides together. There they'd drawn up the Covenant Laws that all were bound to obey to this day.

Yet it was little salve for the innocent souls still crying out for mercy in the prison's halls.

CHAPTER NINETEEN

Jean-Paul stood in his kitchen, bewildered by the sudden warren of cupboards and drawers surrounding him. He'd lived in the château for three years yet had never cooked or prepared a meal. Not even a late-night snack. Madam, he realized, had taken care of his every need. Sometimes before he even knew he needed it. And now he could strangle himself with his own ignorance when what he needed to know was where to find a box of *allumettes*.

He had no idea where Madame had gone. One minute she was rummaging through the storage room in the cellar, upset over Elena's arrest, and the next she was grabbing her umbrella and storming out the front door, mumbling about charlatans and madmen. She'd said not to worry, to take care of the place while she was gone. Or was it *when* she was gone? At any rate, she hadn't returned. And now he couldn't find a damn thing, just when Elena was counting on him.

He banged his head against the cupboard, one thunk followed by another. How could he lose Elena now? He'd only just found her.

He straightened, gave his suit vest a good tug, and forced himself to think logically. He was a trained attorney, for God's sake. He ought to be able to reason out a witch's kitchen. Matches would be on a shelf near the stove in any normal setup, but as he thought about it now he couldn't recall Madame actually striking a match. Ever. He turned on a hunch and opened the drawer beside the icebox where the odd bits of twine and broken paraffin candles awaited their usefulness. Miraculously he found the elusive *allumettes* buried beneath a tin of leftover anise candies. He slipped the box in his trouser pocket, buttoned his suit coat, and donned his gray homburg. He'd just tugged the hat snug on his head when a loud and persistent knocking banged against the front door.

He debated ignoring whoever it was, but they would see him in the courtyard. And he couldn't delay any longer. The prison was twelve miles away, and the first court hearing was in the afternoon. If he wanted to have a proper visit with Elena first, he needed to leave within the next few minutes. After a glance at his pocket watch, he opened the front door just as a fist prepared to pound out another round of insistent knocking. The fist might as well have hit him straight between the eyes.

"Well, are you going to invite us in or just stand there lollygagging all afternoon?"

Marion Martel stood on the threshold dressed in an ecru skirt and jacket ensemble and wide-brimmed hat—a little showy with the white plume and two hydrangeas cocked on the side, but subdued enough for daytime wear, at least for a woman as wealthy as the widow of Monsieur Philippe Martel.

Jean-Paul kissed his mother on both cheeks. "What are you doing here?"

"That's a fine hello." She pushed past him and plucked off her linen gloves one finger at a time as she took in the château's modest salon. Jean-Paul's uncle, tall and thin but with a complexion suggestive of peptic upset, followed inside.

"We caught the first train out this morning. As soon as we heard." Georges Martel removed his straw boater and gave his hair a quick comb to the side with his fingers.

"Heard what?"

His uncle fumed. "Good God, how do you think this looks? Bastien du Monde was one of the firm's most important clients. He turns up dead, and an employee of yours is arrested for his murder? Of course I had to come straight down."

"She's not an employee. She's . . ."

"She's what?" His mother folded her gloves in her hand and peered at him the way she had when he was a child and suspected him of something. He looked away, and then she had him. "Oh, not another trollop from the country."

He shot his head back up. "It's not like that, *Maman*. She's a . . . vigneron." He held back the word "witch," still too uncertain to trust its verity on his tongue.

"A woman winemaker?"

"You have a case of her prized pinot noir sitting in your cellar. Yes, she's the one who coaxed that spectacular Renard vintage you love to serve at dinner parties to life. Now, if you'll excuse me, I was just about to leave so I may see her. There's a hearing this afternoon, and I need time to speak with my client."

"Your client?" The color in his uncle's face went slightly orange. "You can't be serious. You're representing Bastien's murderer? This is outrageous. We didn't send you to law school so you could defend that unscrupulous woman."

"On the contrary. It's the first noble thing I've done with my degree."

"Jean-Paul, be reasonable." When he clenched his jaw, daring his mother to say another word, she settled like a mourning dove tucking her feathers back. "Are you saying you actually care for this one?"

"I do. Of course I do. She's an invaluable asset to the vineyard," he said. "And I know she's innocent."

"Nothing more?"

He faltered then. Damn his mother and her intuition. She might as well be half witch herself, the way she could read him. He'd not said it aloud. He'd barely admitted it to himself. But, yes by God, he was falling for Elena, and happily so.

The admission must have shown on his face. His mother gave him one of her intuitive nods before her mouth broke into a half smile.

"It's not too late to come home on the evening train," she said. "Save your reputation in the city."

He took her hand and held it between his own. "Yes, *Maman*, it is."

Her eyes teared up at the gentle rebuff, but she shook it off. "Well, I suppose anyone that valuable in my son's eyes deserves, at least, the benefit of the doubt." His uncle was about to pile on more accusations, but she put her hand on his arm to silence him, much the way she'd reined in her husband when he was alive. "Come along. I think it only proper we prepare a small care package for your client, don't you?"

She hooked her arm through her son's, and, despite his need to leave, she packed a well-thought-out basket containing a loaf of crusty bread, a wedge of newly ripened cheese, and a handful of dried apricots she'd discovered in the pantry. Like a magician, she covered it all under a plain black wool shawl taken from a hook in the hallway, which she folded into a neat triangle.

Three hours later, after seeing his family to a respectable hotel so they might return to the city on the next day's train, Jean-Paul unhooked the basket from his saddle and stood on the curb outside Maison de Chêne. He tied off the reins and then scratched the back of his head where a headache was hatching. He'd thought of nothing but the law on his ride out—the prosecution's strength, the grounds for his defense, and the complication of dealing with a crime committed with magic he didn't fully understand. Yet she was innocent. He knew it. And so he would do this for her. He would go back to the law and step into his father's shoes once more to see Elena free, and then this vigneron would be done with motions and writs and *corpus delicti* for good.

Elena was sitting alone at the table with her head down when he entered. She stood when she saw him, her eyes full of hope. And for a second he believed it too. And then the chains binding her wrists clattered against the edge of the table, enough to snuff out any false notions this would be an easy visit.

"Are you all right?" It was a dumb question, but she nodded bravely. The tainted smell of confinement lingered in her hair and on her clothes. "Of course you're not. How could you be?" He reached out and took her hand, damn the consequences.

The jailer who had let him in the room cleared her throat. "I was told you are her *attorney*, monsieur."

He gave Elena's hand a squeeze to let her know everything would be fine and then stiffened his manner to more accurately reflect his position. "Yes, I am representing this woman, so you will kindly wait outside the door while I confer with my client in private."

Jean-Paul closed the door behind the guard, then sat across the table from Elena as the runes on her cuffs glowed an iridescent blue even his eyes could see.

"Tell me this isn't real," she said, peering at him with those golden eyes of hers as he removed his hat. "Have I swallowed a dreaming potion? Did someone feed me the underside of a bad mushroom?" She sat back in her chair and looked up at the ceiling while holding up her bound hands in a cupped position.

He didn't have an answer for her. He barely understood the context of her complaint. But he did know she was in terrible danger of losing everything, including her life.

"I'm going to do my best to get you out of here." He paused, catching himself before he added *my love*. How quickly the words nearly leaped to his lips of their own free will.

Elena stood instead and began to pace. "Where is Grand-Mère? Did she come with you? Is she well?"

He cleared his throat and brought out his notepad and fountain pen. "She went out first thing this morning and hadn't returned by the time I left." When he saw a look of alarm in Elena's eyes he added, "I'm sure she's fine." But then he hesitated. He couldn't imagine where the old woman had gone. She hadn't left the house without him for an escort into town the entire time he'd known her.

"Didn't she say where she was going?"

"To be honest, she didn't make much sense. She kept muttering about 'that crazy man.'"

"What crazy man? Nettles? Bastien? Who?"

"I don't know. She went into your workroom in the cellar, and when she came out she told me to take care of the place. I offered to bring her, but she said there was something she had to do, and then she headed for the footpath leading over the hill."

Elena dropped into her chair and stared at the wall behind him as if dumbfounded by the account. A moment later, eyes back on him, she asked, "How confident are you that you can get me released?"

He set his pen down. "If I'm going to defend you, we must be completely honest with each other." He leaned in closer and set his hand on hers again. "I'm going to do everything in my power to get you out of here, but if I fail you will have to remain until your trial, which could take months. The prosecution has indicated they wish to make an example with your arrest to show the community they've got the situation under control."

"But they don't. And if we fail later at trial, I proffer my neck before the guillotine for a crime I didn't commit while the real killer goes free."

He saw the truth take hold in its merciless way, yet she forced a brave face when he confirmed everything she'd said. It was then he realized she might doubt his abilities.

"I can try and find you another lawyer," he said. "There must be someone who specializes in cases of the supernatural, if you're not comfortable with me representing you, but I'd have to put the vineyard up as collateral for payment. I have no more money left, and no one to borrow from." His uncle had said as much when he dropped him off at the hotel. *Defend her if you like, but there will be no association with the law firm. Ever.* The confrontation had bruised him harder than he'd thought. Cut loose of the family business, he was left as pocket-poor as any beggar on the street. If his flailing attempt to make wine didn't improve, he was finished. And without Elena it never would.

"No, I want you," she said. "Only you."

Her words, as strong as any spell she could have conjured, rallied his confidence again. He picked up his pen, and they spent the remaining time together preparing for her court hearing. When they'd gone through all the charges and how he wished to proceed with her defense, he knocked on the door to alert the guard he was ready to leave. As the keys jangled in the lock, he slipped a tin of cigarettes and the box of *allumettes* from the kitchen drawer in her pocket.

"What is this?"

"Think of it as currency. At least in the city that's how it worked. I assume it might be the same in a witch's prison without access to your . . . ability."

"Ah, yes," she said, patting the tin and matches in her pocket. "Thank you for thinking of this."

He wished then to embrace her, to feel her hair in his hands. They had only a moment left together. But already the door had opened, and she would soon be whisked to the courtroom.

"One more thing," he said as the guard searched her basket of food for contraband one more time. "I've arranged to interview Gerda du Monde in the morning to get her account. I want to see for myself what she thinks of the charges. It's possible Bastien was involved in something he shouldn't have been that got him killed, something she might be able to shed some light on."

Elena's face tightened in concern as she nodded. "All right, but take care not to upset her. And see if you can learn anything more about those witch sisters I told you about. There's something not right about them."

And with that she was gone, and he felt once more the pinch of his shoes as he walked toward the courtroom.

CHAPTER TWENTY

Elena sank with her back against the wall, landing in a defeated slump on the floor. She'd maintained her composure in front of Jean-Paul, the judge, and even the guard who'd escorted her back to her cell, but now anger and frustration had frayed her resolve. Bail had been denied. She wasn't getting out. She'd be stuck inside these walls for months. Trapped once more in Old Fox's teeth. She dug her fingers in her hair and tugged at the roots until she wanted to scream.

"Doesn't mean you'll be convicted," Yvette said.

The young woman chewed on an apricot and glanced expectantly at her from the opposite wall. She no longer made threats with her hairpin, but Elena couldn't be sure if that was a permanent change or they'd merely struck a silent truce after she'd given away her basket of food.

"I can't do this again."

Yvette spit out a sliver of pit. "What'd they say in court?"

Sidra was better at keeping her thoughts from her face, but she looked up from cooing and petting the little sparrow perched on her bent knee, eager to hear.

"The prosecutor called me a deviant and said it would be a crime to release someone so dangerous onto the streets. Apparently the magistrate agreed."

"You? A deviant?" Yvette's mouth fell open. "Believe me, I know deviant, and the only thing weird about you is that missing toe of yours."

Mortified, Elena quickly covered her bare feet with the hem of her skirt, proving the young woman's point. The reaction elicited a chortle out of Sidra, whose gold and ivory teeth gleamed in a wide smile. It spread to Yvette, who giggled before falling over on her side in a fit of laughter. Finally Elena succumbed as well, chortling like a madwoman until tears leaked from the corners of her eyes.

A moment later, out of breath yet relieved of the pressure like a newly opened bottle of champagne, she sobered and dabbed at her eyes with her sleeve. She could still smell Jean-Paul on her skin. She inhaled, feeling herself calm. With luck the scent would last the night so she might dream of him instead of the nightmare her life had become.

"You got to see your man in court?" The kohl smudges under Yvette's eyes had turned to watercolor streaks of black across her cheeks.

"He's my lawyer."

The young woman sniffed, as if trying to catch his scent too. "That's convenient. I'll have to keep that in mind next time a lawyer comes to me for *my* services. We might just have to make a trade."

Reminded of trades, Elena reached in her pocket for the cigarettes. They were no use to her as currency. Other than the basket she'd brought back with her, there was nothing to buy—no extra food, no spare blankets, no shoes—but if the cigarettes encouraged small talk, they would at least help pass the time and make life easier.

She drew the blue tin and box of matches out of her pocket and waved them at Yvette. "Here. A small consolation for the deviants."

"Cigs!" Yvette pounced in that sprightly way of hers, crossing the floor with a dancer's lightness at the sight of the tin. "How did you sneak them past the guards?" she whispered.

"They're not allowed?" She held the cigarettes and matches in her palm.

Yvette snatched them away with one swipe. "Shhhh!" she said and twisted around to see her cellmate's reaction.

Every muscle in Sidra's body tensed. Her mouth drew into a hard line. Her eyes, dark and hooded now, checked the corridor for signs of Matron with a predator's gaze.

"Matches," Yvette said to Sidra. The word had a bite to it Elena didn't understand. Then the young woman rattled the *allumettes* inside the box, teasing. "Come and get them."

The sorceress leaped, but Yvette was quick-footed and scurried back to her side of the cell. Sidra's leg iron had stopped her just short of reaching the woman. She lunged and swiped with her long nails, but Yvette merely grinned, taunting her by shaking the box again. Confident she was untouchable, Yvette took out a cigarette and slid a match from the box. Her lips pressed into a hard smile as she dragged the tip of the match against the strike pad with a hard swipe. The phosphorous ignited in a flash of orange, and Sidra's eyes flared in sync. Then she curled her lip at the young woman while she watched her draw the flame through the tobacco with a long inhale.

Elena thought Sidra might cut off her own foot to be free of her chain as she watched the smoke swirl from the end of Yvette's cigarette. She knew tobacco was a powerful herb. She even knew a potion or two that called for adding the stuff, but she'd never seen anyone so ravenous for the taste.

Sidra thrust her hand out. "Give them to me, *sharmoota*!"

"They're Egyptienne Luxury brand too," Yvette said, reading the label. "Isn't that made to measure?"

"Give her the cigarettes," Elena said. "They're for everyone."

A trail of smoke snaked out of Yvette's mouth as she tilted her head. "Want to know why ciggies aren't allowed in our cell?" The young woman bared a fiendish smile. "Watch this," she said and tossed the lit cigarette toward Sidra.

The sorceress sprawled on her stomach on the filthy floor, her hand open, fingers spread wide to catch the half-smoked cigarette as it rolled toward her. Once it was in her hand, she no longer prostrated herself. She raised herself up as if in a trance and walked back to the spot where her chain was bolted to the wall.

Her desperation evaporated. And yet she hadn't inhaled. Hadn't even held the tobacco to her mouth. Instead, she closed her eyes and thanked her god, as though she were eternally thankful for the cast-off stub.

"Just remember who gave that to you," warned Yvette, lighting a fresh cigarette for herself.

"Why can't we have cigarettes?"

Elena waited for an answer, but the young woman merely blew smoke and pointed at Sidra. The desert witch held her arm out to let her silk robe drape to the floor. Her eyes widened in fanatic-like anticipation as she pressed the smoldering tip of the cigarette against the fabric. A black hole rimmed with orange bloomed alive, burning through the silk until it ignited into flame.

"What is she doing? Sidra, no!"

"They can block magic and spells," Sidra said as the fire climbed up her arm, glowing with an unnatural intensity, "but they cannot strip the essence of who we are." Sidra's gold and ivory teeth gleamed in a triumphant smile, then she raised her arms as if welcoming the fire, begging the heat to burn her clothes, her skin, her hair.

Elena reached for her blanket to smother the flames, but it was too late. The fire had spread too fast, as if Sidra had been drenched in oil. Fully engulfed, the desert witch glowed within the flames before bursting into a fiery tornado.

The heat grew so unbearable that Elena had to back away and shield her eyes with her hand. Helpless, she watched the flames consume Sidra's body until it crumbled to the ground, disintegrating into a pile of waxy ash. The fire fizzled, and a column of smoke rose from the metal leg iron, coiling upward as if directed by an unseen force. Yvette stood, her eyes lit in amazement. A ghost of a laugh echoed off the walls, followed by a whiff of frankincense, and then the smoke trailed out the window and was free.

"Wow! She did it. She got out." Yvette spun in a pirouette. "I'd heard about it, but I never thought I'd ever see one combust in front of my very own eyes."

Elena hugged the blanket to her chest. She'd thought she knew every kind of magic there was, but clearly she was wrong. "How could she survive burning without a protection spell?"

Yvette picked up the cigarettes and matches and stashed them behind a loose stone in the wall. "Thought you vine witches were all educated. You didn't know she was a jinni? They're made of fire. Of course she survived."

"A jinni?" Grand-Mère had always made them out to be more myth than real. Wisps of smoke carried on the wind. The scent of premonition. A streak of madness in an otherwise calm mind.

"One joined the carnival after the last World's Fair," Yvette said, taking a last, deep inhale of her cigarette. "He'd traveled across two continents to see the wonders of the new age and then ended up fascinated and in love with our fire juggler. Craziest thing you ever saw, the two of them. Sparks flying every time they held hands."

A door slammed in the corridor, followed by the sound of running feet. Yvette scuttled into her corner, waving a hand to clear the smoke. Elena stood frozen over the burn mark on the floor, still clutching the blanket.

The prison guard bolted for the cell bars. "Oh, no, no, no!" He reached for his whistle and sounded the alarm. Matron waddled in two minutes later, her robe flowing out behind her.

"What happened? Where is our third prisoner?" The matron cast a spell to illuminate the cell and saw the black char pile in the center of the floor. "She escaped by fire? How did she get access to a flame?" She nearly rattled the teeth out of the poor young guard as she shook him by his lapel, demanding an answer.

"That one," he said, pointing at Elena. "She had a visitor." Matron shook him again, so he added in his defense, "It must have been her attorney. They don't get searched."

Matron narrowed her eyes at Elena. "You'll regret this," she said and snapped her fingers at the guard. "Sound the tower alarm. Notify the mayor. We have a killer on the loose."

Elena sat up and counted the stars through the bars on the window. More than a thousand of them flickered in the black space within the narrow frame. She wrapped her blanket around her shoulders, inhaled the trace of incense left behind by its previous owner. To be made of fire in a world full of fuel—a whirling dervish of controlled rage, spinning beneath the eye of the All Knowing—the notion sent a chill rippling over her skin.

To burn until even your bones turned to ash, yet survive the transformation without aid of a spell . . . Sidra had been right. For a person's essence to survive, it had to be so entwined with the core being that chains and counterspells couldn't impair it, which was why she'd been able to hold on to just enough of herself to stay yoked to her intellect and escape the curse. Her second sight had opened a pathway that allowed her to survive because it was intrinsic to who she was. Just as a jinni was made of fire. And a murderer was drawn to blood.

Yes, that too was something that resided within. She'd once thought herself capable of committing murder, dipping her hands in the blood of revenge to be free of the pain of her curse, but it was a stain her hands would not wear. When faced with the deed she proved no murderer. Yet whoever killed Bastien must bear that brutal streak in their skin, in their hair, and on their breath. They would be imbued with the stench of it, because blood and death were a part of their essence. But what would make a person turn to such depravity? She understood the mind exploring the thrill of the risk, but to leap to the act?

A warning crawled up her back one joint at a time to perch on her collarbone. The archaic rules of blood magic tumbled over in her mind. What value was there in spilling the blood of a fox or cat? Or Bastien's for that matter? And what spell would allow for either one? For all her powers of second sight, she was blind to its meaning. And without her freedom she was as helpless as any stumbling mortal to figure it out.

She knocked the back of her head against the wall in frustration. "I shouldn't be here."

"What, you should be at the cabaret drinking champagne?" Even after Matron's threat, Yvette smoked a defiant last cigarette after lights out, blowing the smoke high into the air, daring the guards to catch her.

That one was trouble. Too young to foresee the consequences of her rebellion, yet too savvy to claim ignorance in how she might also take others down with her actions. The stars said as much. Emboldened by the dark phase of the moon, the constellations twisted round in their infinite sky, slowly corkscrewing into the future, divining immutable futures for those still awake and gazing up.

"You'll get us both shackled to the floor if you don't get rid of that thing."

"Oh là là, aren't we feisty tonight." The young woman stubbed out the butt of the cigarette on the floor near the place where Sidra had incinerated herself. "Happy now?"

"Not at all."

She ignored Yvette's rude flick of the fingers under her chin and stretched out on her side to rest her head on her folded arm. The guards had scraped the surface ash from the floor earlier to gather evidence, but a sooty stain remained. Elena stared at it with a stab of jealousy before closing her eyes.

Not even three breaths later she smelled smoke again and propped herself up on her elbow, ready for an all-out fight. "I said put it out."

"I did!"

Elena sniffed the air again, and her nose filled with the scent of frankincense too strong and immediate to be coming from the blanket. She sat up, eyes searching the darkness. As she traced the cell for the source, she spotted a seam of smoke snaking between the cracks in the overhead beams. More sweet smoke sank between the joists, and then the first of the flames begin to lick the underside of the beams.

"Get up, Yvette."

"Why are you such an uptight bitch?"

The young woman rolled over, brandishing her sharpened hairpin like a dagger as a booming series of footfalls rattled the roof. Her eyes shot to the ceiling. A ribbon of smoke wafted down, deliberately wrapping around her neck like a noose. Properly panicked, she covered her mouth with her thin blouse and escaped to Elena's corner of the cell.

"Guard! Fire!" Yvette shook the bars as the smoke drifted toward her again. "Fire! Open the door, you bastard!" She stepped back and desperately tried a spell on the lock. It fizzled the moment the words fell off her tongue.

"It's no use," Elena said, looking for something—anything—that might help them escape. Finally she picked up the blanket, started a tear at one end, and then ripped it into three pieces.

"What are you doing?"

"Thinking like a mortal," she said and tied the pieces of blanket together so that she had one long piece. "Give me that hairpin." The young woman handed it over, and Elena knotted it to the end of the blanket and gave it a hard tug. Hefting the blanket in her right hand, she slipped her arm through the bars and swung the blanket at the alarm bell on the wall. The knot in the blanket glanced off the metal, making a pitiful muffled noise.

"Harder!"

"I'm trying!" She took a breath and aimed again. This time the silver pin struck the bell, clanging out a note loud and clear. She did it again and again and again until the guard entered the corridor ready to curse them both for waking him.

Two trails of smoke snaked down the hall, twining around the guard's head and neck.

Yvette banged on the bars to get the guard's attention back on them. "Open the door, you fool! Let us out before we die in here."

The guard hesitated, blinking as much, it seemed, against the blinding smoke as he did against the strict rules. At the last moment he relented and put the key in the lock. The door swung open, and they ran through the sweet cloud of burnt incense.

"That way," the guard said, pointing to the stairs. Their feet skipped down the steps, hurrying toward the exit. They reached the ground level, eager to run for the door, when the guard ordered them to halt. Matron stood at the other end of the corridor shouting out dousing spells, but the flames licking the beamed ceiling only grew, her words hitting like water thrown on a grease fire. Even the stone foundation appeared to catch fire as the flames clung to the walls of the old fortress.

"It's no use," she called. "Evacuate the witches. I'll see to the mortal prisoners in the east wing."

The guard fumbled for his keys in a mad panic. "You two, in here." He gestured toward a small room where metal restraints hung in rows along the wall.

Yvette balked. "You heard her—get us out of here."

"Not until you're shackled."

"The whole place is going to burn down and you want to restrain us?"

"I'm not risking any more escapes," he said and shoved them both face-first against the wall.

Vibrations from the rune spell buzzed along Elena's skin as the guard snapped a shackle around her left wrist. Hope sank as the other cuff went around Yvette's right wrist, binding them together. If she'd had a notion to run, it had just been pruned to the nub.

The giant oak door of Maison de Chêne opened. The guard escorted the witches down the steps and under the brickwork arch at the bottom of the hill. Free from the clouds of smoke, they sucked in deep gulps of fresh night air as they clung to the stone pillars holding up the arch. Fear dissolved into awe as Elena turned to stare at the massive flames crowning the roof of the ancient castle. Below, at the main entrance, Matron herded a dozen panicked women through the doorway, ordering them to stay calm as she waved her wand. But before she could spit the incantation out, the beams over the main entrance caved in and the shackled prisoners scattered down the stone steps like a stampeding herd of gazelles, tripping and tumbling over each other. The guards, including the one watching over Elena and Yvette, ran to contain the chaos and corral the mortal prisoners.

A familiar laugh echoed off the walls of the prison, prickling Elena's supernatural instincts.

"It's Sidra," she whispered to Yvette. "She's doing this."

Yvette's face lit up. "I knew she wouldn't forget who gave her that ciggie. Come on, now's our chance."

"What, you mean run?"

"Yes!"

"And how far do you think we'll get, bound together and unable to do magic?"

Yvette wrinkled her nose at the logic and yanked her arm, forcing Elena off balance. She tugged back, and a column of smoke rose up beside them. An overpowering cloud of incense prompted them to wave their free hands in front of their faces, while the shape of a human emerged from the smoke.

"Thought you'd be halfway to your desert by now," Yvette said.

"And maybe I was. But a debt is a debt." Sidra, now fully reanimated, grinned and flashed her gold-inlaid teeth at them, then shook her head at their shackled wrists. "This complicates things, does it not?"

Yvette raised her arm, hauling Elena's up with it by the chain. "Can you get these things off us?"

Sidra shrugged. "It is a thing I can do. I owe you each for my escape, and therefore a favor is due to both. And yet I did not expect you would be chained together."

"What difference does it make?" Yvette squealed before stealing a look over her shoulder. "Just do it before that damn guard comes back."

Sidra trailed her fingers through the air, and a screen of smoke cut them off from view of the guards.

The jinni met Elena's eye. "Your fates have been bound."

"What's that mean?" Yvette asked.

"It means you both must want freedom for me to grant such a thing."

"Of course we do!"

Sidra thumped a knuckle against Yvette's forehead and then pointed her finger at Elena. "Did you ever stop to think this one might actually be innocent? If I grant your desire and set you free, I make her a fugitive too. I cannot decide another's fate for them. She must choose her path."

Yvette dropped her arm and glared at Sidra.

Elena felt the pinch of the shackles against her wrists. Running meant guilt, but she feared staying would end in a sure date with *la demi-lune*, innocent or not. She was trapped again by the same wicked hand of fate that had stripped her of her freedom once before while the real murderer still wandered the lanes and hills of home. As did the witch who'd cursed her seven years earlier.

Her desire for justice reignited. She raised her wrist before the jinni. "Set us free."

Sidra raised an eyebrow and nodded. "As you wish." A second later a flash of sparks encircled the magical shackles binding the witches together. The cuffs glowed as if they'd been thrust in a blacksmith's fire before disintegrating into a pile of ash at their feet. The witches rubbed their unburned wrists, kissed the jinni's cheek, and ran.

The crescent moon slipped loose from the clouds as the baying of hounds and the shrill of the alarm bellowed over the embankment. A layer of smoke, meant to conceal movement and confuse the bloodhounds, thinned to reveal distant torchlight moving in their direction. Elena crouched lower in the ravine beside the impish girl. She was a fool to have fled, escaping into the night like a common criminal. But her desperation to find the truth and exonerate herself had outweighed her better judgment. She'd followed an impulse, a witch's natural instinct, and one that had rarely let her down before.

The dogs were near enough that she heard the snuffling of their breath against the earth.

Yvette stretched her neck to listen. "Why are they getting closer?"

"The guards must be using counterspells to disperse Sidra's smokescreen."

"What do we do?"

"Give them what they want." Elena scanned the ground and plucked up a fuzzy dandelion by its stem. She swiped the delicate puffball over her exposed forearm, then held it to her lips. "Scatter these seeds upon the ground, and with them shall my scent be bound." She blew on the seed head to scatter its hundreds of pappi on the prevailing breeze. The tufted seeds shimmered briefly in the dark as they carried her magic over the ravine and into the woods to create a separate scent trail.

"Let's hope it's enough to confuse the dogs. Come on."

With Yvette on Elena's heels, the two ran for their lives in the opposite direction. Thorns, twigs, and stones ravaged their unshod feet as they cut through a meadow. They crossed a shallow creek lined with silver birch, then clawed through mud and weeds to climb the opposite bank. When they emerged from the water they followed a dirt road as far as they dared, then ducked beneath a stone bridge to catch their breath.

"Are they coming?"

Elena listened, watching for the flicker of torches. An owl hooted. A frog croaked in the reeds. A firefly blinked above the meadow. "I don't think so."

"I haven't run like that since I was a kid stealing bread from the *boulangerie* on the corner." Yvette leaned her head against the stone, breathing hard but smiling.

Elena tried not to think about how deep her life had plunged into disaster. Instead, she eyed the weeds that clung to the patch of ground beside the bridge. Spotting a familiar stem, she plucked gray-green mallow leaves off by the fistful.

"Show me your feet," she said.

Yvette pretended to be annoyed but did as she was told, peeling her stockings off. Elena inspected the cuts on the soles, then rubbed the mallow leaves over both feet while whispering a quick healing spell to seal the skin for the long walk still ahead.

"How'd you know how to do that? Or that trick with the dandelions?"

"The healing spell? I've known about that since I was eight. Got my share of slivers running around a vineyard in my bare feet, I can tell you."

"Is your *maman* a witch too?"

"I'm told she was. A country hedge-witch who made potions and wine. I barely remember. She died when I was a young girl."

"Who taught you all those spells, then?"

"Grand-Mère . . . well, she's not really my grandmother. She took me in and raised me. Trained me how to be a vine witch."

"Didn't know my mother, neither."

The frogs croaked again, making them jump.

Elena craned her neck to search for signs of searchlights or dogs. "Would we have a better chance if we split up?"

"Are you kidding?" Yvette rolled her tattered stockings back on and tested her feet against the soil, ready to move again. "You wouldn't last the night without me. Come on. I know which way to go."

Their pursuers hadn't yet picked up their trail. And her primitive calculations of the stars confirmed they were headed in the direction of the answers she sought. With nothing to stop her, Elena quickly rubbed the mallow over her bare feet and then chased after the young woman who darted, lithe as a pixie, through the meadow grass.

CHAPTER TWENTY-ONE

Jean-Paul arrived ten minutes early but knocked anyway. A servant in a black dress and white apron answered the door of the grand château and let him in. He waited in the foyer, hat in hand, while the servant walked to the back of the house to announce him. In her absence he stared at the floor. He could hardly do otherwise. But the black-and-white contrast of the harlequinesque marble soon gave him a bout of vertigo, so he lifted his eyes to follow the hand-carved mahogany banister leading to the upper floors. It curved in graceful sinuosity, like a woman's back arched in the act of lovemaking. Art nouveau style at its grandest. Intrigued, his eye climbed even higher to where a gas-fed chandelier, adorned with a hundred teardrop crystals, gleamed fully bright directly above his head. He took three instinctive steps to the left in the off chance a bolt should suddenly come loose. The house, he reflected, was old and graced with envious prerevolutionary bones, yet it reeked from the scent of new money. What his mother called *nouveau riche*. He wondered, briefly, if the newly widowed owner was planning to sell.

The servant returned and escorted him to the rear of the house, where a domed solarium overlooked the south slope of the vineyard. The addition was typical of other well-to-do homes he'd visited, with its copper-green metalwork and arched glass. Though this one bore a distinct difference on the inside. A bureau Mazarin, carved from ebony and walnut, sat against one wall. It resembled one he'd seen in a museum, only this example was much more elaborate in scale. The ornate desk had to be hundreds of years old, yet dried herbs and dead flowers dangled by their muddy roots from a rack suspended above, raining dirt onto the bottles, tincture jars, and row of ancient-looking books arranged on top. He wished to peek inside the drawers, but the servant snuffed the impulse by offering him a seat in one of four damask chairs arranged around a mahogany table in the center of the room.

He thanked her and tossed his hat on the chair as he admired the remarkable vigor of the plants growing in pots near the windows. Exotic palm fronds arced toward the ceiling, and tiny succulents were perched under glass domes, along with containers of foxglove, belladonna, and one beautiful ornamental bush he didn't know. Reddish leaves and spiky flowers were just coming into bloom. He saw no lilacs among them, though the air hung heavy with their heady scent. Then he remembered the scent of her perfume. He turned to his left to find Gerda du Monde standing at a potter's bench behind one of the massive palms.

She was dressed in black mourning lace as she stood before a row of white orchids. The effect was as stark as seeing a raven in the snow. She snipped a piece of twine with her shears, then tied it around the neck of a bloom-heavy flower head, securing it to a wooden stake in the pot. "Well, well, well, Monsieur Martel," she said without looking up. "The attorney for my husband's murderer."

"I hope to prove otherwise." She laughed without humor at his claim. "Thank you for agreeing to see me," he said. "As my telegram stated, I hope I might ask you some questions about that night."

"You're free to ask, though I've already given my statement to the police and that twaddling fool agent from the Covenants Regulation Bureau."

"Yes, I've read your remarks. After discovering your husband's body, it was you, in fact, who demanded the police contact Agent Nettles to report a supernatural crime had taken place. It's one of the things I'm curious about. I don't wish to make you uncomfortable, but can you tell me what it was about the scene that convinced you it was a crime involving witchcraft? Was there a mark? A scent of brimstone in the air? Some kind of aura?"

She turned the potted orchid from side to side as if deciding which angle suited it best. "Do you have much experience with the occult, monsieur?"

"No, not really." He had even less experience with murder cases, but he wasn't about to advertise that.

"Never sat in on a séance? Never had your palm read? Never bought a love potion at a carnival?"

"Doesn't everyone play those games when they're young?"

She finally turned her head and peered at him with those ice-chip-blue eyes. "You don't consider those to be part of the supernatural arts, then? Is it possible you already understand that real magic isn't about parlor tricks? Perhaps you're further along than I thought."

Jean-Paul thought back to his conversation with Brother Anselm on the night he'd seen the beast materialize in the vineyard. It pricked his palms with sweat even now to recall the image, knowing it was real. Or at least knowing the gargoyle existed in some unseen plane of existence. The experience had profoundly transformed his view of the supernatural.

"I mean to defend Elena—that is, Mademoiselle Boureanu—to the best of my ability. I'm willing to learn whatever I need to about the occult to make that happen. I'm aware it will require a deeper acquaintance with magic than I have now."

"Not just any magic." She turned the orchid once more and tapped a finger under its delicate petal chin. "Blood magic is a very old and revered form of sorcery. Also quite gruesome. Most witches today don't have the stomach for it," she said, picking up the potted orchid and crossing the floor to the desk.

To deflect from his own discomfort with the subject, he took pen and paper out of his jacket pocket and vowed to keep a professional demeanor for Elena's sake. "Can you tell me how blood magic is different? What it's used for?" And even as he said the words he had to fight off a shiver that warned him he was trespassing on dangerous ground.

Her back was to him as she ran her finger over the tincture bottles on the desk, yet he sensed a smile in her response. "Blood is the fuel that powers certain spells," she said and took down a bottle of aquamarine liquid. She unstoppered the cork and passed the solution under her nose. "Bloodletting releases the energy so it can be harnessed and used. Not unlike petrol in an automobile."

Despite the macabre subject, the comparison made sense. Magic could work much like chemistry, or physics, or perhaps even mathematics, only on a grander scale. It must follow its own set of rules, a formula, or some exotic principle, the same as any science, albeit taken to an extreme beyond what the normal human could do or comprehend.

And then the reality of what Gerda had said struck his conscience. Bloodletting. The severing of a vein or artery, that's what she'd meant.

She spun around as if reading his mind, her brows pinched together as tears formed in her eyes. "My husband was killed for his blood. If you'd seen the body, you'd understand the difference between a ritual murder and a mortal wound. The heart was cut clean out."

He nodded as if he understood her pain, yet there was no comprehending something so heinous. He expressed his condolences again and then thought it best to veer the conversation back into the more mundane aspects of the investigation lest she shut down and refuse to answer any more questions.

"I know this is a difficult time, but can you recall your husband's movements that day? Did he have any unusual visitors or appointments?"

"Unusual?" Gerda poured a drop of the blue liquid on a square of cloth, then dabbed it over the orchid's leaves and petals. "Bastien was a popular and powerful man. People were here all the time. Everybody wanted something from him."

"Elena didn't."

"She wanted him dead. That's something."

Taken aback by her directness, he fought for a response but was interrupted by the servant, who'd returned bearing a tray with a silver coffee service for two and an envelope.

"This just arrived, madame. The courier said it was urgent."

Gerda finished applying the liquid on the orchid—blue vitriol, in all likelihood, the same mixture he used to treat fungus—then set it in the center of the coffee table before snapping up the envelope and flicking it open with her fingernail. Her left eyebrow arched in interest as she read its contents. "Thank you, Marguerite. You're dismissed for the day. You may go to your room."

"Shall I pour the coffee first?"

"I'll reserve that pleasure for myself."

The servant bowed her head as one wise to the consequences of lingering and turned on her heel. Gerda stuffed the note back in its envelope, then gestured for Jean-Paul to sit.

He'd rather thought it was time to be on his way. Given her mood he doubted he'd gain as much useful information as he'd hoped, and he still needed to inquire with the Bureau about the black-market witches Elena had mentioned, but he didn't wish to appear impolite. Reluctantly Jean-Paul sat in one of the damask chairs. At any rate, he could certainly do with a jolt of caffeine to get him through the research that lay ahead of him.

He'd just settled, crossing his leg, when Madame dropped the note she'd been delivered. He bent forward to retrieve it, awkwardly stretching his arm under the table.

"Tell me, do you know if the inspector tried to get a confession out of your client?" Gerda asked as she sat on the chair opposite and poured the coffee. "I've heard he can be quite rough, once the door is closed."

His eyes locked on the note as he handed it back. The return address was for the prison at Maison de Chêne. "She was questioned, of course," he said distractedly, "but she has nothing to confess."

"Cream?"

"Please." He accepted the coffee and took two sips, curious about her urgent news.

Madame stirred sugar into her cup and smiled. "Are you in love with her?" She blew gently on her coffee, then took a drink. The orchid swayed slightly, as if her breath had carried over the cup. The peculiar scent of the flower hit him full in the face along with the bluntness of her question. "I'm curious because I saw you spit out the tarts at the bakery that day we met in the village. Tilda rarely gets it wrong, so I wasn't quite sure what to make of your reaction."

Jean-Paul tripped over a series of "ums" and "ahs" as he set his cup down. "I don't know how—"

"You see, so much of what I do as a witch is reading the tea leaves of a person's life after it's been drained of pretense. Interpretation truly is the greater part of the art of magic." She set her cup down and leaned forward. "So let me ask another way. Does Mademoiselle Boureanu feel the same about you, full of 'hmms' and 'ahs' and blushing denials?"

God, what was in that note? "What is this about? Has something happened?"

Gerda clicked her tongue behind pouted lips three times. "It seems your client has escaped."

"What? Are you certain?" She held out the note long enough for him to get a glimpse of Inspector Nettles's signature. His body tensed, ready to fly to Elena. "I must leave at once."

"Oh, I don't think so." She fanned the letter at the flower so that a cloud of pollen-like particles wafted toward Jean-Paul's face. "Wouldn't it be much more fun to see how long it takes for her to come to you?"

He'd had enough of this woman, despite her tragic circumstances. He reached for his hat and stood. Or at least he thought he'd risen out of his chair. Instead, his legs seemed to float beneath him, watery and weak. He fell back against the damask. His head swam as if caught in a whirlpool. The floor undulated, the light dimmed, and a final thought drifted through his brain.

That wasn't blue vitriol in the bottle.

CHAPTER TWENTY-TWO

Elena woke to the smell of camphor. She opened her eyes to find her nose pressed against the side of a wooden trunk, the decorative type used to store blankets and clothing against the threat of hungry winter larvae. The medicinal scent of the wood worked like smelling salts to revive her, and she rolled onto her back. Above her hung a kaleidoscope of colorful fabrics embellished with feathers and sequins, confirming she'd spent the night on the floor of a carnival wagon.

"Good morning, free bird." A smudgy-eyed Yvette grinned down from the sleeping berth above.

Something pointy dug into Elena's backside. She reached down and removed a red lace-up boot, its toe slightly squashed. "What time is it?" she asked and tossed the boot aside.

Yvette had sworn in the middle of the night that she knew a safe place only a few miles away where they could hide. Where exactly, Elena hadn't asked. All she knew was at the time she was cold and damp from tromping through the waist-high grass moist with dew and would take any bolt-hole, so long as it was dry. Yvette had led them straight to the carnival following an instinct a bloodhound would envy.

The young woman shoved her thumb between her teeth and began chewing madly against the nail. "We overslept. Place is already humming. God, I'm dying for a smoke."

"Not in here, you won't."

The challenge came from the front of the wagon near the door, where a petite brunette sat on a cushioned built-in bench. She wrestled with a pair of white stockings as she secured them to a garter beneath a gold-fringed skirt that barely covered her thighs. "My bad luck, you catch whole place on fire." Her words were lacquered in the strong dialect of her native language.

"Missed me, didn't you, JuJu?"

"Like a snake misses shoes."

While the women traded friendly barbs, Elena sat up to peek through the curtain of a small window. Half a dozen men in work clothes sat under a tent with its flaps rolled up, eating at a table consisting of a sheet of plywood placed atop a pair of sawhorses. The number of people who might have heard them arrive worried her. "You're sure it's safe here?"

"Don't mind her. These are my people. We're as snug as a bug in a rug."

JuJu nodded, adjusting her breasts upward inside her red-and-gold corset. "We just having a laugh. Yvette is my best roommate. Only snores a little. I didn't even throw her things out while she was gone. I not tell anyone you're here."

"Come on, Ju. I'm just dying for a smoke."

"No smoking here. Too many pretty things."

Elena glanced up again at the assortment of costumes lined neatly along one wall, each like a tropical bird, feathery and iridescent.

"Oh là là, from one jail to another." Yvette threw off the blanket and swung her legs over the side of the raised bed. "So what's the mood out there? Anyone new I need to know about?"

JuJu held up a mirror and dabbed a dot of rouge on each cheek. "New sister act does magic trick with small dogs. Not as good as me on the unicycle, but it's okay show. A man joined the crew a few towns ago. Replaced old Antoine." She reached for a kohl stick and filled in dark lines around her eyes. "Everyone else the same."

Yvette jumped to her feet and arched her back in a catlike stretch. The cramped wagon seemed to shrink even more, once everyone was awake and moving. Elena shifted off the floor and took a seat on the edge of the bed. When they'd arrived in the quiet predawn hours, Yvette had knocked on the window in a pattern that roused the wagon's owner. Without question they'd been allowed inside, each left to find their corner of space to sleep. Now that the sun was up, Elena could see it was a small but cozy nest of self-contained essentials: stove big enough for boiling water, single cupboard for storing dry goods, a fold-down table for two, a camphor trunk, and a rack custom built to hold a dozen colorful costumes.

"All right if we make some of your great tea, JuJu?"

"Help yourself, but no smoking," she answered and secured a feathered tiara atop her head.

JuJu kissed Yvette on both cheeks, waved at Elena, then stepped out of the wagon with every curve of her body on display for the world to see.

"I can't stay in this cramped wagon all day," Elena said, letting the curtain drop.

Yvette stoked the tiny stove with wood kindling, then struck a long matchstick. "Well, you can't leave. You're not getting me arrested again because you can't stay put until dark," she said and blew out the match.

Elena wondered if it was possible to cast a spell big enough to stun an entire carnival. Obviously not with what little supplies she had to work with. Still, she wasn't above muttering a bruising spell in such stifling quarters. All it took for that was a reverse spell and a little comfrey leaf, which any witch should have. The temptation made her fingers itch to open a bottle of the stuff.

But on a secondary search of the wagon she noticed something was missing. "Your roommate said she didn't throw out any of your things, so where are your stores? Your herbs, your charms, and amulets?"

The young woman shrugged. "Don't have none of that stuff."

"But you must have a Book of Shadows. How do you do your spellwork?"

Yvette crossed her arms and shifted her weight to one hip. "Not everyone's as fancy as you vine witches. I know the spells I need to get by, and that's been plenty good enough for me so far."

Elena suspected the young woman had little training, but she'd never run across an illiterate witch before. She sank on the cushioned bench. She'd assumed Yvette would have a spell book she could use, a book of the occult, something that might give her a head start in unraveling how the blood magic was used in the killings. It was one reason she'd agreed to spend the night squeezed between half a dozen pointy shoes and a trunk that smelled like an undertaker's basement. If she had to lie low, at least she could spend the time trying to understand how and why she'd been framed.

There was nothing for it. She had to leave. Elena ran her fingers through her hair, twisting it into a respectable updo. "I'm sorry, but I don't have the luxury of waiting until dark."

Yvette banged the kettle down on the stove. "Do you want to get caught, is that it?"

"You obviously can take care of yourself, but there are things beyond my knowing that I need to figure out. Now rather than later."

"What sort of things?"

"Theories about animal killings and blood magic for a start."

Yvette rubbed the gooseflesh on her arms. "What the hell are you involved in?"

Elena explained about the murder and her arrest, and about the cats, the blood, and the witch that was still free to kill again. Yvette listened as she prepared the tea. To her credit, she never flinched, even when Elena admitted at one time she had meant to kill Bastien.

Yvette handed Elena her tea. "Like I said before, I didn't know my *maman*. If she had a spell book, she never left it to me. That doesn't mean I don't know how to get my hands on one, though. I'm not the only witch traveling with this bum carnival."

She'd thought Yvette was an isolated case, someone who'd fallen through the cracks too early to know where she belonged in the world of magic. Carnival life had a way of attracting those who'd shrugged off conformity. A place where the odd duck could find its flock. She supposed it made sense there would be others, but would they know anything more than the young woman?

"So how do we find this other witch if we can't leave the wagon?"

Yvette eyed the racks of pretty costumes lining the wall. "Maybe there's a way we can go out after all." She set down her mug and pulled out a sparkly green outfit, leveling a lopsided grin at Elena. "How do you feel about peacocks?"

An hour later Elena stepped out of the wagon in borrowed shoes. They were soft and flat heeled, made for performing on acrobatic mats. She rather thought they were an improvement over the toe-pinching shoes most women wore. The outfit, on the other hand, would take some getting used to.

She'd successfully protested the cape of peacock feathers but was unable to fend off completely the outlandish taste of her cellmate. The price of leaving the wagon early meant donning a pair of risqué harem pants, a feathered turban, and a silver-beaded bodice that thankfully covered most of her stomach, though her arms were left bare. The silky trousers swished as she walked, mimicking the familiar flow of a skirt, yet she found they provided far more freedom. Her legs absolutely dared to leap off the last step. But the silver veil draped from cheek to cheek was what ultimately gave her the most freedom. Only her eyes, which were now rimmed in the same dark kohl as Yvette's, showed above the silk.

She gave each end of the veil a secure tuck under the band of the turban as Yvette shut the door to the wagon and skipped down the steps.

"This way."

The young woman didn't seem to be the least bit self-conscious about strolling out in broad daylight wearing a skintight harlequin bodysuit. If she had any shame, it was well hidden behind the black eye mask as she led the way, quickly adjusting to the freedom of her own immodest trousers.

After squeezing between a pair of wagons, Elena got her first proper look at the carnival grounds. Two enormous red-and-white-striped tents rose in the center of a grassy area encircled by a dozen or more caravans. Many of them had their sides painted with symbols for luck and good life—a star, a moon, a five-petal flower. Something about the images ticked open a memory in Elena's mind, but it slipped away with the morning mist.

Not many stirred outside their cabins yet, but those who did inhabited the world as if they were creatures from a fairy tale come to life. A man with a twirled mustache tromped the ground on three-foot stilts, towering over a wagon to stow sleeping gear atop the roof. On the far side of the green a tattooed woman stoked the flames of a cook fire, while a young girl did a backbend in the grass with a boa constrictor draped around her middle. The woman smiled approvingly while spreading honey on bread for her breakfast.

Elena's stomach clenched at the sight of the food, but even hunger couldn't distract her from the specter of a clown passed out drunk under a wagon wheel. His white face paint had smeared in the dewy grass, creating a grotesque swirl of mouth, nose, and eyes. Whatever whimsy he'd worn the night before, the morning had unmasked a ghoulish face lurking beneath. He roused to stare bleary-eyed at her.

"What're *you* looking at?" He raised a gin bottle to his lips. Finding it empty, he tossed the bottle into the grass, grumbled, and rolled over.

"Don't mind him," Yvette said with a flip of her hand as they stood over his prone body. "Jacques might look a mess now, but he'll be sober by showtime and smelling like a daisy again. He's a lovable Pierrot when he's on his feet. A regular Doctor Jekyll and Monsieur Hyde, that one."

Two beings living inside one body. Elena had to shrug off the convulsive shiver that followed, recalling her cramped view from behind the toad's eyes.

Yvette nudged the clown's foot with her shoe to get his attention again. "Which way's Rackham's trailer?"

"What you want with that shriveled old prune?"

"He's got some books we need to borrow."

Jacques growled animallike deep in his throat. "Got a whole fucking library, but he ain't never cured my headache."

Elena lifted an eyebrow at him. "Try massaging the bottom of your left foot just below the third and fifth toe. And drink a few cups of willow bark tea. Your head will clear soon enough."

"She one of your lot?" he asked with a chin-thrust aimed at Yvette. She nodded, and he shrank back a fair few inches behind the wagon wheel. "He's on the back end by the snake charmer," he said and then crawled off in the other direction.

Yvette pulled Elena aside by the arm. "Listen, don't do that with Rackham. Best if you play it dumb with him. He knows what a piss-poor witch I am, but that's why he helps me. He likes being all superior and reminding me how much I don't know."

"So you're saying he's a man?"

Yvette smirked. "Right, and the way to get what you want from him is to keep his bread buttered on the right side, if you know what I mean."

Elena knew what she meant and agreed to slather him with just enough praise to distract him from her motives.

The Amazing Professor Rackham, Seer of the Other World! The hand-painted lettering on the side of the wagon shimmered in gold. The paint had been magicked, of course. At night, under the flickering torchlight, it would shine like an electric sign in the city, drawing the lovelorn, the forlorn, and the simply curious like moths. The entire spectacle had a tawdry commercial quality that had Elena doubting this Professor Rackham was a real witch. The "third eye" painted above the door practically winked at her as they climbed the stairs.

Yvette knocked on the door bordered, naturally, in the requisite astrological symbols.

"Matinees begin at ten," replied a male voice. "You may come back then."

"It's Yvette, Professor. My friend and I need your help with something. You know, *magic*." This last part she said in a hushed, secretive tone, like honeyed bait.

A man wearing a shimmering green-and-gold robe and matching turban opened the door. Hawkish eyes rimmed in black kohl stared out under a pair of pasted-on eyebrows that shot up in devilish exaggeration. The glue adhering the similarly pointed mustache and cone-shaped goatee in place oozed out below his bottom lip. He stood back and held the door open. "Of course. I'm always available for students of the craft requiring professional assistance. Come in."

Elena took a seat beside Yvette on the built-in sofa as instructed, while Rackham reclined in a plush velvet wingback chair and crossed his legs. The scent of ambergris, fragrant yet animalistic, stirred in the cozy space, awakening in her an odd sense of déjà vu. She knew better than to ignore the feeling, but she found nothing about the wagon familiar.

Well, except for the nature of the furnishings. Rackham did indeed own an entire library. Old books. New books. Some bound in leather, some in cloth, and one or two wrapped in the scaly skin of some long-dead sea creature. They filled the shelves behind his chair. And where there weren't books there were herbs, charms, a scrying mirror, and tiny soft-bellied frogs bottled up in formaldehyde displayed in built-in nooks. And in the center of it all, propped up by a pair of golden hands, sat an expensive crystal ball atop a small mahogany table. A touch out of reach for a carnival psychic, she thought, but perhaps he was better at his art than his sham stagecraft would imply.

Rackham seemed to absorb her appreciation of his things, showing the bare minimum of a smile when her eyes met his. "Terribly rude of me to bring it up, I know," he said, turning to Yvette, "but aren't you supposed to be incarcerated?"

Yvette pushed her mask up on her forehead. "Got out early on account of my good behavior."

"Ah." He gave a slight flinch of his shoulder, dismissing the subject as no concern of his. "So, what sort of help may I offer you and your acquaintance today?" His hawklike eyes traced their silhouettes as Yvette pointed her thumb toward Elena before reaching for the deck of tarot cards on the side table.

"I'd like to borrow a book," Elena said. She kept her face covered, preferring to address the professor from behind her veil. He could stare at her aura all he liked, but he'd not see beyond the purple veil there either.

"Any particular volume you're interested in?" He folded his hands in his lap, his long fingernails yellowish against his pale skin. "Love potions, luck amulets, or moon magic perhaps?"

"May I?" She leaned forward and tilted her head to the right to read the titles on the spines: *A Compendium of Herbal Magic; Lady Everly's Grimoire; Shamanic Practices in the Southern Hemisphere; Book of the Dead.* There were treatises on voodoo, necromancy, shadow vision, and one palm-size book entitled *Curses and Maledictions* that made Elena blink twice. In truth, his collection rivaled Brother Anselm's library of magic at the abbey, save for a copy of *The Book of the Seven Stars*, though as she examined the lower shelf it was apparent Rackham's taste skewed much more toward the dark end of the spectrum. A fortunate omen for her particular need. She pointed to a black-and-red leather book labeled *Sanguinem Artes Ocultus*. "That one would make a good start."

Rackham did a double take, his eyes shifting between her and the book. "Not the usual fare for a young woman on a beautiful summer morning." He plucked the volume from the shelf, though he didn't hand it over right away. Instead, he casually flipped through the pages, as if reacquainting himself with the subject matter. "Might I inquire what this is about? It's rather complex magic, requiring a firm mind."

Despite her promise to Yvette, she didn't have the time to play the coy dumpling, not with so much rich information just outside her grasp. "Exsanguination, to be precise. I'm interested in how it works in ritual spellcraft, and to what purpose."

Yvette tapped the cards against the table and stared at her with angry owl eyes.

Rackham, on the other hand, no longer tried to control the smile that had lodged in the corner of his mouth. "Ah, if this is in reference to the cat mutilations and recent murder in the valley, you wouldn't be the first to speculate on the subject. It's been the driving talk among magic folk across the countryside for years. Though I hear they've made an arrest to spoil all the fun of guessing who the culprit might be." He handed the book over. "At any rate, chapter thirteen likely has what you're looking for."

Elena turned to the pages, scanning quickly, feeling him watching her as she read.

"Blood," he said, "is neither good nor evil in spellcasting. It's simply a highly concentrated conduit for energy. Blood *is* life, after all. Where and how one directs that energy is what determines its effect."

"None of these spells have any continuity to them," Elena said, looking up from the chapter. "They're one-offs with specific outcomes in mind. But the cat killings present themselves as ritualistic, repeated over and over. Perhaps timed with the moon or some other cosmological signal."

"You seem rather well informed on the subject."

Elena felt a pinch on her thigh. A signal to dumb it down. "Just curious how it works."

"Bit of dabbling in the dark arts, is it?" He ran his tongue over his eyetooth. "Everyone comes around to shadow magic at one point or another. No harm in appeasing one's curiosity. After all, without the dark the good would never shine."

"I'd never keep body and soul together if people didn't get curious about the dark side now and then," Yvette added, adjusting the exposure of her cleavage before shuffling through the tarot deck again.

Rackham's eyes lowered perceptibly. "Quite."

"Why would there be so many animals involved?"

"Several deep thinkers on the craft, myself included, believe the cat killings may have been a mere flourish, a setup for the real murder. To establish a ritualistic pattern, as you noted." Rackham ran his hand over the shelf and then slid a folded page out from between a pair of books. "Others suspected a timed relationship with the moon or Saturn or even Jupiter," he said, spreading the paper open to reveal a list of dates and locations. "But you can see by the entries of when each known animal corpse was reported in the valley, there's no precision to the killings. And as I said, they've already arrested the guilty party, so there's little point in dredging the matter all up again. It's been solved. All we can do is hope she reveals her methodology before she's executed."

Elena gripped the edge of the bench and fought back her own grim urges. "You honestly believe all those cats were killed to cover up a single premeditated murder? Nothing to do with a blood ritual? That's a lot of dead animals, Professor. Half a dozen would have been enough to form a pattern and get tongues wagging, if that's all the murderer had wanted."

Rackham shifted his weight in his chair uncomfortably. "There are others who entertained the idea there was something more sinister going on. But there was never any real proof."

"Sinister how?" she asked and thought again about the Charlatan sisters and their appetite for hoarding dead animal parts.

He narrowed his eyes at Elena. "Do you mind removing your veil?"

She supposed this was dangerous talk. Not the sort of thing discussed in polite company. Or with a stranger you'd just met. Yvette put a hand on her arm to stop her, but there was no real harm in showing her face to Rackham. He didn't know her. And she'd be gone by nightfall anyway. If that was the price for the information she wanted, it was a paltry sum. She pulled the corners of her scarf loose from her turban. "Sinister how, Professor Rackham?"

He stared at her lips as they moved in the dim light, and his throat convulsed in a hard swallow behind his fake goatee. His brow puckered ever so slightly as he twisted the ring around his finger. A toadstone, Elena noted. Just the sort of useless amulet a carnival witch like Rackham would put his faith in. Though she wondered who he thought might be out to poison him.

"I really couldn't say." He released the ring and twisted his neck to look at the clock on the wall. "And it appears I've run out of time. The gates will be opening soon, and, as you may suspect, I am often besieged with people seeking their fortunes."

There was more behind what he'd hinted at, she was sure of it, and she wasn't going to let him get off that easy. "Sinister how?" she repeated, bleeding any submissiveness out of her voice.

He hesitated, avoiding her eye. Something about their conversation had spooked him. Whatever he knew must be disturbing indeed.

He checked the clock again and then relented. "There are said to be spells that have never been written down in any book," he said at last.

"Old magic. Bound in the earth. Held in a crevice of time. Some call it conjuring the Devil, because to see the spell rendered, one must enter into an exchange. It's the blackest of magic. The kind that can eviscerate the soul if even a word is out of place."

"Démon dansant." Elena's mouth watered at the feel of the words on her tongue. "But it's just a childhood rhyme. Are you saying it's real?"

"More than one witch has expressed that belief. Do you think your little valley is the only place to have found a trail of dead creatures? I travel all over the Continent. Everywhere I go there are other stories. Theories. Suspicions. The police don't keep track of such things, but witches do."

"What's *démon dansant* mean?" Yvette asked, hugging a pillow against her middle.

Elena recited the rhyme she'd learned as a child, then explained. "It's magic that hides in the shadows, outside the view of the eye of the All Knowing. And the covenants."

Rackham added, "To engage in magic with a demon is to flay your heart, mind, and soul open to him on the promise of an exchange of immense power. In what form, I'm not sure. Money, authority, or perhaps even immortality would be my guess."

"Which would explain the extensive trail of dead animals."

Yvette flipped over the Queen of Wands. "*Merde*, you two are giving me the creeps."

"With good reason," Rackham snapped, asserting his air of authority once again. "But if that's what this murderess was up to, they won't need a trial. Without more blood for her spells, the pact will be broken. That's how dark magic works. She'll wither to a strip of leather like the beasts she's killed."

"But what if the person hadn't been caught yet," Elena ventured. "Would there be a way to recognize them? A dark aura around the pupil? Or maybe a mark left on the skin from the exchange?"

"A smell. That's what some scholars have surmised. One telltale mark would be the scent the demon leaves in the exchange."

Acrid, foul, sulfuric—it was something, however vague.

Rackham shook himself loose of her sharp gaze. "Now, if there's nothing else, I must realign my chakras and prepare for my clients."

Yvette glanced at Elena out of the corner of her eye before slipping her mask back down over her face. "Thank you for seeing us, Professor," she said, stacking the tarot cards back on the side table.

"Certainly. Though I would ask that you keep this conversation just between us," he said. "A little mischief in the dark arts is a fine thing for the reputation, but I don't want any of this demon business, if that's what it is, being associated with my work as a medium. Most mortals are flustered enough when they enter my wagon without talk of devils."

"Of course, Professor."

He reached out to retrieve the book from Elena. Instead, she made the effort to replace it herself on the bottom shelf. She lingered a second longer, her finger trailing over the other spines, before she twisted around to look at Rackham over her shoulder. "You have a wonderful collection," she said and tucked her veil back in place.

He attempted a civil nod, though his eyebrows knitted together in a worrisome expression. "I hope you found it helpful, mademoiselle . . . what did you say your name was?"

But Elena was already out the door, a palm-size crystal hidden in the pocket of her harem pants.

They kept their heads down until they rounded the corner of the nearest wagon. The pace of the carnival had picked up as workers scrambled to get ready for the impending crowds. Yvette took Elena by the arm and led her to a quiet space where the outhouses were lined up behind the snake charmer's tent. There, the younger witch pulled out her cigarettes and struck a match. She sucked in a deep breath of smoke, then let it out slowly. "You've got sticky fingers," she said when she'd calmed down.

"You saw that, did you?"

"You might be good at spells, but I'm very good at stealing." Yvette sat on a bale of hay and flicked the ash off her cigarette. "No one survives on the street without knowing how to snatch a bit of this and that to get by."

"I've never had to steal anything before."

"Lucky you. So why now?"

Elena took the crystal out of her pocket. "I could sense the strong protection aura emanating from it. *If* I can find the real murderer, I'll need all the protection I can get. You won't tell him, will you?"

"No one survives the streets for long if they snitch, either." Yvette took a deep puff on her cigarette.

The faraway look in her eye when she exhaled stirred a sisterly instinct in Elena. She had to restrain herself from smoothing the girl's hair back from her face and telling her it would all be okay. Instead, she sat beside her, feeling the morning sun warm her face through the veil.

"You said there wasn't a pattern to the killings, but there is," Yvette said after a pause. "I didn't want to say in front of the Professor, but I've seen the same thing before."

"You recognized something?"

"It's the craving. That's why they keep doing the same spell over and over again. To feed some hunger," Yvette said, as if staring at memories. "Only after a while whatever they're doing isn't enough anymore, so the next score has to be a little bigger to get the same result. Ever been with a gent who can't wait to put the white powder up his nose? Trust me, you don't want to get between him and his next hit of madness. Or a drunk and his next bottle," she said with a nudge of her chin toward Jacques the clown, who exited the outhouse wearing his pointed hat and white blouse with the black buttons.

"A pattern of addiction?"

Yvette nodded and tossed her cigarette away. "Worst kind of habit."

Immortality. Power. Money. They would all qualify as powerful drugs. If Rackham were to be believed, it's what the murderer killed for, driven by a compulsion so strong it defied law and logic.

A vision of a fiendish obsession flashed across her mind. A slathering craving. The murderer would be wide-eyed with madness. But then Jacques, who she'd seen wrapped around an empty gin bottle only an hour earlier, sauntered by and waved, thanking her for the remedy to his headache. There wasn't a stagger in his walk or a tremble in his speech. Even his face, which had been an abstract mess, was now covered in fresh white greasepaint.

If addiction were the motivation behind the killings, would the murderer vacillate between extremes too? Between the craving and the satisfaction? Between living a life and taking a life? Yes, of course, but the mark of the demon would be permanent, just as Jacques's costume remained whether drunk or sober. The stench of bonding with a demon would be imbued in the host. It must.

Elena's head snapped up. "The smell."

"Yeah, the back end of a carnival always smells like that."

"No, I mean the demon. You could hide the behavior of addiction, but you couldn't cover up the smell. Not without a potent fix."

"I'd just drown myself in a bottle of L'Origan. Ha, I'd do that anyway. Divine stuff."

"Perfume . . ."

Elena saw again the image of a scented gift box dangling from a feminine wrist as her scent-memory recalled the odor of rotting meat, so misplaced at the time. Realization coursed through her, every nerve alert to the truth.

"How could I have been so stupid?"

CHAPTER TWENTY-THREE

Jean-Paul woke in the dark. His back rested against rough-hewn boards, and his legs would not move. Could not move. His arms, too, were useless to him, tied down at right angles to his body as if he were prostrating himself to God. A six-foot-square pallet rested against his chest, leaving off just enough pressure for his lungs to expand. Above the pallet, restrained by the mercy of a single rope attached to a steel crank, hovered a giant metal wheel on a helical screw.

He took a reflexive breath to calm his fear of suffocating. The heavy musk of oak, earth, and fermenting fruit overrode the stench of his sweat and fear. He was in a cellar, though not his own. And yet there was a familiarity to the surroundings. He tried to turn to get his bearings, but his head spun with a nausea-inducing bout of vertigo. He steadied himself and swallowed. The taste of black coffee furred his tongue.

And then he remembered.

The swish of a long skirt on the flagstones forced him to turn his head and suffer through the dizziness. The smell of decay, like cut flowers that have sat too long in their own water, wafted toward him, making him ill. A flicker of candlelight erupted in the dark, and Gerda's face came into focus.

"The effect of the sleeping powder was shorter lived than I'd expected," she said. "I must have misjudged your weight." She placed the candlestick atop a polished wood table, one that guests to the cellar might stand at to sample the latest vintage, or perhaps a cherished bottle of vin '99, opened for a special occasion. Of course. He was in Monsieur Du Monde's coveted wine cellar. It housed a hundred barrels in the catacombs beyond. And, as he uncomfortably recalled, it also retained its original sixteenth-century press, on which he now lay helplessly constrained.

"For a city-born elitist, you're in surprisingly fit form," she said and removed the bung from a barrel of wine.

He lifted his shoulder, testing the strength of the medieval contraption and finding no give. "Why are you doing this?"

"It's nothing personal." She smiled out of the corner of her mouth, revealing a row of perfect white teeth. She sunk a wine thief inside the barrel to obtain a sample, suctioning up a vein of red into the tube.

"This is absurd. Untie me."

"I think not."

Angered, he thrashed his body against the wood, but it did nothing to loosen his restraints.

"I really do need you to stay put, Monsieur Martel," she said, filling the silver tastevin hanging from her waist chain with the wine from the barrel. She gave the cup a slight swirl and studied the contents.

Jean-Paul stared at the ceiling. His shoulder hurt from the dull ache of a bruise, and his temples throbbed from the lingering effects of the drug, but it was his growing fear that disabled his mind. He squeezed his eyes shut and pleaded with God for all of this to be a wicked dream. But when he opened them again he saw once more the face of his unlikely captor. Only something had changed. Was it just a trick of the candlelight, a smudge on his glasses, or was there something different about her face? He lifted his head to see her at a better angle. Yes, he thought, her skin sagged jowl-like around the mouth now, and her eyes appeared heavy and hooded. Even her hair had lost its luster, frizzing and dulling as strands came loose from its tight updo. The change so intrigued him he lost his fear long enough to recoup his wits.

The witch, for he remembered in earnest that's what she was, sniffed the wine in her cup. "I was always better at brewing ale," she said after running her tongue over her teeth. "But this red will have an enviable life once it's had time to mature." She stepped up to the press and held out the cup. "Care for a taste, vigneron?"

The wine, a deep red that clung to the sides of the silver tasting cup, had the hue and vigor of blood. He recoiled with new understanding as his mind made the connection. "It was you, wasn't it? The cats, the blood, Monsieur Du Monde."

She stuck her finger in the wine and stirred. "It's always been me," she said, then licked the wine off and straightened. "And will be again."

She picked up the candle and carried it to the center of the cellar floor. The light from the candle illuminated a circle of symbols drawn on the flagstones in chalk. He didn't recognize any of the marks, though they set off a tremor in the roots of his instinct when he saw them for what they were: symbols of wicked, illegal magic.

He was not going to live through this. She was going to kill him and drain him of his blood. Bile rose in his throat at the thought. But then why hadn't she done so yet? What had she been waiting for? Was there some ritual she must perform?

And then he recalled the note.

"Before. In the conservatory," he said as she incanted words so foreign to his ears he thought them gibberish. "You said Elena escaped."

"Mmm." The witch didn't bother to look up from her work as she drew three new symbols above the rest. "Which is why you're going to be my staked lamb."

Just as he feared, the witch knew Elena would try to find him. "But why? Why involve her? Why not just escape? Get as far away from here as you can."

"Because she knows who I am now and how to find me. And I have ever so much more living to do."

The witch knelt in the center of her macabre scribblings and then poured the wine over the stones as if in offering. He squinted at the circle of candlelight. Her hair had been bleached of its blonde sheen, paling to dull silver, and her hips had lost their curve. She smiled, knowing he was watching the transformation, and let out a sly laugh as her knuckles gripped the wine cup with knotted joints.

Terror shuddered through his body, knowing he was at the mercy of a murderer's magic.

CHAPTER TWENTY-FOUR

Yvette watched Elena draw a circle with a stick in the dirt. She added a cross in the center and then stood back to judge the balance of the four quarters.

"You're sure you can find him this way?"

"I have to try." She knew the chances weren't good, but it was all she could think to do. She had to warn Jean-Paul before he went to see the bierhexe.

"A circle in the dirt doesn't seem like very good protection."

Elena tossed the stick aside. "No, it isn't." She felt in her pocket for the crystal. "But I'm hoping it's enough to let me slip in and see what I need to see without being noticed. Keep a watch out while I'm . . . away."

Cradling the box of *allumettes* and cigarettes in her hand, Elena knelt inside the circle. She closed her eyes and concentrated on the items. The sensation was faint, a single thread floating on the wind, but it was there, an imprint of his aura. She took a deep breath and sank below consciousness until the shadow world closed over her head. A whisper of "good luck" reached her ears just as she slipped from the physical world into that of shadow.

The trace of his energy was nearly imperceptible. She worried he'd not held the matches in his possession long enough to get a bearing on his location, but she persisted, widening her focus to concentrate on Jean-Paul's warm brown eyes, the scent of his skin after he shaved, the way his hair fell forward when he plowed the field without a hat. And how his palm electrified her skin when they held hands.

It worked.

The emotional pull she could no longer deny drew her senses deeper until her shadow-self emerged in a cold room swamped by darkness. The stone beneath her feet and the echo of space around her made her think of the abbey's cloisters or an underground cave, but the smells were wrong. Her nose detected oak, vanilla, and fermenting wine. And something sulfuric. She was in a cellar, a large one, but the silence made her fear she had miscalculated.

She was too late.

But then a spark of candlelight flared at the other end of the room, and the Gothic ceiling, with its arched ribs and center posts, came into view. She knew the space at once—Bastien's famed cellar, a series of caverns and tunnels begun eight hundred years earlier by the same ambitious monks who'd planted the first vineyards. She knew if she touched a finger to one of the supports she would still hear their workaday chants droning in the stonework. Yet she dared not move lest her spirit disturb the air and cause the candle to flutter. Instead, she tilted her head and listened for a heartbeat.

In the corner near the light, two of them. No, three. One beat at the frantic pace of a panicked human, one with the cold tick-tock of a serpent on the hunt, and the third tapping out a frenzied rhythm like wings battling a storm. It was not the heartbeat of a creature of this world. Then a head bent forward into the light, the hair gray, and the skin creased and flaccid with age.

It was the face of an older woman . . . but the eyes . . . they flashed in a familiar glittering blue as they stared out over the flame. Then they narrowed to peer into the darkness, and the nose twitched, seeking out her scent.

Elena let go. She reeled herself in, hurling backward through the liminal space to reenter her body. She woke from her trance with her head spinning and her heart galloping.

"Thought I'd lost you for a minute. You went all creepy quiet and still," Yvette said.

Elena pulled her veil free and sucked in deep gulps of air. "I saw her." She shuddered recalling the wrinkled face that stared out at her with those piercing eyes. They were the same stunning blue she'd remembered and yet full of malice. As if a mask had been ripped away.

"You saw her? You mean the cat killer murderer witch lady?"

"I'm too late. She has him. In the cellar tasting room. I think he was tied up."

"Merde," Yvette said, covering her mouth with her hand. "You don't think she'll kill him too, do you?"

The thought fish-hooked Elena right in the heart. "Yes, but not yet. She's waiting for something. Me, I think. But why do it underground? Why hide in the dark?"

Yvette looked over her shoulder at the carnival coming to life. "Because she feels safe there. It's familiar. Just like the carnival is the first place I run back to."

Elena's head snapped up. "She gets her energy from the damp and the dark. Things underground. Unseen. Out of the light."

"Like a—"

"Like a demon."

Elena got to her feet and passed Yvette the crushed box of *allumettes* and cigarettes, apologizing absentmindedly for the damage.

The young woman tossed the useless tin to the ground. "Never mind those. What are we going to do?"

"We? *We* aren't going to do anything." Elena retrieved the crystal shard from her pocket and thought about the meager herbs she might gather for a spell. It would never be enough.

Yvette lifted her mask. "Like hell we're not." She stepped in front of Elena, blocking her path. "You can't let her get away with it."

"I don't intend to."

"Look, I know you don't think much of me, but I want to help."

"No offense, but how is a carnival worker who runs a kink trade on the side going to help me confront a power-addicted witch who, in all probability, is bound to a demon? You can barely read a spell book."

"Right, I'm shit at magic. I'm shit at life. But I'm still a witch, and you're going to need my kind of help."

"Really? And what kind is that?"

Yvette straightened. "Let's just say, between the two of us, I'm not the one claiming I'm innocent."

The confession sent a shivery dart through Elena's conscience. She'd known the young woman had been locked up for murder, but she'd let herself half believe it was a false accusation like her own. "Yvette . . ."

"It's true. According to the rule of three I'm already damaged goods. I didn't have much learning growing up, but I know that much about magic. If it comes to it, if she tries to do to this man what she already did to the other, you'll need me. Maybe snuffing her out for good is the thing I can do that you can't."

And you might also die in the process, Elena thought. But before she could dissuade the young woman, a commotion on the other side of the fairground erupted. Performers who ought to have been in position to greet customers for the carnival opening hightailed it for their wagons. And somewhere men shouted as an argument broke out.

"That's Gustave, the carnival owner," Yvette said, craning her neck toward the noise. A shrill whistle followed, sounding a warning. "Uh-oh."

"What is it?"

"*Les flics.*"

"The police? They found us already?"

"Not yet they haven't." Yvette turned back to Elena. "Take me with you, and I promise to get you out of here in one piece."

"Why are you doing this?"

The young woman shrugged. "I don't like people who hurt cats."

"And if I can't protect you?"

Yvette pulled a small but deadly hairpin out of her updo. "Witches still bleed, don't they? I can protect myself."

The air went out of Elena as she finally relented. "We haven't got much time."

"Good thing I know a trick or two of my own, then." Yvette slipped her mask back down and took off for the other end of the carnival. "Go back to JuJu's and wait there. I'll meet you in five minutes," she called over her shoulder before disappearing behind a trio of stilt-walkers.

Elena threw her hands up in surrender. She was beginning to think the curse had bonded with her blood and bones, affecting everything she saw or touched or loved. Grand-Mère included. She must be worried sick. There was precious little time, but she couldn't have her mentor fretting over her again. Not after what she'd put her through the last seven years.

Scanning the distant trees, she uttered a quick summoning spell. A rock dove and a stork swooped out of the sky, landing at her feet. "*You* might send the wrong message," she said to the stork and shooed him on his way. To the rock dove she explained in the simplest terms about the bierhexe and that she was well but unable to return home. The bird cooed, and she sent him on his way with a spell to help home in on Grand-Mère's location, wishing she could fly away with him. She might yet be cursed with bad luck, but she still didn't want to get caught. Covering her face with the veil, she headed for JuJu's wagon, battered once more by the whims of the All Knowing.

CHAPTER TWENTY-FIVE

Though old and obsolete, Jean-Paul knew the ancient wheel was still capable of twisting lower on its Archimedes's screw with enough pressure to macerate fifty tons of grapes to release the *vin de presse*. He'd seen it demonstrated with pride three years earlier when he'd toured the cellar at Du Monde's insistence. As if reading his thoughts, the wheel winked at him in the candlelight and descended its first inch, forcing the pallet that much tighter against his chest.

"Not long now." Gerda walked up the steps at the base of the old press. "She knows you're here."

"You'll burn in hell for this."

The witch scoffed. "What makes you think I haven't already?" She knelt beside him holding a knife, an almost tender look in her eye. "A little insurance," she said, then slashed a two-inch cut into his exposed forearm.

He cursed her, spat at her, and writhed against his restraints as she held the wine cup to his skin to collect his blood.

"Come now, we haven't even started," she said, walking back to her circle. "You should save your strength for when the screaming really begins."

She stirred the blood with her finger while speaking more gibberish. His stomach tugged at his throat as if he might retch, but he held it down, terrified of choking to death in his restraints. She finished whatever spell she'd formed with her evil words and then came at him again carrying a small bowl. He braced for more bloodletting, but instead of cutting him she dabbed a poultice onto the cut, relieving the pain of the knife's sting. Was she doctoring him now? She had to be deranged. Insane.

"Get away from me, you fiend."

His blood rimmed her fingernail. She sucked at it and smiled. "Oh, you have no idea," she said, then turned the crank on the windlass to let the wheel twist down another punishing inch.

CHAPTER TWENTY-SIX

Elena squeezed between a pair of show ponies decorated with feathered headdresses and sequined saddles. JuJu's wagon ought to be straight ahead, but it wasn't. She'd gone the wrong way, and now she was terribly lost in a maze of angry show people in a panic to avoid a police shakedown.

"Check it again! Check every closet, trunk, and storage space. They're here somewhere, I know it."

The inspector.

He was searching for her two wagons down on the right. The timbre of his voice as he shouted commands shook Elena out of her confusion. She backtracked behind the ponies and skirted left, keeping to the rear of the wagons to get as far away from him as she dared. It was safe for the moment, but it was only a matter of time before the police spread out and searched that area too. Could she run and make it to the trees without being caught? Was there a spell that could produce a distraction big enough to fool an army of officers?

She racked her brain for a spell that might mimic fireworks or gunfire, anything to create a commotion to confuse the inspector, when she heard an engine purr like a lion. A bright-blue two-seater convertible rolled up beside her. Behind the wheel, having donned a pair of driving goggles, sat Yvette.

The young woman revved the engine and nudged her chin toward the passenger-side door. "I thought you were a goner for sure when you weren't at JuJu's."

"I got turned around."

"Lucky you. They're all over her wagon looking for us. Come on, get in."

There was no time to argue. Despite her reservations Elena jumped in the passenger seat of the diabolical contraption and held on. Yvette shoved the stick shift into gear, then pressed her foot on the gas pedal, and the car sped off. Elena dared a quick look over her shoulder. The inspector ran out of JuJu's wagon, waving frantically at his men to return to their horses and pursue, but the newfangled automobile hit the dirt road and took off at an exhilarating speed.

Yvette pushed the car to thirty-five miles per hour, sending gravel churning under the tires as they sped down the country road in the jaunty two-seater. Elena's hair flew out behind her, and she grabbed the solid-brass fittings on the side of the windshield to hold on.

"What's the matter? Haven't you ever ridden in a car before?" Yvette winked through her driving goggles and grinned.

"Never," Elena shouted over the roar of the engine. She braced her other hand against the dashboard as they swung through a curve. The acceleration blew the veil loose from her face, sending the silk flapping on the wind. She hurled a quick spell with it to create the illusion that a silver birch had fallen across the road in case the inspector's motorcycles tried to catch up. The trick wouldn't stop them, but it might confuse them long enough to fall behind.

Yvette patted the side of the door. "She's a beaut. Best little *bébé* I've ever driven."

"Or stolen."

"*Borrowed*," Yvette corrected. "It's Gustave's pride and joy. He'll get it back in one piece . . . eventually."

There was no arguing it was the fastest way to escape even if it was by way of mortal mechanics. If the inspector's men had followed, they were nowhere in sight. Grown confident that the vehicle wouldn't fall apart every time it hit a rut in the road, Elena relaxed her white-knuckled grip on the windshield, though she couldn't let go completely the feeling of careening toward danger.

But what choice did she have? Jean-Paul hadn't asked for any of this. He'd said from the beginning he wanted no part in magic and witches. Yet he'd jumped feetfirst to defend her from the false charges. He'd put himself in danger, and now she had to douse her fear and do the same for him. Newly resolved, she muttered a protection spell under her breath while she held the stolen crystal in her hand. It glowed warm against her palm, and when she looked down after the third incantation his name had been engraved into the quartz. She kissed the crystal to seal the spell before putting it back in her pocket.

Yvette slowed the car as they approached a sign. "Which way?"

They'd come to the Y in the road where one lane led straight to the village and the other curved through the lower vineyards—the safer but longer route. Elena peered at the abbey steeple looming over the village, feeling its compass point tug her forward.

"The village," she said.

Yvette looked over her shoulder at the direction they'd just come before reluctantly putting the car in gear to climb the hill. There was danger, of course, in entering the main street. An automobile still attracted attention in the small town. Especially one with two women wanted for escape and murder sitting in the leather seats. But a witch was nothing without her instinct, and Elena's was telling her to stop at the abbey.

"Wait here," she said once Yvette pulled over to the curb. "I won't be a minute."

The young woman revved the engine for emphasis. "I hope we have that much time."

The warning was met with a firm nod as Elena pushed against the abbey's heavy wooden door. The thousand-year-old apse greeted her with spears of colored light that shot through the stained glass at the top of the vaulted space. A balding monk in a blue-and-white robe looked up from his sweeping at the sound of the door closing behind her.

"Elena?"

"Hello, Brother Anselm."

He set his broom aside and approached from the altar, confusion building on his face as he noted her harem pants and silver bodice. "Good heavens, I've heard several stories about your return, but none included a career in the circus."

"I don't have time to explain. I need your help."

"Certainly. What can I do?"

"Air, fire, water, and earth."

The monk paused, considering. "A spell?"

"A man's life is at stake. Jean-Paul's. Mine as well, if I'm honest."

"Right," he said and began a flurry of movement. "Help yourself to the candles. And there's water in the font. I'll collect the other items."

"May I take the oil instead?"

Anselm's eyes narrowed in concern. "Of course," he said and then hurried off through a door that led to the outside cloisters.

A moment later he returned bearing a small over-the-shoulder satchel. "I procured a little incense. It's basic frankincense, but it should be suitable for air. And will salt do for earth? There's a goodly amount in there. Plus a little cheese wrapped in cloth."

"That'll do." Elena accepted the bag and slid the candles and stoppered bottle of olive oil inside with the other items. "Thank you," she said and made the sign of thanks to the All Knowing. "I'll explain someday, if I can."

In return the monk crossed himself. "By the way, Ariella stopped by earlier. She seemed to know you were . . . free."

"I sent a dove to find her and let her know I was okay."

The monk considered that. "Yes, well, she lit a candle, then left a twenty-year-old bottle of wine on the altar. On her way out she dropped a rather healthy sum of coins in the orphans' fund box. In forty years she's never done that."

The report made little sense, but there was no time to sort it out. Baffled, Elena promised to send another dove later and then thanked Brother Anselm as she rushed out the door to the sound of Yvette gunning the engine.

The property at Domaine du Monde stood abandoned. No workers walked the vine rows, no maid peeked out through the curtains as she dusted the upstairs windowsill, and no attendant came out to greet them and escort them inside Bastien's grand home. Elena also noted the protection spells surrounding the property had been removed.

But there were ghosts. Memories from Elena's past floated up to remind her of when she'd once looked forward to visiting the vineyard and flirting with the handsome vigneron who'd taken the helm from his ailing parents. She'd admired his certainty, his drive, and his dream for creating a brilliant future in a bright new age. He'd plied her with praise and sweet honey kisses. How intensely they'd gone from believing they were in love to accusations of curses and murder. He'd been an innovator and successful businessman, yes, but he could be cruel too. Manipulative. Self-centered. Vindictive. It's why she'd been so certain he was capable of having her cursed. Just another loose end to clean up after a failed proposal. But she'd misjudged everything, and now he was dead.

Yvette killed the engine, and Elena felt a shadow of malevolent energy brush up against her.

"So what now?"

She took a cleansing breath and recalibrated her thoughts. "They're in the cellar."

"Right, so how do we get down there?"

"We don't. Not yet. There's something we have to do first." She stepped out of the car, the satchel over her shoulder, and walked to an outbuilding to the left of the main house.

Yvette followed her inside and stared up at the knives, picks, and hammers hung on hooks along one wall of the workspace. She took down a short-handled saw and tested the grip. "Since when does someone need one of these to make wine?"

"It's the cooperage," Elena said, dropping the satchel on a workbench. "They make the barrels in this building."

Yvette whistled low as she walked along the wall. She removed an ax from a peg and juggled the tool in one hand, tossing it blade over handle as comfortably as flipping a coin in the air. "There's enough hardware here to slice through ten bad-seed witches."

If only it were true. "I'm going to need an athame," she said. "See if you can find something suitable while I clear a space."

"That's the fancy knife, right?"

Elena rebuked her with a look of disbelief.

"Oh là là. We weren't all raised to be so high and mighty, remember? Some of us work the carnival for a living."

"Yes, it's the ceremonial knife. The sharpest you can find."

Yvette blanched. "You mean to do a real proper spell? Here? While she's down there?"

"I do. Now hurry. We haven't much time."

While Yvette explored the hardware on the wall, Elena took a broom and swept the floor clean of the wood shavings between the workbench and the fireplace.

Yvette returned a moment later offering a round-handled *cochoir*, a wicked-looking knife with a curved steel blade used to plane wooden staves. "Fancy enough for you?"

"That will do," she said and tucked it in her costume at the small of her back.

Together they emptied a crate and turned it over in the center of the floor. Elena opened the satchel and removed two candles, both white with clean wicks, and set them aside. Then she placed the salt, oil, and incense on top of the crate. To her surprise, Brother Anselm had included something he neglected to mention. The cheese, which he'd wrapped in cloth, was tied up with string. A sprig of dried lavender and bay leaf had been secured in the center with a knot. She nearly cried at the gesture, knowing he'd meant it as a protective charm.

Her resolve reinvigorated, she took a deep breath and motioned to the young woman. "Come stand beside me."

For once, Yvette obeyed without comment, seemingly awestruck at the prospect of participating in a full ritual. If life permitted, Elena vowed to find a way to mentor the young woman later so she at least knew a few simple spells to begin building her own Book of Shadows. But first they had to survive the witch in the cellar.

Setting her doubts aside, she concentrated on the small tin of frankincense and rubbed her thumb and fingers together. Tiny sparks danced on her fingertips, then fizzled. "*Merde.* I'm perspiring too much to hold a flame. Hand me the *allumettes*."

Yvette patted her pocket and shook her head in alarm. "I left them with the ciggies back at the fairground."

Elena dabbed her upper lip with the back of her wrist and pretended not to panic. She wiped her palms against her harem pants, though the sequin and silk did little to absorb the moisture.

Concentrate!

She took a deep breath and rubbed her hands back and forth, ready to try again, when a whirlwind swelled to life in the courtyard and slammed against the cooperage. A cyclone of dust and debris twisted through the doorway, crashing against the workbench and ravaging the shop in a fury of raw energy.

"It's her," Elena said, scrambling to protect the paltry items on her altar. Around them barrels splintered, saws and iron tongs stabbed the ground, and the window glass shattered before the energy spun out and dissipated in a small gust that billowed their hair off their necks. "She knows we're here. We must finish. Quickly now."

Fear was no longer a luxury. Elena planted her feet, centered her thoughts, and rubbed the base of her palms together. There was heat but no fire. She closed her eyes and opened her mind until she felt the prickly sting of fire against her fingers. She opened her eyes, and soon an orange ball of flame bloomed to life like a poppy in her hands. With more than a little relief she set it down atop the incense, then watched as the frankincense began to glow. Maintaining her focus, she aligned her thoughts toward her purpose and held the cooper's knife over the rising smoke. Asking the All Knowing for its blessing, she purified the crude athame by passing it through the sweet incense three times. The metal shimmered as if coated in oil, and she began her ritual.

"I want you to still yourself, close your eyes, and concentrate on the shape of the star," she said to Yvette. "The top point is straight in front of you." While the young woman closed her eyes, Elena picked up the sack of salt and judged the weight of it in her hand. It ought to be enough if she was careful. Trickling the salt out in a thin stream, she traced a faint line around them on the floor, encircling the points of the invisible pentagram contained inside. She closed the circle at the top of the star and still had a spoonful of salt left. She returned it to the makeshift altar and raised her hands to thank the All Knowing.

She was working too quickly, but there was no time for a proper spell. If Gerda's patience were stretched too thin, there was no telling what she might do to Jean-Paul. Elena's instinct would have to carry her over the gaps in preparation.

Standing before the altar, she raised the tin of frankincense and let the smoke trail over her head. "Blessed be," she said and placed the incense on the floor at the head of the invisible star. With the lavender and bay, she first trailed the herbs under her nose, inhaling their calming scent, and then placed them at the left point of the star. "I'm going to anoint us both," she warned Yvette before smearing the young woman's forehead with the olive oil. She repeated the gesture on herself, said a quick "blessed be," and then positioned the vial at the right point of the star.

Yvette appeared to be in a near reverent trance as she observed in awe a ritual that should have been a normal part of her childhood. A flicker of worry for the young woman's safety tried to invade Elena's thoughts, but she cast it out. She had to be a tyrant against doubt now. She handed one candle to the young woman and kept the other for herself. Eyes wide with uncertainty, Yvette seemed to ask what she was supposed to do with hers. Elena snapped her fingers against the wick, lighting it with a quick spark. A sign her power was back under her control.

"Hold the candle in front of you and envision the energy of the universe converging around you. Draw it in like breath. Like sustenance. Let the energy build inside you. Fill yourself with light."

The young woman took in several deep breaths, and Elena eased her into a sitting position, coaching her to keep breathing, to keep focusing on the light as she crossed her legs. The circle's energy began to coalesce around them, shimmering in growing intensity. Yvette had finally entered the meditative state of semiconsciousness. The preparation was nearly complete. It was a sloppy job, but the All Knowing seemed to accept and approve her intent. Buoyed, she tipped her candle into the flame of the other, letting the wick catch. She dripped a pool of wax on the floor at the star's left foot, then secured the candle upright within it.

For the final placement, she picked up the remaining salt from the altar and set it on the right foot of the pentagram. The young woman's head drooped forward and Elena exhaled. Five points, five elements: spirit, air, water, fire, earth. And a hotheaded naïf sat square in the middle of it all.

With her offerings set in place, Elena recited a silent spell, directing her thoughts outward and upward.

Smoke, candle, oil, salt. Cone of energy form a vault. Safe within, safe without. Protect the one who sits devout.

Satisfied she'd done all she could, she slit open a doorway at the back of the circle with her athame and slipped out, closing it up behind her. The veil of energy appeared to hold. Yvette should remain protected inside the cone. With that burden off her shoulders, she tucked the athame at her waist and walked out the door.

The witch seething in the cellar could no longer wait.

CHAPTER TWENTY-SEVEN

Jean-Paul could taste fear coiled in his mouth like a length of old rope, a dry knot he couldn't swallow down. The winepress had inched another notch closer. The wooden boards pressed against his rib cage, bending but not yet breaking him. He eyed the mechanical wheel that controlled the pressure. He wasn't sure he could survive another three clicks.

Gerda stirred the lees inside the barrels, doing the cellar work as if it were just another day at Domaine du Monde. But she'd seen him turn his head. The witch set down her stir stick and approached. He refused to look at her.

"Do you hate me?" She didn't wait for an answer. "You know, if you'd come to the valley just a year or two earlier, I might have fancied you instead of Bastien." Her fingers combed through his sweat-dampened hair, chilling his body. "We might have made a beautiful wine, you and I."

He nearly choked on the thought. Why didn't she just kill him and be done with it? Elena wasn't coming. She'd disappeared before, and she would again. He tugged at his restraints, desperate to strangle the witch. "Get your filthy hands off me, you goddamned hag."

"Hate it is," she said with a sigh.

The wheel turned another click.

He shut his eyes against the pressure as the heavy timbers shifted lower, like an elephant squatting atop his lungs. But when he opened his eyes and gasped for a breath, something had changed. A shaft of natural light cut a swath through the cellar's darkness. He had to twist his head around to find the source, straining to see through the stinging sweat that dripped into his eyes and fogged his glasses. After so long in the dark he doubted his sight, but then he saw her descend the stone steps.

Elena glowed in his vision, encircled by a veil of energy, as if she attracted all the light in the cellar, from the finger of daylight seeping through the crevice under the door to the unnatural flame flickering above the witch's candle. Even her odd outfit sparkled as though it had been beaded with precious stones.

God, she was beautiful.

He didn't want to die. He wanted to hold her, to tell her love had no real weight or value until he'd met her.

But he had to warn her. He had to tell her about the witch. If only he could keep his eyes open. If only his mouth would form the words. Instead, he seemed to drift away on a gentle wave. Sunlight warmed his face, and the pain that had racked his chest, head, and teeth slipped loose from his body, floating away on tiny filaments of radiant energy.

He no longer had a care in the world, only a trancelike memory of an exciting and alluring love that made life worth living.

CHAPTER TWENTY-EIGHT

She had conjured a temporary hypnosis spell to alleviate his suffering. To see him in pain would reveal her weakness. She had to eliminate the distraction of wanting to run to him and cool his fevered body. All her energy, all her focus, had to be reserved for what waited in the dark.

Elena took the final step into the cellar. Cool air infused with the scent of oak and fruit drew her in like a familiar hand, leading her into the darkness, though the tinge of sulfur still hung in the space, as if the empty barrels had recently been cleaned with the stuff.

Only the two sconces above the press and the three-pronged candelabra flickering inside a ritual circle on the flagstones provided any light. She peered into the dimness, watching for movement. This one, she knew, liked to hide in the dark and damp. Though she couldn't yet see her, she sensed the witch's eyes watching from the shadows.

"Now, now, a sleeping spell like that might be interpreted as interfering with a mortal," Gerda said. She stepped to the light's edge, letting the sweep of her long skirt brush against a cat skull positioned on the eastern point of the pentagram. Her face remained half in shadow. "Wouldn't want the covenant police locking you up for your little infraction, would you?"

"Release him and I'd be happy to reverse the spell." Elena took a cautious step toward the candle, hoping to lure her adversary farther into the light. "He's no danger to you."

"Oh, even a lovesick mortal can be dangerous when provoked. And I rather thought I'd save him for later."

"He came to see you in good faith."

"To help you."

"Let him go. I'm the one you want to hurt, not him."

Gerda scoffed. "Spare me the martyrdom. You were merely a convenient scapegoat for my little indiscretions. Though I admit I underestimated your training. It's been years since I've encountered another witch with shadow vision as developed as yours."

Gerda lifted the hem of her skirt and turned from the circle's edge to ascend the steps to the winepress. Elena, fearful of what she might do to an unconscious Jean-Paul, clasped her hand tighter around the crystal in her pocket and ventured nearer. The energy from the protection spell still radiated warmth against her skin, calming her.

"You can't hope to get away with this," she said.

"Oh, but I already have." The witch kept her back turned as she stroked Jean-Paul's exposed arm with her finger. "And I will again."

Elena's skin rippled with gooseflesh at the sight. "You enjoy this, don't you? Hiding in the shadows. Uttering your blood magic spells. And now you've strapped an innocent man to a machine that looks more like it was invented for torture than winemaking."

Gerda hissed between her teeth. "And what would *you* know of torture?"

"I see the pleasure you take in hurting others."

"You know nothing." Gerda twisted her neck to look up at the monstrosity of wood and wheel and rope overhead and raised her hand. The wheel on the press groaned. The rope squealed against the windlass, and the wooden pallet shuddered lower as if it had been magicked. A gush of air left Jean-Paul's lungs with a sound like a pillow being punched. "If I'd desired it, you would have found his body split open like the skin of a grape under that weight. I do admit a certain curiosity about what sort of juice comes sluicing out of a man subjected to that much weight and pressure." Gerda lifted her arm again.

"Wait!" Elena's hands involuntarily reached out as if she had some power to hold up the weight of the press. She didn't yet understand the game they were playing, only that she must keep moving on the board long enough to keep Jean-Paul alive. "Just tell me what you want."

Gerda pivoted away from the press. She finally showed her face to Elena, but the shadowy light from the oil lamps seemed to play tricks on her skin, as if she wore the wrinkles of a woman twice her age. And her lustrous hair, normally held in a tight chignon at the back of her neck, had dulled to gray, frizzling in long strands that stood on end. There was little left of the elegant young bierhexe who had come to Elena's aid in the village street. The witch before her was in the process of some transformation. But what kind of spell could strip a woman's youth from her face as if it were a coat of varnish?

"Whatever is the matter? You look as if you've seen an unfortunate future." Gerda bared a grin, revealing a row of teeth brown with rot.

Elena gripped the crystal for strength. "What's happening? Why are you doing this?"

"It's nothing personal. But I'm quite set on having my way." A cool draft swept through the cellar as the rafters creaked overhead. "This 'hiding in the shadows,' as you call it, has kept me alive for a very long time, and I intend for it to continue."

Gerda stepped off the platform and strode past Elena, and the curve of her spine bowed against the lace of her mourning dress. She seemed to be shrinking, yet the aura of her power only intensified. Then Elena noticed the witch's legs. They'd seemingly warped beneath her skirt, forcing her to walk crab-like to her magic circle. Once inside her cone of power, her metamorphosis accelerated, doubling the age of her appearance yet again.

Professor Rackham had said the lure of influence, money, and immortality created a pitfall for magical folk. Power craved power, leading some into dangerous alliances. The sickly sweet scent of lilac water churned in Gerda's wake, barely masking the underlying whiff of decay. But why change into this hideous creature? What ability did she gain from decrepit disfigurement?

And then it struck her. The bierhexe wasn't transforming into something new. She was reverting into herself. Hidden beneath the veneer of a powerful illusion lay her true form, one possibly testing the limits of immortality, a body rotting at the fringes from the unnatural extension of life.

"How long?" Just asking the question made her stomach queasy.

The witch stood hunched and balding as a shriveled foot protruded from under her skirt. "Oh, I've seen kings and conquerors come and go. Dauphins, emperors, prime ministers, presidents." Gerda retrieved her black-and-silver walking stick from atop a barrel. "Mark my words—fashions change, causes change, but men's ambitions never do," she said and leaned heavily on the cane.

Elena found herself horror-struck at the rate of the transformation yet also drawn in by a curiosity shaped by years of studying magic. "What spell allows a person to endlessly cheat time and fate?"

Gerda stared back through eyes now veiled with cataracts. "When I learned you had escaped from prison, it confirmed an earlier suspicion. You see, I'd already begun to think we had more in common than most," she said. "It's why I decided to bring you here. To show you a glimpse of what life can be for those brave enough to grip it by the throat. If you want to hear."

Elena wanted to scream they had nothing in common, aside from this unfortunate crossroads in time and place. But she'd do anything to keep the murderess talking and distracted from lowering the press against Jean-Paul another breath-stealing inch.

The witch gripped her cane with care and bent to pick up the tasting cup she'd placed at the west point of the pentagram. She sniffed its contents as she waited for an answer. If not for her grotesque appearance and taste for murder, she might have been mistaken for a wise elder, a teacher, a mage. But even the monsters of the world can prove a flashpoint of enlightenment to those stuck in the dark.

Elena agreed with a nudge of her chin. "Tell me about this shadow magic of yours."

The witch's teeth had disintegrated to nubs so that she spoke with a gummy, wet inflection, and her eyes had lost their midrange focus, suggesting she'd sunk into blindness. Even so, Elena suspected Gerda's magic still carried the sharp swipe of a falcon's claw. Though the crone appeared easy prey, only a fool would attack a bierhexe in her domain.

"When the secret was first revealed to me I was still young enough that I blushed when a man looked at me with a mischievous smile. A complete innocent, aside from a strong curiosity about the world that didn't conform with the nature of my sex. I wanted to know everything."

She stirred the liquid in the tasting cup with a rhythmic, almost hypnotic, gyration of her wrist. "I came from a good family. Direct descendants of the bierhexe who discovered the magic of adding hops to beer. Changed beer-making forever. The brewers benefited from more reliable batches, and the hexen stopped being blamed for every natural disaster that destroyed a field of grain or ruined an unstable vat of beer. Because of my lineage, I was apprenticed to the renowned braumeister Hans Steinacher. The secrets he knew about fermentation!

"But I soon learned secrets too. I saw how he cheated his customers, slipping their change into his pocket when their eyes blurred from too much alcohol. And once I watched him conjure a hex to ruin a rival's crops with mildew." She shrugged, as if it wasn't the worst offense. "But the day I learned about his ungodly appetites was when things changed." The old witch whispered as if relating a whiff of gossip she'd heard at the fish market. "I'd spied on him, you see, with the barrel boy in the cold room. So many fingers and mouths where they shouldn't be."

"He knew you'd seen them," Elena said, drawing Gerda back in when she'd begun to spool off in distant thought.

"Mmm, I would have looked the other way to keep learning his magic, but . . ." A shudder ran through her, a convulsion perhaps brought on by those thoughts she'd revisited. "I was too green to know what lengths a man with power would go to preserve what he'd attained. Oh, but the child doth learn."

The old witch paused and stuck a crooked finger in the red liquid of her tasting cup. She stirred it once, then licked her finger, smacking her lips before setting the cup back down on the pentagram and turning the handle to the north.

"To punish me and protect his secret he had me cursed," she continued. "He'd offered me a sample of his latest brew under the guise of wanting to know my opinion." She "hmphed," as if ashamed of being taken in by such a notion. "The 'brew' turned out to be a barbed potion. It stitched up my voice with a thousand unseen hooks that worked their way into my throat, binding the vocal cords immobile. I couldn't speak a word, let alone utter a spell, when he was through."

Elena had read about similar concoctions in old grimoires—dated, dusty books that reeked of mold and damp from sitting in cellars and crawl spaces for too long. Such sadistic spells were illegal in the Chanceaux Valley and most regions beyond, though things were possibly different in the northern forests.

Gerda cupped a hand over her saggy neck as if reliving the pain. "We didn't practice in the open the way they do now. It was a different time. The world was caught in a riptide of corruption and cruelty. Accusation was all it took to create a cloud of guilt. After the braumeister stole my voice, he publicly accused me of witchcraft, knowing I'd be swept up with the hapless mortals being rounded up like sheep. And then it was off to the *drudenhaus* for me."

Elena tilted her head as if she hadn't heard right. She understood there were still places where witches had to practice with discretion. But the *drudenhaus* were northern prisons erected during the height of the witch hunts to house those unfortunate mortals accused of malefaction. They were older than the castle that had held Celestine. "But there hasn't been a *drudenhaus* for—"

"Two hundred and seventy-eight years."

"That's impossible."

A wave of dizziness swept over Elena as logic and reason struggled to make sense of the time gap. If the witch's claim were true, she would have to be nearly three hundred years old. And yet looking at the shrunken, grotesque figure Gerda had become, Elena could almost believe it was true.

"It wasn't all mortals, despite what you were taught." The witch took the femur of a small animal from her pocket and set the bone on the southern point of the star. "Do you remember the frailty you felt when you woke from your curse? The feeling that your head was filled with a thousand bees and your skin had turned colder than an eel fished out of black water?" She nodded, seeing Elena understood. "They hunted witches then, but it was like wolves chasing after deer. The strong got away while only the weak and old were taken. Hex-weak. Feebleminded. Those of us who fell behind were just as pathetically vulnerable as nonmagic folk. And just as susceptible to pain."

"Was there no mercy to be found?"

The witch reached in her other pocket and brought out a black feather, which she placed on the southeastern point of the star. "Mercy? There was precious little of that to be scraped off the floor of the *drudenhaus*. No one left that place under their own power. Including me." She gave the feather a turn so it sat horizontal on an east-west axis. "They had a room, built two stories high, made of stacked white stones. There was a window at the top where thin northern daylight grazed the ceiling." The witch cast her eye on the medieval winepress. "It had a windlass with a rope attached to a beam and pulley in the high ceiling. The rope wriggled down from on high to a reddish-brown stain on the stone floor. The smell of copper, salt, and piss was so strong it embedded itself in the walls, the rope, and the clothes of the men who worked in the room."

Elena knew what came next. "You wouldn't confess, so they tortured you."

"They confused my silence for the Devil's obstinacy. They'd already burned off my hair, shredded my clothes, and debated the wickedness of a mole on my left thigh, and still I had not told them what they wanted to hear. So up, up, up I went, hoisted by arms tied behind my back and blocks of wood lashed to my ankles. I swung like that for hours while cloud after cloud passed over the sun and bitter winds howled above the roof. Shadows crept along the walls as the men ate their supper. And then down, down, down I came like an egg cracking on the sidewalk." Gerda lifted her skirt and tapped her cane against her bent right leg. "They broke this one on the first try. It took two more falls to break the other."

Elena closed her eyes against the horrific image in her head. "How did you survive it?" But even as she asked the question, she knew she'd already allowed too much sympathy to enter her heart.

"They dragged me back to my cell, showed me where they'd inked my mark on a written confession, and told me I would burn in the morning with the other confessed witches." She shifted her weight uncomfortably from foot to foot. "I closed my eyes, hovering on a wave of agony, and wished for death to take me. But first I begged the All Knowing to smite those men who would set me aflame. After that I drifted in and out of a delirious sleep, stumbling into one nightmare after another. Just before dawn I awoke shivering with fever. I curled up in a pool of my own sweat and urine, listening to the sound of breaking wood as they built the pyre outside my window. I knew I'd be dead within hours. The All Knowing had forsaken me."

Elena had been cursed, stripped of her powers, and accused of murder, but she'd never been violated so deeply it left a void empty of hope. "Even in death the All Knowing is watching, ready to reclaim its own," she said, the words coming out awkward and misshapen in the wake of the witch's account.

"And yet where was that benevolent eye when it was *my* blood staining the tower floor? Was it watching then for one of its own? Or when I begged for justice against my tormentors?"

"It doesn't work like that. You know it doesn't. You can't make demands."

"More's the pity for you, then."

Gerda turned her back to Elena. On the final two points of the star she placed a gold coin and a small bag of mixed herbs. Elena didn't need to hold the sachet to her nose to know it was filled with ginger, fennel, turmeric, and garlic, medicinals that ebbed the tide of aging.

The air grew thick with the scent of building magic as the last of the ritual items had been laid out on the stones. The witch reached for her athame. If Elena didn't keep Gerda grounded in conversation, the witch would speak her blood magic incantation and seal it to the deed. And then what would happen to Jean-Paul?

"But you escaped," she said, desperate to keep the bierhexe talking. "How did you get out of your cell with two broken legs? What magic is strong enough to overcome that much pain and suffering? Tell me."

The witch cocked her head ever so slightly, as if her ear had been tugged to the left. She looked over her shoulder, the corner of her wrinkled mouth twitching. "There is glorious magic to be found in the darkness," she said, as if she had the secret tucked safely up her sleeve.

"Tell me. You said we had more in common than I knew. Is this what you meant?"

Gerda twisted full around. The smile faded. "So it's true what they say," she said under her breath. "At night, all the cats are gray." She considered Elena for a moment, then nodded. "Very well."

The witch tucked her ceremonial knife away. "There is power in dreams. You know this. But the bad ones attract a different energy than the good or the merely odd. That morning I awoke feverish, chilled, my legs broken and swollen. Certain I would die. But then a weight, solid and warm, pressed against me like a dog resting its head against my chest. I opened my eyes, and there it was grazing on the remnants of my nightmares, the smell of brimstone burning my nostrils."

A memory flickered to life like a motion picture—a painting of a diminutive demon sitting on the chest of a sleeping woman. Elena had seen it as a child reading at Grand-Mère's elbow as she flipped through the pages of a spell book. Fear had lodged like a stone in her young throat to know that such a thing existed.

"A demon revealed itself to you?"

Gerda's eyes glittered bright once more in the candlelight. "He never spoke, and yet I knew he had come to save me."

Elena's mind raced ahead, recalling the little she'd dared to learn about the ill-natured creatures. The one thing that let her sleep as a child was the assurance they only showed themselves to a willing heart. "You made a pact? That's what the blood is for?"

"They're quite generous beings," Gerda explained, taking a deep, shuddering breath before releasing it in a gush, as if exhaling all the pain she'd felt. "But they need a conduit so they can travel from their world and ours. Someone who can straddle both."

"A witch who can see in the shadow world between."

"They're more than willing to pay for the journey. They'll give you anything you desire. Money, sex, immortality."

"Freedom?" Elena saw the deflation in the witch's shoulders before she ignored the question.

"He showed me how it was possible to escape my prison. All it required was a small gesture to establish trust." Gerda rubbed her arms as if she shivered inside her skin, remembering. "The midwife in the cell with me was as good as dead already. Once they'd ruined her hands with thumbscrews she confessed to sleeping with the Devil. For hours she knelt, hands pressed palm to palm like two bloated fish, uttering her nonstop apologies to the heavens. It was a mercy, truly, to spare her the fire for such a lie."

Elena swayed on her feet and reached for the nearest column to steady herself. "You killed her?"

"Mmm, yes, but I'd bungled it by strangling her. I was supposed to draw blood. So elementary in demon magic. But I'd had to crawl on my elbows to get to her, and by then I'd forgotten my purpose. He made me go back and do it again."

Elena leaned against the column with her hand held over her stomach. She feared she would be ill, and the reek of sulfur coming off the barrels was only making the sensation worse. If there were some spell she could speak to obliterate this woman—this lunatic—from the world so she could be free of the stench of her, she would do it. But the source of that magic resided on the other side of a dark line she knew she could not cross. Instead, she swallowed a gulp of air and continued listening to the mad confession, knowing every minute the crone kept talking was another moment Jean-Paul remained alive.

"He'd been following the Allfather on the Wild Hunt when he sniffed out my fever dreams and dropped from the astral plane to the earthly realm. Once he was satisfied I was in earnest, he anointed me in blood. Then he turned me into a blackbird, tied a small stone around my leg to keep me tethered to him, and whisked me out of the cell. We climbed the stars until we emerged within the astral plane, and there we joined the pack of hunters as they stampeded over the forests, scooping up the spirits of the dead and undead." Gerda centered her cane before her, gripping it with both hands. "So you see, I owe him for the long life I've enjoyed."

"And this transformation"—Elena gestured to the witch's appearance—"is why you need so much blood? You transfuse it inside yourself to replenish your youth?"

"It only takes a spoonful for the spell."

"But all those animals. And Bastien. They'd been drained. Why bleed them out if all you need is a little? Why kill them at all?"

"My dear, you haven't been listening. The drops of blood are for me, but the deaths are always for him. Large or small, animal or human, whatever his appetite demands."

She followed the direction of the witch's pointed finger to the top of the medieval winepress. There, hunched over the wheel, half-hidden in shadow, sat an apelike creature covered in coarse hair, with pointed ears and clawlike nails. Golden eyes gleamed in the dark, hungry with curiosity as the being stared down at the sleeping Jean-Paul.

Gerda's demon.

The creature inhaled through its puggish snout as if sniffing at one of Tilda's pastries. It paid no attention to Elena as it crawled out of its hiding place, following the scent of Jean-Paul's dreams with its nose. The demon crept with deadly intent, eyes focused on its prey. Not knowing what it might do to satisfy its appetite, she had no choice but to rouse Jean-Paul and shake off the beast. She rubbed the stone in her pocket and uttered the quick rousing spell, delivering him from a sleeping nightmare and into a waking one.

CHAPTER TWENTY-NINE

He'd dreamed he'd been tied to a stake and set on fire for making wine no one would drink. Jean-Paul shook his head to chase off the last threads of the bizarre images, but then panic rose when he remembered it wasn't all a dream. The press had come lower, squeezing against his chest so he could not take a full breath, and what air he could get reeked of sulfur. He coughed and tugged his wrists against the restraints. His head thrashed to the right, and he saw Elena standing across the room. It hadn't been an illusion. She shimmered in the candlelight, and it wasn't just due to the peculiar silver-threaded clothing she wore. Her very skin radiated with energy. His heart nearly broke from the desperation to hold her just once before he died.

"Run!" he tried to warn her, but his voice came out a hoarse whisper. "It's her. Gerda is the killer," he tried again, but she didn't even turn.

Instead, she covered her mouth with her sleeve to keep from breathing in the same foul stench he choked on as her eyes tracked some invisible movement. But then something in the room shifted. She raised her arms against a threat he couldn't yet see, while an ancient woman, bald and toothless, grinned from inside the circle drawn on the floor.

The black dress with the draping sleeves. The black-and-silver walking cane. It had to be Gerda. Or some corrupted version of her. He tugged again at the leather straps tying him to the press. There was slack building on the right. If he could just gain another inch of space he might slip loose.

He banged his head against the platform in frustration. When he turned his neck again to find Elena, a fairylike creature caught his eye instead. No, it was a young woman with pale-yellow hair, crouching in the shadows of the cellar stairwell. She, too, was dressed strangely, clad in a harlequin costume with red-and-black diamonds. He craned his neck to see her face. Her eyes were smudged with black kohl, and her cheeks had been rouged like the women he'd seen working the cabaret district in the city. He'd never been a great reader of women's thoughts, but there was no mistaking the murder in this one's eye.

As if sensing his stare, she turned her gaze upon him, held a finger over her lips, and winked. He decided then he must have transcended into hallucination, because there was no other explanation for seeing a harlequin imp toting three glinting axes in her hands while lurking inside a world-class wine cellar. She pointed to the space above the wheel, and he braced himself, certain the press would squeeze the last breath out of him. He looked up to the ceiling to say a prayer to God and instead saw the thing. It watched him from above, drooling and sniffing. Like the gargoyle in the vine row, the brutish beast sat hunched, observing him, nostrils flared. Jean-Paul flinched and tried to shrink beneath the pallet, but there was nowhere to hide. Then the thing twisted its head and shifted its weight to stare at Elena, and he pulled with all his strength against his restraints.

CHAPTER THIRTY

Waking Jean-Paul out of his bad dream had slowed the diminutive devil only a fraction. Once drawn in by the nightmare, its fixation on the flesh seemed to intensify. She stood between the demon and the bierhexe, a hand held up against each as if she could hold back the tide of their intentions.

"Call that thing off," she yelled, ignoring Jean-Paul's hoarse warning. She hoped he was strong enough to bear the weight of the press a little longer.

Gerda removed her ceremonial knife and waved it over the tasting cup on the ground. "You wanted to spill Bastien's blood in the road the day you two met again," she said. "Your will to murder vibrated in your heart so loud it drummed along the ground until I couldn't help but tap my toe beneath my skirt to the rhythm."

Elena recoiled at hearing the truth come from such a foul mouth. Meanwhile the demon trained its golden eyes on her as if assessing before returning its attention to the prey on the press.

"I knew then you'd be the one to take the fall for me. After all, there's only so long one can get away with killing people's pets before the blame piles up. Toss in a mortal and it's definitely time to move on. But then you escaped. And I secretly hoped you might aspire to be more than a country vine witch. I can teach you the spell for immortality. Here. Now. If you desire it."

"And be chained to a devil for eternity?" Behind her the demon unfurled its tail and crawled headfirst down the side of the wheel and onto the pallet above Jean-Paul.

"Come, be my sister. Let me show you how. You have the talent; I can see that you do."

Anger and repulsion churned until Elena could no longer suppress her hatred. "Sister? You're a murderer. A bloodthirsty killer. A . . . a . . ."

"I was going to say nasty old bag of crone bones." Yvette stepped into the candlelight. "I can't believe you just left me there."

"Yvette, no! Go back outside!" Could the girl do nothing she was told to do?

In her hands were three axes from the cooper's shop, two in the left and one in the right balanced perfectly by its wooden handle. The first left her grip with such ferocity it made a whirring noise in the air. When the blade landed it hit with a hard thud, cleaving the tasting cup at Gerda's feet in two and sending wine and blood splashing across the witch's skirt.

"Sorry, old habits." Yvette cocked her arm again. "We're taught to just miss our targets in the carnival, you know."

She tossed off a second ax just as violently. It struck with exact precision, the blade slicing through the end of Gerda's foot before she could hobble out of the way. The old witch let out a cry to rival a banshee. She twisted her body, tugging her deformed foot free of her shoe, leaving a bloody trail behind.

Yvette cocked her arm. "The next one goes between your eyes if you don't call off that beastie of yours."

Gerda hissed and raised a knobby arm to signal the demon. "Kill them!"

The demon pricked its ears and curled its lip. Defying gravity, it leaped from the winepress to the ceiling, where it crawled bat-like along the stone arch above Yvette's head. Too late she ran for cover behind a wine barrel. The demon pounced, landing on her shoulders. It clamped its teeth on her throwing arm and yanked, dragging her into the open. She released the remaining ax in a painful spasm, and it scuttled across the flagstones.

Yvette's scream awakened an animalistic fear in Elena that begged her to run, but she held firm, even as Gerda slunk off down a shadowed passageway deep in the cellar. She could not abandon the young woman to that thing. Feet planted, she rubbed her palms together as vigorously as she could until a blue vein of electricity arced in her hands. Infused with the energy of her anger, the lightning bolt shot out at the beast, striking it in the spine. The demon arched its back and grinned as its hair singed and smoked. It released an ungodly howl of laughter that pierced the ear. Cunning Yvette didn't waste the distraction. She grabbed her silver hairpin and stabbed the creature in the torso. The fiend squealed as if amused by the fight in its prey and then flung her against the wall with one hand. She crumpled like a soggy playing card, a streak of blood trailing from her nose.

The demon drew back its lips, revealing a pair of canine teeth, as it skulked toward Elena. Across the room Jean-Paul groaned as if in agony. From the corner of her eye she saw him pull one hand free from its restraint. She stepped to her left to keep the devil focused on her. If she could lead it far enough away, Jean-Paul might have a chance to free himself. She didn't dare speak but held eye contact with the beast, luring it toward her. Back, she must lead it back. Her foot nudged the cooper's ax on the flagstones. The bloody shoe lay nearby. The beast hissed and crept closer.

On instinct she backed inside the witch's circle, hoping it held some protective energy against the thing. But the moment she stepped across the line, tendrils of murky energy crept up her legs, seething with dark magic. A current of energy ran over her skin, sleek as snakes. The demon held back, studying her, watching for what she would do with the magic.

She took the gamble. Elena drew the bierhexe's magic into her hands as a thread of saliva slipped out of the demon's mouth. Miraculously, the magic held together like a ball of static that bit at her skin. The beast crouched, legs ready to lunge. With fingers quivering, she unleashed the sphere of crackling energy. The blast hit the creature full in the muzzle, but instead of setting it afire as she hoped, the energy enveloped the demon's body in glowing green light.

The thing's hair thickened, its snout elongated, its teeth and claws curved and sharpened, and then it stood on its hind legs, displaying the full height of a grown man. The fiend roared at her, its breath reeking of spoiled meat.

Her mouth convulsed as if to scream. It merely grinned back. And though the demon didn't speak aloud, she understood every word directed at her as it inched closer. "That old hexe's instincts were right about you," it said, unfurling a pair of leather wings. "Your cursed blood only enhances the dark energy." It licked its lips, tasting her magic in the air. "Pity you won't be joining us in everlasting life, but you're going to taste deliciously wicked when I tear your throat out."

Jean-Paul let out an agonizing yell as he scraped his chest against the press to free himself of its grip. She heard a rib snap. The demon heard it, too, and just for a second seemed to consider which was the better of two meals.

Her eyes darted from Jean-Paul to the beast. It growled low and hungry. She pulled the *cochoir* from the small of her back and waved the curved blade in front of her as she inched backward. There were no more magic spells. "Get out," she shouted to Jean-Paul, not daring to take her eyes off the demon a second time. "Take Yvette with you."

"Elena!"

The beast pounced, fangs bared. It pinned her against a row of barrels, its teeth sinking into the triangle of flesh above her collarbone.

She'd thought she'd known pain when Old Fox took her toe, but it was nothing compared to the electric stars that flashed in her eyes. Jean-Paul's voice shouted at her to hold on. *Fight, Elena, fight!* She swiped the curved edge of the knife against the thick hide of the demon, and it answered by sinking its teeth deeper. A strangled animallike shriek crawled out of her throat. She tried to push the thing off, to wriggle loose, to flee, anything to be free of its bite. But its grip was too strong, its teeth too practiced at their purpose. Her blood was being drawn into its mouth.

She would be drained like a cat to feed the desecrated body of a demon.

But as sudden and vicious as it had struck, the hairy devil abruptly let go. Its tongue thrust in and out of its mouth, as if trying to rid itself of the taste of her. White froth foamed on grotesque lips. It clawed at its face, gagging for breath, spitting her blood on the floor. Elena shoved the beast away, thinking it possessed, when a putrid stream of yellow bile oozed out of its mouth. The demon dropped to its knees in a spasm that racked its body in marionette-like contortions. The golden eyes dilated in disbelief.

"What have you done to me?" it begged. And then the monster slumped into stillness, leaving her bewildered and without answer.

Jean-Paul, finally free, limped madly toward her from the wine-press, one hand clutching his ribs. "Christ, is it dead?" he asked.

The demon was definitely dead. But how?

Rivulets of blood trickled from the puncture wounds near her neck. She wiped a smear of it on her hand and rubbed it between her fingers. Could it be? For seven years she'd ingested toxic toad skin to break the curse. Was it possible the bufotoxin still swam in her blood after all this time? It must have, though the realization gave her no comfort.

"It's been poisoned," she said and wiped her hand on her costume.

"You're bleeding," he said. "Are you hurt badly?" He reached up to her collar, groaning from the pressure it put on his ribs to raise his arm.

"I don't think so." Though if it was possible for her to infect the beast, she had to wonder if it could have done the same to her with its vile, hell-born mouth. No fire burned inside her veins, and her head and eyes were clear. Still, she would need to visit Brother Anselm to be sure.

"Can you ever forgive me?" Jean-Paul asked.

"What for?"

"For not being able to protect you."

"Stop." She held a finger to his lips. "There was nothing on your mortal earth you could have done."

He removed his shirt and pressed the cloth against her wound to stop the bleeding. "Can you at least tell me what in hell just happened?"

"One of its denizens used a human bridge to pay us a visit," she said. "Oh, Yvette! Is she all right?"

They hurried to the other side of the barrels and found the young woman lying on the floor, unconscious. Elena thanked the stars there wasn't much blood except for the small trickle coming from Yvette's nose and a scratch on her arm.

"I performed a protection spell on her before we entered, but she wasn't supposed to come down here."

Jean-Paul tapped the woman's cheeks and got no response.

"Let me try a little of this," Elena said, digging in her pocket. She'd saved a bit of lavender and bay from Brother Anselm's bundle. She passed it under Yvette's nose several times. The young witch's eyes fluttered open, and Elena held her hands in the sacred pose to thank the All Knowing.

"What happened?"

"You were knocked out. I'm afraid you're going to have a terrible headache later."

"Where is she? And that devil? Did they get away?"

Elena glanced over her shoulder at the cellar passageways cloaked in darkness. "The demon is dead, but Gerda is still here. Hiding in one of the barrel rooms."

Yvette sat up. "Let's get her. Where's my . . ." The young woman swayed unsteadily and fell over to the side. Jean-Paul caught her shoulder, gritting his teeth to keep from crying out at the cost to his ribs.

"You've had a nasty bump to the head," Elena said. "It's best if you rest."

She stopped and put a finger over her lips. The clatter of horse hooves beat upon the cobblestones. She crept closer to the steps leading out of the cellar and heard the rumble of motorcycles. "They're here."

Jean-Paul helped the girl to her feet. "Who?"

"The inspector. And, I imagine, the matron."

"You have to get out of here. They'll lock you up. Both of you."

"I'm not going back," Yvette said. "There has to be a way out. A window or something."

The authorities would search the house first. Only after finding it empty would the men expand their hunt to include the outbuildings and cellar. She and Yvette had a moment, albeit a brief one. Elena had no choice. She had to get Yvette out. She owed her that much.

"Right. No windows, but there is one other possible way out. At least for you."

Elena took a step back and raised her arms in the sacred pose again. She closed her eyes and brought the image of flames and incense into her mind, the nearest she could align with the jinni's spirit. Then she called out Sidra's name three times.

"What! No, not her. Anyone but her. She hates me."

After a long pause, the scents of charred citrus and frankincense trickled into the cellar. As the aroma grew stronger it infiltrated the space, pushing out the odor of death and sulfur. A trail of smoke seeped in through a tiny crack in the cellar's foundation, a passageway only a spider ought to know of. The smoke built into a column, and the jinni stepped out, her skin still shimmering with magic.

"What is this place?" she demanded. "It's as dark as Jahannam in here. Did you summon me inside the walls of a jail?" Sidra wore a scowl that would have frightened the demon back to hell if it were still alive. "If this is a trick, I will curse your offspring for all eternity."

Jean-Paul's mouth fell open at the sight of the jinni in her shiny silks and gold jewelry.

"It's a wine cellar," Elena assured her. "And I'm in need of a favor, if I'm still due one."

"Already? You didn't get very far." Sidra's eye traveled down the length of Elena's costume. "Prophets protect us, what are you wearing?"

She'd forgotten about the unfortunate apparel. "Never mind that," she said, fighting the urge to cover her partially exposed midriff. "We have only a minute."

Ignoring the threat of combustion from Sidra, she explained the need for a quick escape that only her magic could provide.

"Are you sure this is what you want?" the jinni asked. "Leaving this one with the authorities would save you a favor for a more worthy moment."

"Oh, that's gratitude for you." Yvette crossed her arms. "And maybe I should have tossed the matches out the window and let you feel the kiss of *la demi-lune* against your neck."

"Ladies!" Elena pointed to the cellar door as a reminder of what was at stake.

Sidra rolled her eyes. "Fine, but I choose the method of her escape." Elena and Yvette grudgingly agreed, and the jinni pushed back the sleeves of her robe and raised her arms. "You know, I could take you both," she said with a glance at Elena.

"I know. But I have to stay and settle this. I can't have a shadow of guilt trailing me for the rest of my life. I have a home at Château Renard that I hope to return to. If its owner will have me."

Jean-Paul slipped his hand in hers as his answer, and she gripped it with all her might.

"Very well. Peace be with you both."

"And with you."

Sidra narrowed her eyes at Yvette. "Come, let's get this over with."

The young woman stepped forward, still woozy but able to stay on her feet. The jinni removed the sash from her caftan and tied it around Yvette's wrist, singing her magic so that the melody echoed through the cavernous space. Outside, the inspector's voice rose in irritation, shouting orders to search the outbuildings. Soon he would discover the door to the cellar. Sidra finished her singing. Her body shimmered like a heat wave above a desert until she disappeared, taking Yvette with her. In their place a gray sparrow flapped its wings in a cloud of smoke as it perched atop the winepress, waiting for the cellar door to open. A red string trailed off its leg. Whether the transformation was real or merely an illusion planted in the mind by the jinni, Elena did not know, but she raised her hands in the sacred pose, thankful to see both women on the cusp of freedom.

Jean-Paul hugged his ribs and sat on the cellar steps to wait. He was still gaping, hand over mouth in amazement at what he'd witnessed, when Elena left him. Taking the witch's candlestick, she followed the smeared blood trail on the flagstones. Bastien's cellar was a vast catacomb of interconnecting corridors and individual rooms that had stood for centuries. Perhaps a thousand years. Each generation of winemakers had dug deeper into the earth, searching for the ideal temperature and humidity to perfect the aging process. The result was a warren of irregular rooms and narrow passageways.

And Gerda could be hiding in any one of them.

The blood loss had slowed, but an intermittent line of drops and dragged-foot smears pointed toward the oldest part of the cellar. Elena followed as it led under an ancient lintel with a wedged keystone. The corridor sloped noticeably downward, growing narrower than the main cellar. Cobwebs heavy with dust laced the ceiling. She lit a wall sconce to mark the way, leaving it to burn as she descended into the passage that bore more resemblance to a dungeon entrance than a storage space for wine.

Holding the candlestick out in front of her as a weapon as much as a torch, she ducked her head into each anteroom she passed. Some were no larger than a niche with a dozen dusty bottles; others held several racks of wine, where the air was half-damp from the expended breath of the bottles. To her recollection there were perhaps five or six similar rooms this deep in the cellar. She moved cautiously, knowing each one she passed left fewer places for the witch to hide. A moment later she held still. Breathing. Listening. There was a subtle shift in the air. The scent of dead flowers just below the exhale of the wine. Then a muttered whisper rose out of the darkness in a pattern every organ in her body recognized. Gerda was casting a spell.

Elena let the sound lead her as she crept forward on the balls of her feet to a small crypt-like alcove on her left. The room held two racks of very old wine. The bottles were caked in mold and dust, and white spores grew out of the corks with tiny tentacles that wafted on the slightest air current. Though decrepit looking, she knew the wine inside would be perfectly protected.

Unlike Gerda, whom she found slumped against the back wall between the shelves.

The witch's leg was bent akimbo so that her mutilated foot rested in her lap. Remarkably, her hair had filled in again. Though still gray, it hung in waves to her shoulders. The cataracts, too, had vanished from her eyes, though she did not look up as she continued chanting her spell.

"Blood of vigor, vitality, and life. Whether suckled by tooth, or drained by knife. Transfuse your grace into the vein. Till the verve of youth be all that remain." The witch dipped her finger in her own blood, then wiped it on her tongue. "You can use your own if nothing else avails, but you have to keep doing the spell over and over again until it takes hold." Her eyes closed as she leaned her head back against the wall. "Quite exhausting."

"I'm not sure your spell is working." Elena trailed a finger over the dusty bottles and then blew the dirt off with a puff of breath. "My guess is you'll be nothing but dust yourself soon."

The witch kept her eyes closed and began the chant again, dabbing her finger in the bloodstain on her skirt.

"Your demon is dead, by the way."

Gerda's eyes opened, calculating truth or lie. "Impossible."

"Apparently the cure to my curse left my blood poisonous," she said, raising the candlestick to show off the bite wound on her collar. "But I'd be happy to donate a few drops to your cause."

The witch managed a defeated laugh. "Your spiteful side is why I thought you might be one of us." A pain hit her and she grimaced, sucking in a breath. When it passed, she swallowed hard as a faint blush returned to her cheeks. The wrinkles on her face smoothed out and her teeth reappeared, polished and white. She turned her hands over front to back, checking for age spots, pleased with the results.

A vague thud echoed at the far end of the corridor. Elena adjusted her stance to lean against the wall, shifting the candlestick to her other hand as a distraction. There was precious little time left. "Was it Bastien who had me cursed?" Even now she needed the certainty.

Gerda touched her face, delicately probing the tautness of her skin. "Have my cheekbones filled out?" Elena nodded, and the witch gave a half smile before letting it fall again, as if the weight of it was too heavy to hold in place. "He often wondered what happened to you. I believe . . . he was still in love with you." It cost her to admit it, as if revealing the shadow of a vulnerable and childish heart that had once coveted love above all else. "Your absence carved a hole in him. That piece of him was still missing when we met. It's what made it so easy to reel him in. I merely molded myself to fit the shape you left."

The candle flame blurred as tears rimmed Elena's eyes. "Why kill him like that? Why kill him at all?"

The bierhexe's face hardened into a Medusa stare as she spit out her venom. "Because after you returned, he never looked at me again."

The blood magic seemed to pump through Gerda's veins quicker, encouraged by the heat of her temper. She suffered a last bout of pain, and then her youthful appearance was fully restored. She stretched her leg out straight, turning the bloody foot from side to side. "I thought it might grow back after the change, but it must require a different form of blood. A rabbit perhaps." Gerda licked her lips and stood with surprising agility. "Never mind that. It's all for the best anyway."

"How's that?"

"Now that you've ruined everything, I'm going to take great pleasure in making sure what remains of your life is nothing but misery. This foot shall be my evidence," she said, limping toward Elena to make her threat face-to-face. "If I'm not mistaken, that's the authorities I hear coming, and I can't wait to show them what you did to me with your fiendish devil magic."

On cue Inspector Nettles showed himself, stepping out of the narrow passageway, his face flushed from the chase. "Make one move and it will be your last," he said, waving his torch at them. The flame glowed eerily blue, burning with a ferocious desire to leap at them.

Gerda crumpled, feigning weakness. "Oh, Inspector! Thank the All Knowing you've come. She forced me down here and nearly killed me." She backed away from Elena and revealed the ghastly foot.

Elena dared to meet the inspector's eyes, uncertain what he would do next. He made no move toward her, but perhaps uncertainty kept him rooted to his spot, despite his flamethrower. After all, what charm could he possibly possess that could deflect a demon's sorcery?

"Reeking, foul magic it is," he said, choosing wiles instead of amulets. "Can you walk to me? You've nothing to fear from her while I'm here." He held out a hand to Gerda as if she dangled off a high ledge.

She went to him, limping and sniffling. He cooed at her with comforting words, wrapping a protective arm around her shoulders as he escorted her safely out of the storage room.

Elena waited, wondering if she should have fled with Sidra after all. If she'd miscalculated, misjudged . . . and then he beckoned her forward with a stern look and a tilt of his head. She inhaled the scent of the old wine one last time and walked out of the room.

The snap of handcuffs followed.

Matron had been waiting in the hallway. She clapped a restraint on Gerda's right wrist the moment the bierhexe got caught between her and the inspector. The left wrist evaded her, however.

"What is this?" Gerda yanked and twisted, trying to get free. She screamed like a fox with its foot caught in a trap. "What are you doing, you fools? She's the murderer. Arrest her. I am Madame Du Monde. You're making a terrible mistake." She hissed and tried to sink her teeth into Matron's arm. The inspector pinned her against the wall with his body and finished handcuffing her other wrist. The blue light of the runes glowed to life, sapping the witch's magic. Both Matron and the inspector exhaled in relief.

"How much did you hear?" Elena asked once they had their prisoner under control.

The inspector held up his seashell listening charm. "I caught the confession. Your man upstairs showed us the demon and the summoning circle. Hell of a mess this whole thing, but you ought to be granted bail while it gets sorted out in court." She thanked him, and he gave her a grudging nod, adding, "We'll discuss the disappearance of your cohorts later."

She remained silent and dutifully followed as they frog-marched Gerda through the narrow corridor to return to the main barrel room. They'd walked only a few feet when Gerda stumbled, writhing in pain, her back arching as if caught in a spasm. It appeared a trick. A stalling measure to buy time or sympathy. A way to slither free through a feint of injury. Elena braced herself for a confrontation.

"I didn't do it." Gerda pleaded with Matron, tugging on the handcuffs. "Whatever deal she's made with you, I can give you life. Immortality. We could live forever. You and me. Just take these damn things off!"

Matron rolled her eyes and prodded Gerda forward again. But the witch's outburst was more than prisoner dramatics. The aging metamorphosis had begun to reverse again, but at a freakishly fast pace.

"The cuffs," Elena said, remembering the sensation of having her magic severed by the restraints. "They've cut off the spell that's been keeping her alive."

Gerda's eyes widened in horrified realization of what was happening to her. In seconds her hair turned gray and fell out, her skin sagged, and the eyes clouded over. She'd transformed into the same old toothless woman she'd been before, but then her body recoiled even more violently. She cried out in agony, shriveling to an impossible thinness of bone and skin, like a twisted strip of leather withering in the sun. Seconds later, desiccated as an ancient mummy, the skull crumbled and the body disintegrated into a pile of dust and bone beneath a layer of black mourning lace.

Time had finally come to collect the death it had been cheated for three hundred years.

CHAPTER THIRTY-ONE

There'd been no midday fire in the stove. The grate was cool to the touch. No bread crumbs on the table, no plates drying on the dishcloth, and the delivery of eggs still sat on the back step beside the geranium pots. Madame had not returned home.

"She's not upstairs or in the sitting room," Jean-Paul said, returning to the kitchen.

Elena tried to hide her concern, but the way her eyes and fingertips checked for details beyond his vision told him the prolonged absence wasn't normal.

"She's probably still upset over all that's happened," he said. "Perhaps she stayed in town to see a friend."

"She went to see Brother Anselm, but that was hours ago. I'll get another message to her later."

Jean-Paul hung up his jacket and homburg on the rack near the back door. His button-up shirt was covered in blood and sweat, his and hers. He'd tried to hide it, but she noticed him flinch as he slipped his arms out of the jacket.

"Come to my workroom. I need to put some salve on those wounds."

There was a pause as he bit his lip. He held back from saying what was on his mind, but she'd guessed anyway.

"Yes, it's magic. Good magic. You won't feel a thing."

He doubted that. Nothing this woman did left him without feeling. He followed after a compliant nod. Regrettably the workroom was located in the cellar, a space neither wished to revisit so soon, but he propped the main door open to add air and light. He'd not entered her workroom before. The times he'd tried to get a look inside it had been locked, jammed, and seemingly blockaded from the other side. Now, as she held her hand over the lock and whispered a spell, he suspected it might also have been secured by an enchantment. The door swung open without so much as a squeak.

He had to confront his privileged standards of normal when he saw the smallness of the space she'd been living in. The single bed, the trunk, the desk, and the shelves overflowing with bottles containing bits of leaf, fur, and animal bone—Madame had been closer to the truth when she'd called it an old storage closet full of brooms.

She selected several bottles, shaking their contents and considering, before replacing them back on the shelf. Her finger paused at an empty space, a toothless hole in an otherwise full smile of apothecary jars. Her brow tightened. Her lips pressed together in concentration as she searched the desk.

"Something wrong?"

"Strange, there was a bottle here and now it's gone."

"Madame was in here earlier."

Elena considered it and then shook her head as if setting the thought aside. She reached for her mortar and pestle, then began crushing a handful of dried leaves. "You'll need to unbutton your shirt," she said, adding the grindings to a jar of sweet-smelling cream.

He obliged, ever more aware of the impropriety of the two of them being in her room alone together. He decided he didn't care and opened his shirt to let her fingers probe his tender ribs. He sucked in a short breath at her touch.

"Breathe," she said and applied the cream, smoothing her hands over his side while she whispered soft words of healing and mending.

"What happened to you?" he asked, feeling slightly dizzy from the nearness of her. "Before. To make you go away?"

She looked up at him with those cat eyes of hers, only this time she didn't turn away or change the subject. "Someone put a curse on me. A bad one. It took seven years to break it so I could free myself. That's why I was gone so long."

"Someone? You don't know who?"

"I was convinced it was Bastien. But it wasn't. Now I don't know."

He wanted to put his arms around her. He wanted to protect her. It was absurd to think someone with her supposed powers might need his protection, but he remembered the desperate look in her eye as she'd faced Du Monde in the street. Trapped like a wild bird fighting to get out of a cage. Now he knew why. And now he understood that whoever cursed her was still out there.

She handed him the jar of cream and turned her head so that her neck was exposed to him. "Just dab it on the worst of it."

"Do I say something?" She smiled and had him repeat the incantation. As he applied the salve and spoke the words, he felt the familiar static run over his skin. He didn't think he'd done any real magic by saying the spell—he understood his place on the spectrum—but an enchanted energy seemed to envelop them just the same.

In the luster of that magic he studied her face. Her golden eyes, which on another woman might advertise a sultry nature, held only warmth and wisdom. Her hair, her skin, her lips—he was bewitched by his need to caress the supple feel of her. He felt the pain in his ribs subside, only to be replaced by an even stronger ache to hold her. He lifted his hand to cup the soft edge of neck and cheek. She didn't pull away. When the urge to press his lips to hers grew so strong his chest heaved from the craving, he stole his chance and kissed her. And when her body yielded, as hungry for the taste of him as he for her, he let passion guide his hands, pushing off the silver-beaded bodice.

CHAPTER THIRTY-TWO

She absorbed the weight of his bare arm draped over her hip and the warmth of his breath on her neck as he slept beside her on the bed. Love magic, she was learning, could be a powerful curative. As it spread through her body, filling in the last tiny crevices left cold and empty from the curse, her instinct led her to ruminate on the melancholia infecting the vines. It was as if the roots had suffered an injury. Like a stone bruise or ulcer of the stomach. But that wasn't quite right. It was more emotional. Like the pain of a broken heart. And yet the cause evaded her. In the morning she would pull out Grand-Mère's old grimoire from the early planting days and see if there was anything to be gleaned on the emotional state of plants.

Satisfied with her thoughts, she nestled in closer to Jean-Paul. She'd just settled into a dreamy state of happiness when a scratching at the door made her lift her head.

Jean-Paul stirred awake and kissed her neck softly. "What is it?"

"I think there's someone at the door."

He sat up, listening. "Stay here—I'll get it," he said, grabbing his glasses. He tugged his trousers on and then opened the door a crack. His shoulders relaxed as he looked down. "It's only a bird."

Elena lifted her head to see a pigeon bobbing back and forth. "No, it's a message. It must be from Grand-Mère." She propped herself up on one elbow and called to the bird. It obediently flapped its wings, landing on her hip. "Odd she used a pigeon," she said, looking over the dingy gray bird. "Grand-Mère swears by doves."

"Naturally," he said. He picked up his dirty shirt and shook it out. "But where's the message? I don't see any note tied to its leg."

She gave him a pitying stare before coaxing the bird to speak by rubbing her finger under its beak. It cooed its message like a perfect gentleman, until Elena sat up so quickly she startled the bird into retreat. It dropped a pair of feathers as it flew back out the door.

"The pigeon spoke to you?" He shook his head as though the exchange were just another bewilderment to add to an already rich pile. "Is something wrong? Is it from Madame?"

"No, it's from someone else." But she hardly knew how to explain. She collected the feathers and kicked off the blanket. "It was from the barkeep at the tavern. I have to go," Elena said as she dug through her trunk for something to wear.

"Tavern?" Jean-Paul shrugged on his shirt. "You're going out? Now?"

She paused as she rolled up her stockings. "Yes. May I borrow your horse?"

"May I come with you?"

She clipped a stocking in place. "It would be better if you didn't."

He opened his mouth to protest, but she kissed him before he could speak. When she felt the argument go out of him, she pulled away, ready to acquiesce. "Very well," she said, wondering how she would ever deny him anything he wanted again. "Get the horse."

The sun had faded to a gauzy pink over the hills as they stood outside Grimalkin & Paddock's. Her heart fluttered with the intensity of a moth's wing against a lantern, knowing what had brought her there.

Jean-Paul tied the horse's lead to a post with an iron frog for a finial. "How is it I've never seen this place before?" He looked around as if to get his bearings.

"Did you feel spiderwebs against your face as we rode up?"

"Yes. How did you know?"

"Spellwork often feels like walking through a web for a mortal. This end of the road is protected by enchantments to make it less interesting to nonmagical passersby, but since you're with me you're seeing it as I do."

"The rats aren't enough to keep the curious away?" He stomped his foot in the face of a large rodent that had come to inspect him from the alley.

She nudged her chin at the rat and pointed, and it scurried away. "This is a witch's tavern. I let you come this far, but it really would be best if you wait outside while I do this."

"I can't let you go in there alone if it's dangerous. Not after everything we've been through."

She tried to peer through the window, but the usual dingy, yellowed grime coated the glass, obscuring the view. "I'll be all right," she said, patting her pockets. "I'm prepared." And she was. She'd brought every protective talisman, amulet, charm, and herb she possessed. This time she would not be blindsided.

Jean-Paul began to protest, but in the end he had no choice but to trust her. He kissed her cheek and said he would wait with the horse. He was learning. Still, she was grateful to know he would be nearby as she opened the door to the seedy tavern.

The main room, normally half-empty on a good night, bustled with customers. There wasn't a seat to be had. Elena threaded her way through the crowd, ever more aware that it wasn't the usual locals. A group of sorcerers who looked as if they'd just disembarked a train from the other side of the world shook their turbaned heads and blew smoke into the air as they debated the number and meaning of the dead cats. She gave a wide berth to the cloud of tobacco and gin hovering near them and emerged next to the table by the window, where a sagging cobweb hung precariously low over the patrons' heads. Two young witches sat across from each other studying their tarot cards. The one with the city accent tapped her finger on the Empress and smugly noted she'd foretold the death of the demon-dancing witch a week earlier. The other pointed to the Wheel of Fortune and said it was pure luck. Elena stood on her toes to look for Madame Grimalkin and ended up bumping into a man whose face was tattooed with black swirls and dots that she was sure contained its own type of magic. He took her measure with a curious glance, one absent of attraction yet fully inquisitive, then inhaled. His eyes widened with excitement. "You're a winemaker. Like the evil-hearted one," he said. "Did you know this woman? Is it true she drank the blood of a mortal man?"

He was talking about Gerda. They all were. Everyone in the room, it seemed, had come to revel in the details of her crimes and death. How many doves had been busy flapping their wings over the countryside to spread the news?

"No, I didn't know her," she lied, suddenly struck by the realization that any one of the strangers in the room could be the one who had cursed her. And then she saw them. The long ringlets of gold hair and the embroidered jacket with the faded flowers. The Charlatan sisters were there, raising their glasses with everyone else and cheering Gerda's death. Or perhaps her accomplishments.

She was about to confront them when a bony hand grabbed her by the arm. Before she could protest she was shuttled into a dark corner. Her hand went to her knife.

"Thank the All Knowing you got my message." Madame Grimalkin checked over her shoulder, then looked straight at her. "It was just like you said. A green dragon's eye."

She released her grip on the knife. "You saw the watch?"

Her gray head nodded. "It's a gentleman that owns it."

"Gentleman?" She glanced again at the Charlatan sisters, laughing and dancing across the room. "Are you sure?"

"Well, that's how he presents himself, though I wouldn't say it of a man who goes around cursing his own kind, if it's him."

A man? Of all the times she'd fantasized about this moment, it had never occurred to her she'd be facing a male witch. But who? Why? She felt as if she'd drifted even further from the answers she'd been looking for.

Grimalkin set her serving tray on top of the bar and held up two fingers to her husband as she shouted for beer. "So what are you going to do?" she asked. "I don't want any trouble. No more than the usual anyway. We've got a good crowd tonight on account of that demon witch dying. People are hoping the authorities'll sell off her bones and ash for talismans. Isn't that right, Paddy?"

Paddock set two frothing glasses of beer on Grimalkin's tray. "If they don't, I've a mind to sweep up the coals from the fire and sell 'em as witch bones myself. I'd make a fortune." He laughed before waddling back to the tap to fill another glass. "About time we had a bit of good luck around here."

"That's why I love you, Paddy." Grimalkin picked up her tray. "So what's it going to be?"

"I'm not looking for trouble. I just need to know why."

Grimalkin nodded, understanding in a way only someone living with the cursed could. "He showed up about an hour ago and ordered supper. We're busier than usual tonight, so it's taking longer to serve people. He kept pulling that watch out, checking the time, and giving me the evil eye. That's when I recognized it. Tried to stall him best I could after that. Then the strangest thing happened. I was set to give him his check when a woman joined him. Older lady. Real proper. Came in a few minutes before you and ordered two glasses of wine. Can't imagine what she wants with the likes of him, but they moved to a private booth at the back."

"Show me," Elena said, her curiosity straining against the leash.

Madame Grimalkin delivered the beers to a pair of conjurers spinning coins three inches above their palms. She snatched the coins out of the air for payment, then pointed Elena to the booth in the back with the curtains half drawn. A man's elegant leg peeked out of the curtain—the trouser perfectly creased, the wing-tip shoe polished to a mirror shine. "That's him," she said. "Probably explaining his services to her right now. Bah. Sooner he's gone, the better."

Elena felt a supportive hand on her back before she was left alone to stare at the half-open curtain. She'd been delivered to this moment on a seven-year tide of yearning. Revenge had been the sweet fruit she'd craved in her sleep, poison the elixir to deliver the dream. But Bastien's death had turned the taste for vengeance to rot. Murder was no longer the salve she'd once sought for her injury. Yet as she gravitated right to see past the curtain and finally know the face of her assailant, she had to temper a rising impulse to strike.

He was an ordinary-looking middle-aged man in a gray suit. Clean-shaven, balding, soft in the middle, and yet he possessed enough vanity to wear an enchanted tie that shimmered with a silver glow. A trick to make his eyes sparkle now that natural youth had slipped away. She tilted her head and looked again. There was something familiar about those eyes, yet not enough to trigger *knowing*.

She lowered her gaze to where a chain looped from the button on his vest to the watch in his pocket. He didn't need to pull the watch out for her to know what the case looked like. The image had never left her mind—a sickly green dragon's eye with a vertical slit overlaid by an elaborate golden eyelid. Tick tock, tick tock, the lid had snapped shut and her life got sucked away. But his ordinary appearance threw her.

What if he wasn't the right person after all? What if the watch was more common than she'd thought?

And then he raised his voice.

"How dare you accuse me of subterfuge," he said, pounding his fist against the table so that it rattled the silverware. "You practically begged me to fix your little problem. As I recall you handed over a pretty stack of cash and told me I was free to do whatever it took so you could be rid of the situation. That's what I did."

The nasal tone, the air of superiority, the twinge of false aristocracy—his identity came flying into focus. The face without the dramatic pasted-on eyebrows and pointed goatee. The eyes wiped clean of their black kohl. A wizard without his flowing robe and false nails.

"You!" she said, throwing back the curtain.

Rackham startled, then narrowed his eyes. "You?" Once he made the connection, he balked at his tablemate. "What is this?"

"Good heavens, what are you doing here?"

Elena pushed back the other curtain. Sitting opposite of the man who had cursed her and left her for dead was the woman who had raised her from a child.

CHAPTER THIRTY-THREE

Was it a chance meeting? Coincidence? The All Knowing's idea of a cosmic joke? Elena's mind grasped for any reasonable explanation for why Grand-Mère would keep company with *that* man.

Then she spotted the brown vial gripped in her mentor's trembling hand. The missing bottle from her workroom. The one she'd filled when deranged with the need for revenge.

Of course. It was the only explanation that made sense. Grand-Mère had sussed out the witch who'd cursed her and was willing to retaliate. Perhaps even commit murder in the name of vengeance.

Elena slid into the booth beside Grand-Mère and put her hand over hers. "Please don't do it. I know what I said before about needing revenge, but it isn't worth it. You don't have to do this for me."

Rackham pushed his glass of wine aside and leaned toward Grand-Mère. "What does she mean you don't have to do this for her? What kind of setup is this?"

The old woman pushed Elena's hand away. "It was never supposed to be permanent, Edmond. You promised me you knew what to do. That she wouldn't be hurt."

"You've always known how I make my living." He took a swallow of wine before pleading his case to Elena. "I did what I was paid to do. Purely business."

Grand-Mère's eyes swelled with tears. "Your lies ruined everything."

Rackham leaned back in his seat, lifting his eyes heavenward as if it were *his* curse to try and reason with a woman about business. To cope, he drained the contents of his wineglass in one swallow.

"How is it you even know this man?" Elena said, turning to Grand-Mère. "He's a shady carnival palm reader who works out of the back of a wagon."

Rackham snorted, indignant at the description. "Oh, Ariella and I go way back. I was the one who sold you to the Gardins after your parents died."

Sold?

He set his empty glass down hard for emphasis. "That's right. I know exactly who you are. You may disparage my carnival work," he went on, "but it was your mother and father who were actually—"

"Edmond, no."

"You knew my parents?"

"Of course I knew them. All those dark magic books you were so interested in—who do you think I procured those from?"

Intuition knows the truth when heard, but the sound can leave a terrible ringing in the ears.

"You're lying."

"Yes, you'll find he's rather good at that," Grand-Mère said.

Rackham paused to cough into a handkerchief. "Clearly Ariella has kept you in the dark about your heritage, but it was your mother who taught me everything I know about curses and poison. Esmé and Raul were my mentors. That is until they were both hanged for selling their poisons to society women in the city who'd grown bored of their wealthy husbands." He made a *comme ci, comme ça* gesture with a wave of his handkerchief before stopping to cough again. "I didn't fully see the resemblance before, but I should have known by the way you were drawn to the book on curses you were Esmé's daughter. But then I expected you'd still be hopping around your swamp, plucking flies out of the air with your tongue. Or giving some stray dog indigestion by now."

"Edmond!"

Hanged?

He leaned in and inspected her more closely. "How is it you're even here in the flesh? That curse was taken straight out of Esmé's grimoire."

For a moment she couldn't breathe. Couldn't think. The world tilted off its axis, spinning into oblivion. A storm of stars and dust expanded inside her head as her shadow vision intruded of its own volition, forcing her to glimpse the past and the parents she'd barely known. Memory whirled her to an apothecary wagon, its shelves lined with bottles that rattled as the wheels rolled down a narrow brick lane lined with shops smelling of red and yellow spices. Jars hung above her head filled with shriveled seedpods, dried animal hearts, and scaly toes with long claws suspended in formaldehyde. One bottle, she recalled a voice telling her, held the sweet-smelling extraction from a red flower that could make a man dream of the past forever. Another contained a jade liquid that fumed with gray smoke when bits of nail clippings and hair were added with a swirl of the wrist—her mother's wrist, which jangled with the music of a dozen gold bracelets as it mixed the poison.

The truth of her bloodline tugged at her. It knocked against the center point of her nature, beyond learning, beyond intuition, beyond instinct. It injected itself into her consciousness until she could no longer deny the truth. She'd been born a potions witch, a conjurer of poisons and curses. A *venefica*.

The sound of harsh coughing broke her meditation. Urgency summoned her back through the liminal space, accelerating her from the past to the present. When she opened her eyes the proof of her lineage stared her in the face. She saw it in the dilation of Rackham's pupils, the beads of sweat on his temple, and the blue tinge of his lips. Her poison was snaking through his veins, looking for his heart. Grand-Mère had already slipped it into his wine. It would have only taken a drop or two. Nothing to taste, nothing to see, and nothing she could do for him, except give him the chance to tell her the truth and clear his conscience before death dropped him at the feet of the All Knowing.

"Apparently my mother didn't teach you everything," Elena said. "That toadstone might protect you from getting sick on spoiled food, but it won't help against a tailor-made poison." She waited while he coughed and gave the ring a twist. "And to answer your question, if you knew half of what you claim to know, you'd have understood that when allowed to build up in the body over time, some poisons—such as self-ingested bufotoxins—degrade the energy holding a transmogrification spell in place. It took seven years, but the bonds of your curse disintegrated. That's how I'm sitting here, Professor. And why you are now dying."

"What?"

"You've been poisoned," Elena said. "It's already moving through your bloodstream, circling your heart, waiting for the right moment to squeeze."

Rackham's head snapped up from his handkerchief. He stared at Grand-Mère, horror-struck. "You poisoned me?"

"Yes." Grand-Mère tilted her glass, savoring the last of her wine.

He blinked at her in disbelief. "You're mad. Both of you." He tried to leave when the first spasm hit. He gasped for air and tore his silver tie loose from his neck. "Help me—damn it, someone help me."

The room was full of witches reeking of healing herbs, but only the Charlatan sisters stopped their celebrating to push through the crowd. The one nearest reached in her embroidered jacket and brandished a useless rabbit's foot, likely with the hope of demanding two coins for it, until she saw who sat at the man's table. She sneered and backed off.

Elena dug in her pocket for the rue amulet she'd brought with her. "Here," she said, dropping a pinch of the herb into Rackham's hand. "Put it on the back of your tongue. It might lessen the pain."

He greedily inhaled the herb, crunching it between his teeth. "Will it stop the poison?"

"Elena doesn't use half measures, Edmond." Grand-Mère calmly set the empty vial on the table and folded her hands together as if her work was done. "She's Esmé's daughter, after all, and my protégé. I'd guess your heart is going to explode in a matter of moments."

Rackham's voice rose in pitch as if desperate pleading might change his fate. "It was nothing personal. 'Take the girl away' she said, so I did." He reached out and grabbed Elena's wrist with surprising strength. "Now give me the antidote!"

How could she tell him there wasn't one? Murder had always been her goal when the poison was mixed. Rackham let go and coughed into his handkerchief, staining it with bright-red blood. Panicked at the sight, he slid out of the booth to beg for help from the other witches. But by then the poison had ensnared his heart. His eyes bulged and his sallow skin drained of color. He clutched his chest, wincing in disbelief. "I am dead," he said and folded to the floor.

One of the young tarot readers screamed, igniting a low-grade panic that spread across the room. Morbid curiosity followed, drawing the crowd nearer to the body. The effect proved temporary, however, as a green-and-black aura formed around the dead professor. The crowd recognized a revenge poisoning when they saw one. Madame Grimalkin shooed the witches back to their celebration, reassuring them a pigeon would be sent to the authorities.

Jean-Paul, however, didn't have the benefit of reading auras. He pushed through the crowd, knocking over empty chairs and spilling mugs of beer to get to Elena.

"What happened? I heard a scream." He paused and gaped at the body. "Is that man dead?"

Elena didn't trust her legs to hold her up, but she took his hand when he offered it.

"Let us hope," Grand-Mère answered.

"Madame. You're all right? We've been looking for you."

"Monsieur Martel, I hoped I might see you again."

He slid into the empty booth across from them. "Of course. Why wouldn't you?"

She gave him a weak smile that was interrupted by a fit of coughing. When she regained her composure, she smiled and patted his hand. "I fear my fate is tied up with the dead man's on the floor. My heart is in retreat, but it can't evade answering for what we did much longer," she said with a *c'est la vie* flick of her hand. "I won't be returning to Château Renard. But know that it was everything to me, and I leave the estate in the best of hands."

"Madame?"

We?

The old woman cleared a tickle in her throat, then unhitched the silver chatelaine, with its keys, amulets, and small tastevin, and held it out to Elena. "I won't ask for your forgiveness. That's between the All Knowing and me. But I hope, in some way, I've given you the peace of mind you needed, knowing the person who cursed you is gone."

"Grand-Mère, no." Vertigo gripped Elena as if she were standing on a ledge overlooking a canyon of secrets too vast to see the bottom. She shook her head, willing the words to be a mistake, even as her mentor laid the silver chain in her hands.

"As for my part, I only wanted you to come to your senses. You were in such a rush to marry Bastien. You couldn't see how he was manipulating you. Trying to steal you and your talents away from me. After everything I taught you? I couldn't allow it. Joseph and I had worked too hard to build the vineyard up from nothing to have it stolen by that man. I just couldn't let you leave to be his vine witch."

"How could you think I would turn my back on you and Château Renard?"

Grand-Mère demurred. "I'm not proud of it, but for a time I worried your blood's true calling had finally churned to the surface. Edmond warned it might happen when he first brought you to us as a child."

Sympathy drained from Elena's voice. "Because he'd sold you the daughter of a *venefica*?"

"Yes."

The word deflated her, and she stared at her hands in her lap. But as much as she hated hearing it, there was a spark of truth in the admission. Hadn't her first impulse been to brew a poison so she could get her revenge on Bastien? Wasn't a man lying dead on the floor because of that compulsion?

"I know what you're thinking, Elena. And, yes, you've always had an impeccable instinct for what deadly root went with which warty fungus. Or which spotted leaf was more potent steeped as a tea versus crushing it into powder. The art of poison has always come naturally to you. It's probably what saved your life in that swamp."

The old woman went silent for a moment but waved off any concern when Jean-Paul questioned if she was all right. The exchange made Elena look back up, and it was enough encouragement for Grand-Mère to reach out and take her hand.

"Even though you were an imp of a child when I first saw you, I recognized your potential. You didn't belong on the back of a carnival wagon. And, I thought, alcohol is its own form of poison anyway. The disciplines aren't as far apart as some might think. And you adapted brilliantly. No one could say otherwise. The art of poison might run in your blood, but never doubt you were meant to be a vine witch." The old woman paused, closing her eyes again as she pressed her hand to her chest. "But then that damn Bastien came along, ambition and greed pulling him to our front door like a team of horses. I was so afraid . . ."

"Of what?"

"Of losing everything to his damnable greed."

"So you had me cursed? Abandoning me to die alone and half out of my wits?"

"No," said Grand-Mère. "I would never have done that. Not on purpose. That you must believe." Grand-Mère removed a silk cloth from her sleeve and dabbed the corners of her eyes. "It was that man," she said, eyeing Rackham's body. "The carnival was pulling up stakes to leave town, and I thought if you just got some distance from Bastien you'd come to your senses. Time apart might help you see the truth. So I asked Edmond to take you with him. Only he said there wasn't enough room in any of the wagons, and the money I offered would barely cover the expenses to take care of you for an entire year so . . . he asked if he could transform you as a matter of convenience. I thought he meant to keep you as a bird, or maybe a cat, just until he returned the next summer, and then he'd release you from the spell."

"What were you thinking?"

"It was horribly wrong—I know that now. But then I was wrong about so many things." She turned her head away to cough. "When the carnival returned to the valley the following year and you didn't come home, I went to his wagon. He seemed surprised to see me. Made some excuse about you meeting someone and running off. I had no choice but to believe him, until you showed up years later and I learned the truth of his deception. I never dreamed he was capable of cursing you and dumping you on the side of the road like that. Not Esmé's daughter."

Grand-Mère held her handkerchief over her mouth, coughing until her eyes watered. When the fit passed she brought the cloth away and found the silk stained bright red. Her eyebrows rose with curiosity at the sight. "Blood and silk, mud and milk, never the twain should meet," she muttered. "No, that's not right, is it?"

Jean-Paul looked sidelong at the old woman, then back at Elena in alarm. "What's the matter with her?"

It was then Elena took note of the empty wineglass. She'd been so focused on sorting out the truth inside the betrayal she'd missed the early signs of poisoning in the old woman. She grabbed the vial and shook it against the light to see how much liquid remained.

Empty.

A shudder of fear ran through her, as if she was falling and her lifeline had just slipped through her fingers. "She's poisoned herself," she said and threw the vial on the floor.

"Can't you do something? Use your magic?"

She emptied the pouch of rue on the table and began grinding the leaves between her palms. "I'm going to try a purge chant to empty her stomach," she said, knowing she'd used a powerful binding spell on the poison to prevent exactly what she hoped to do.

But before she could chant her spell, Grand-Mère winced and slouched in her seat. Her head tipped back so that she stared at the ceiling. "I never meant to cause you any pain," she said, gasping for air. "I was just so scared I was going to lose everything. But it was never meant to be permanent. You must believe me. You were always supposed to come home again."

Elena blew on the herbs and asked the All Knowing to purge the poison, but it was too late. Grand-Mère's body made a tiny rattle as her breath slipped out, then she went slack, the heart cornered at last by the deadly potion.

There were no screams to follow the second death. After an initial collected gasp, there were whispers of concern, a spoon laid gently on a table, and a quick inhale of awe as the mentor's aura rose in a silver cloud, acknowledgment of the wisdom and experience lost when one so old passes. A final hush settled over the witches as Elena, still reeling from the confession, raised her hands in the sacred pose to praise the All Knowing and plead forgiveness for the woman who had taught her the art of the vine, and life.

CHAPTER THIRTY-FOUR

The vines sagged with heavy clusters of fruit. Their broad leaves exalted palms up to the sun while secret tendrils threaded around the hardened canes, seeking their next anchor point. It humbled Jean-Paul to see the vineyard respond with such robust growth. As he walked among the vines, he plucked off a grape, testing the fruit's firmness between his thumb and finger before taking a bite. The sweet juice ran over his tongue. For three days he'd been telling her it was time, but she would put her hand on his and say, "Not yet. Not until the full moon passes." He was beginning to think Elena's patience for the harvest was as much a part of her magic as were her spells.

Each morning she checked her star charts, consulted with the lacewings, the beetles, the moths, and he swore even a lizard once, as they went about their business in the canopy. And then she'd close her eyes and let her fingers trail along the vines. There was some secret communication in it all. A language only she spoke. On the days he felt brave he would ask her to let him listen too. Then she would take his hand in hers, and he would hear the rush of life surging through the vines, see the bright halo of gold and green hover above the rows, and watch the bees buzz through the air toward their ultraviolet destinations. And then he would let go. It was enough to know that other world existed and that she was watching over it.

In the weeks and months after Madame's death, he'd had to return to his law books and the covenant decrees one last time. There was never any real threat of Elena returning to prison, but the law had to officially release its grip on her, which meant a formal hearing. Complicating things was the revelation of her family history. Because two people had died from a poison she'd formulated, she would have to register with the Covenants Regulation Bureau as a *venefica* so that any future concoctions might be monitored for malicious use. The decree required seven pages of official documents, but it was all just legalese, the secret language he spoke, and one he happily translated for Elena so she understood she was free to continue making wine.

Well, mostly free. The death of her mentor had, for a time, clamped a restraint on her confidence. The natural fallout of betrayal and loss. Afterward, she'd spent her mornings walking among the old vines Joseph had planted for Ariella, speaking to them when she thought he wasn't near enough to hear. Whispering words another might reserve for the departed. Words of regret, confusion, guilt, and finally, he thought, acceptance. Until the day she was ready to say yes to his proposal.

He may not have asked to partner with witches when he bought the vineyards at Château Renard, but like the scientist with his microscope he'd discovered there was so much more to the world around him than what his eye alone could see. And more chambers of his heart than he'd ever known existed before he'd met this cat-eyed woman with her charms and spells and bewitching magic.

CHAPTER THIRTY-FIVE

You had to respect the grapes. That was the first lesson. Wine, after all, was a living, breathing thing. Each wine its own entity, each vintage as unique as the heart and mind of the witch who crafted it.

Jean-Paul opened the bottle and set it on the table to breathe. Though still young by some standards, the wine had aged for two years and already had the maturity of a grande dame in the prime of her life. It was time. He poured, and the wine filled the glass like liquid gemstones, catching the light in rubescent brilliance. Elena held it to her nose. Flint and fire, figs, spice, and tart cherries. More than any other, she'd wanted the full expression of the grapes to shine through in this vintage, though even a witch couldn't be certain of which characteristics would be transfused through the roots and vines to settle in the fruit.

She sipped and tasted the complexity of fruit and smoke, earth and oak, as the legacy of the renowned Renard terroir came through. And then the subtle aftertaste hit as hoped with just a hint of melancholia in the finish. It was more memory than infusion, but it was there all the same to remind her. Like the scent of geraniums in winter.

ACKNOWLEDGMENTS

As a writer I've always felt that storytelling was the last true form of magic left in the world. But I may be wrong. For there is also gratitude, which is no less powerful in the right moment. With that in mind, I wish to express my thanks to the many people who helped make the publication of this novel possible. First, a gracious nod to my agent, Marlene, who reads quickly and knows what she likes when she sees it. Thank you for being my advocate. To Adrienne, whose positivity and collaborative style made the work a joy, my sincerest thanks for believing in my story. There are also a number of people whose editorial input on the book made me look like a better writer than I am. To Clarence, Jon, Sarah, Karin, and the amazing team at 47North, many of whom I never had a chance to correspond with personally, I send a hearty thank-you for your expertise and professionalism. It's been wonderful to work with so many dedicated and creative people. On a more personal note, I wish to thank Caitlin for her early reading and revision guidance. And lastly, to Rob, David, Autumn, Brett, Matt, and my parents, Jim and Carol, thank you for your endless support on this long and winding journey.

ABOUT THE AUTHOR

Photo © 2018 bobcarmichael.com

Luanne G. Smith lives in Colorado at the base of the beautiful Rocky Mountains, where she enjoys hiking, gardening, and a glass of good wine at the end of the day. *The Vine Witch* is her debut novel. For more information, visit www.luannegsmith.com.